Daniel Scratch

A STORY OF WITCHKIND

AUTHOR'S PREFERRED EDITION
BOOK ONE

DON JONES

DONJONES.COM

Also by Don Jones

Daniel Scratch, a story of witchkind®

Endless Sky®: Truthsayer

The Never: A Tale of Peter and the Fae

* * *

Free eBooks!

The Achillios Chronicles trilogy, *The Prime Wave Accounting* duopoly, and *short stories of witchkind* are all available by joining the author's newsletter at DonJones.com.

For Donavan,
thank you for being part of the family I chose.

Contents

the world
Bryssi
Lastpointe
Greensea
Great Northern Wood
Rushford
Northsea
Soloton
Farreach
Chiton
Evermore
Landshire
Dvocastella's
Taliesin
Westhead
Fyngershire
Twynsits
Spurham
The Tower of Endings
Lakewood
Withring
Cuppton
Little Bay
Disemstoke's
Carvendam
Meadowside
Hook
Baythwaite
Nworions
Nek
Pease
Harbsmouth
Wisding
Farreach
Thornwaith's
Soysea

Foreword

This book is a "second edition" of _Daniel Scratch._ I had the opportunity to work with an amazing development editor, and made some substantial rewrites to the manuscript—juicing up the action a bit, digging more into the characters' personalities, and tightening up the story in several places.

As a result, this edition of _Daniel Scratch_ doesn't align with the original sequels, _Master of the Tower_ and _The Fifth Axis._ So if you like the story and decide to keep reading, be sure you're grabbing the second edition of _those_ titles as well, otherwise nothing will make sense.

Also, and this is important: while the original _Daniel Scratch_ definitely had a Young Adult-vibe (and was favorably compared to Ursula K Le Guin's _A Wizard of Earthsea,_ a Young Adult classic), be aware that this new edition gets a _bit_ darker. A mature fourteen year-old would likely be totally comfortable with this novel, but the story definitely visits some uncomfortable topics, including the death of family members. If you're considering this tale for your young adult, just give it a quick read yourself (especially the last three or four chapters) and make sure you're okay with it.

Prologue

NO, *I'm quite real. Perhaps not in the way you're used to, but I'm real.*

Well, that's because I don't talk to very many people. You're special that way.

Mostly because they can't hear me. Or don't want to.

Stories? Yes, I have quite a few stories. My own story is quite... Well, I suppose it's interesting, but it's also quite long.

No, I guess you do have the time. What's that?

Yes, I could skip the boring parts. I feel like I skipped them myself sometimes.

You're quite sure?

Well, then let's begin.

The Test

"HERE YOU GO, MASTER DANIEL," Abbygail said, sliding a plate of eggs and sausage onto the rickety table before clambering back down her worn wooden step stool. The house's formal dining room table was far grander—and sturdier—but the room was also dark and foreboding. I preferred the little servant's nook in the kitchen. It couldn't exactly be called *sunnier*, given the grimed-over condition of the thick, warped windows, but it felt less like a mausoleum.

And yes, I know what a mausoleum feels like.

The whole house, in fact, had something of a mausoleum feel. To begin with, it was *old*. Two centuries old, at least, and very probably more. The walls told its history, with wallpaper layered over paint, layered over plaster, layered over the old wood lath. The current wallpaper—probably not the first these walls had seen—was faded and peeling in places. The stout wooden floorboards were time-worn, with the nicks and scratches that are earned only through decades of service. The threadbare round rug that lay under the table—the only floor covering in the kitchen, and one of very few rugs in the entire house—had probably been around since before my parents were born. Probably before *their* parents had been born.

I picked up a fork, smiled, and nodded, careful not to offer thanks. Abbygail was a brownie, and the knee-high, white-haired, blue-skinned little creature had been with the family for decades. After Mother and Father died, more brownies had arrived. Abbygail said her kind simply sensed the need and showed up. They were the house's only servants now, cleaning up what they could and keeping me fed. They were also, frankly, my only friends. But a single word of thanks to any of them would see them all vanish before nightfall, never to return. Mother had taught me that much before... well. Before.

I quickly finished my breakfast as Abbygail bustled quietly about the ancient kitchen, climbing up to the sink to wipe the heavy cast-iron skillet, scurrying down to bank the fire in the ancient wood-burning stove, and then peering through the pantry cabinets, scratching one of her long, pointed ears and trying to decide what she'd make for lunch. The pantry was never full, but also never empty, through some magic of the house itself. It made for a lot of repetitive meals, but at least nobody starved. Mother had always supplemented the pantry's unvarying stock with fresh produce and treats that she conjured from the market in the village.

I especially missed the crisp, tart obuolys-fruit, but I'd never quite caught the runes Mother had used to summon the food, and I wasn't even sure how she paid for it. I supposed she could have sent coins the same way she brought the food.

I was just starting to wonder what I'd do with myself all day. Even before my parents had gone, I'd been a solitary boy, keeping to myself and largely keeping myself amused all day. With no siblings, I had turned to the many books in the house for companionship. With no school—I would learn later that I was unusual in that respect—those books were also my education. If I grew bored of reading and the weather seemed nice, our expansive estate gave me plenty of room to wander. I could visit the dilapidated outbuildings, throw pebbles into the pond, or walk through the abandoned and overgrown horse pastures. If the weather was poor, I might even help the brownies keep the house clean.

I'd almost decided it would be a reading day when an insistent, loud clanging rang from the attic, echoing down through the walls and plumbing. Abbygail froze, looking anxiously at me. "I'm going," I said, resignation coloring my voice.

Great-Great-Grandmother had called.

The house itself was devoid of any living beings other than myself, the brownies, and the kobolds who dropped by almost weekly to handle heavier tasks, like the seemingly continual repairs the creaking old building required. I'd never even seen a spider, although I'd read about them and seen a few sketches of them in some of my books. Great-Great-Grandmother was something... else. Certainly not a "living being." She'd grown up in this house, following at least half a dozen generations before her. But unlike her forebears she'd declined to leave the house simply because she'd died. Instead she'd moved into the attic and made it her domain. When she wanted something from the living—meaning me—she'd make a racket until someone showed up. I always showed up quickly, too: I'd once made her wait almost ten minutes and it had put her in an even colder mood than usual.

I hadn't known about her when Mother and Father were alive; they'd simply forbidden me to wander higher than the second floor where our bedrooms were. It wasn't until Mother was gone that Great-Great-Grandmother had first summoned me, banging and scratching until I'd finally overcome my fear and ascended to discover her. As far as I knew, she never left the attic, although I had no idea what she did up there to while away the days.

But she had called, so I once again trudged up the four flights of massive, creaking stairs, running my hand along the smooth, worn handrails all the way. I'd learned early on that the stairs liked to play tricks. Not so much with the family, although with no other opportunities they'd occasionally get bored and try to trip me up. The handrails never tried such things though, and were always firm and steady under my grip. The handrails were yet another sign of the house's grand past, carved into a comfortable shape and featuring intricate, delicate engravings of flowers, birds, and woodland creatures along the sides. When I was younger, I'd spent hours looking at the little carvings, running my fingers over them and inventing stories about the animals' lives.

As I passed the landing for the second floor, I brushed my fingers over the portrait of Mother that hung there. She'd been much younger when the painting had been made, still unmarried, with the rare, pale skin that she'd gifted me, and the straight, honey-colored hair that she'd always kept in braids when I knew her. My eyes were my father's though, gray and sharp; Mother's were the bright, lush purple that was so common amongst the women in her family. I didn't linger any longer over her picture, though: one didn't keep the matriarch waiting.

Great-Great-Grandmother always heard me coming of course, and the stout wooden attic door flew open as soon as I'd stepped onto the landing in front of it, swinging silently despite its obvious weight. The room beyond the door was dark and murky, and Great-Great-Grandmother sort of *oozed* out of that darkness. She was every inch a witch from human stories: a long, full dress of embroidered black material, including a black knitted shawl that she clutched around her thin, bony torso. Her back was hunched with age. Even her nose, a bit bulbous, attempted a slight hook at its end. Her face was at least not colored green, although it was deeply lined, especially around her eyes. Those still retained their purple color, although they'd darkened and faded to a dull, dim shade. A black mole, complete with two stiff bristles of pure white hair, decorated one cheek. She smelled horrific, an aged combination of butterscotch and rotten flowers. I held my ground on the landing: she'd never once let a single part of her body extend beyond the attic doorframe, and so I kept a good three feet between us.

It goes without saying that I'd never ventured beyond the doorframe into the attic itself. In my imagination, the attic wasn't even a room. It was another dimension, one inhabited solely by Great-Great-Grandmother and whoever or whatever she'd captured.

She sniffed. "You're thirteen today," she said, as if there was a particular odor associated with that age. Her raspy voice was like two pieces of thick, worn leather twisting around each other. "You're to go and be Tested," she added. That last word was uttered with such weight that I knew at once I was to be *Tested*, not merely *tested*. Whatever that meant.

But then I blinked. Thirteen?

I'd been alone in the house since Mother had been dragged off to Witchhold—two years ago? Three?—to be tried and interned. The prison had sent word scant months later that she'd died, still screaming the curses and epithets of whatever madness had taken her. The official letter expressed regret at failing to discover a cure for her ailment, let alone identifying its cause.

It didn't matter, Great-Great-Grandmother had said. *She served her purpose.*

I'd remained in the house, the last living member of a once-proud family. Looking back, I wonder that nobody thought to do *something*. I mean, even the Proctors who'd taken Mother must have known they were leaving a ten year-old alone in the house. *Must* have known, no? And yet I'd been undisturbed for three years. I'm sure now that Great-Great-Grandmother had something to do with it. But with no living adults around to remind me, I'd quite given up on observing birthdays and was mildly surprised to learn I was now a teenager.

I nodded to Great-Great-Grandmother because once she'd made a proclamation, it was far easier, and safer, to go along with it. I'd left the great house only a handful of times since my parents' passing, every time at Great-Great-Grandmother's whim on some errand or another. "Where do I go?"

She extended a frail, bony finger toward me, holding it just short of the doorframe that bounded her world. I stepped forward, closing the distance between us, and leaned my head into the doorframe. Her long, thick yellow fingernail brushed my forehead, she muttered an arcane phrase, and I suddenly *knew* where I was to go. I stepped back quickly, and she retreated back into the inky darkness just as fast. The attic door flew shut, *clicking* closed with surprising gentleness given the force of its swing.

"Abbygail," I called as I trudged down the stairs. "Could you fetch my coat?" I was to go into the village, but I didn't ask if the brownie wanted me to fetch anything for her or the house. When one was on one of Great-Great-Grandmother's errands, one didn't deviate for any creature or reason.

But a short delay wouldn't be noticed. I stopped on the third floor, where the tiny, empty bedrooms intended for the house's staff nestled closely together, lining both sides of a short, narrow hallway. I stepped into the hallway and placed my back against the wall next to the first door. That door had stopped closing properly decades ago, and even now its warped surface leaned slightly inward. Dim sunlight crept through the opening, but there was no reason for me to go in. Instead, I slid down the wall and came to rest on the battered wooden floor.

"Father," I said quietly. "Grandmother says I'm to be Tested."

I waited. Father had died in the vast basement three levels down, but for some reason his restless spirit had taken up residence here. I sometimes told myself that he couldn't bear the thought of leaving his only child alone in this enormous, empty house, but it was just as likely that death had held no more interest for him than his family had. All my life, he'd been more interested in tinkering with his experiments and machines than in engaging with my mother and me.

A scratching sound came from inside the wall. "Don't eat the food," a gruff, hollow voice said, echoing behind the plaster and lathing. The scratching faded, and I stood.

Don't eat the food.

* * *

Our old house sat on the very outskirts of town, mandating an hour-long walk to make it into the center of our little village. Mother had made the trip with me in just a few minutes by using her magic, but she'd never shown me the trick of it, so I was stuck doing it the slow way.

A wrought-iron gate—surprisingly sturdy for its age—provided egress from the estate. A single dusty road stretched from that gate through empty meadows and little copses of trees. There were no other houses on this side of the village; Mother had said the family had once owned all the land leading up the village itself. I didn't know if that land was now all mine or not, but even if the family had sold it, nobody had bothered to build any closer. There was only the house, overgrown remains of farmlands, quiet meadows, and the village. The occasional bird would let out a soft *cheep,* but I'd never seen one. I'd never seen *any* other creatures on the land, for that matter.

It was a clear day, the second moon still stubbornly clinging to its place in the sky even as the sun threatened to blot it out. The weather was mild, as it was for much of the year, and the breeze blew gently through the leafy branches of the trees that lined the road.

As I neared the village, the packed-earth lane gained a cover of fine gravel. This is where the humans' buildings began, starting with rickety wooden farm-cottages and slowly improving into sturdy homes. I passed chicken-coops full of clucking, pecking hens. There were small vegetable gardens, tended by sturdy-looking men and women in simple, home-spun clothes. There were children frolicking in front of their homes, dogs running around and barking, and adults' voices calling to each other across their properties. Notably, this far from the house, there were even birds and the occasional insect, all flitting through the air.

The road then transitioned to tightly placed cobblestones as the old stone buildings of the village proper began. These build-ings were worn and crumbling around the edges, but the remained sturdy, hunkered closely to one another as if for protection from the outside world.

The villagers ignored me: I was just one more child dressed in black slacks, sturdy (if dusty) black shoes, and a long black coat. I seemed to warrant no special attention on their part, although it couldn't have been common for a child my age to be wandering into the village alone. I cast sidelong glances at them:

I'd had few opportunities to see humans up close, but as far as I could tell they were physically indistinguishable from witchkind. Perhaps they dressed a bit plainer, and perhaps they moved with a bit more of a trudge in their step, but then again perhaps that was simply this village's way of doing things.

The village wasn't especially bustling, but it wasn't empty either. I passed the market where Mother had somehow summoned her groceries from, and a small banker's office where two or three people waited to conduct their business. Further down the cobbled street, I knew, was a tiny smithy, a spacious courthouse, and the village's ancient church. I could hear the rattling, clanking sounds of a carriage rolling over the uneven streets, likely carrying goods to some shop or other. This village was far removed from the humans' iron roadway, Father had told me, and relied on carts and carriages to haul in whatever goods the villagers might need.

I made my way to the narrow alleyway that ran between a busy general store and the sleepy post office. Two steps into the alleyway led me to the ancient lead pipe that carried rainwater down from the rooftop gutters. I'd never seen it before, but Great-Great-Grandmother's magic had placed its location and image firmly into my mind.

Witchkind couldn't afford to live cheek-to-jowl with humanity; we'd learned that ages and ages ago. And so when we couldn't have a secluded place to ourselves far from the humans, we crept around in the nooks and crannies they ignored. My heart pounding lightly in anticipation, and my nerves giving a slight jitter to my hand, I gave the old pipe two gentle knocks with my knuckles, on the exact spot where a small rune was carved into the soft metal. It echoed ringingly for a moment, and then fell silent. Then with a *pop,* a small section of the pipe swung open, like a tiny lead door, and I was sucked inside.

* * *

I emerged into a small, crowded office. Great-Great-Grandmother had sent me on a few errands into the village before, and if there was one common attribute of witchkind, it was that we seemed to enjoy clutter. The walls of the office were lined with shelves and cubbies, and each was precariously over-stuffed with books, knick-knacks, trinkets, piles of paper, and more. Glistening little sprites flitted between it all, stirring up eddies of dust that then meandered independently around the room. Presiding over it all was a prim, matronly woman whose pewter hair had been gathered into an elaborately coiffed up-do. Her burgundy-colored dress reminded me of Great-Great-Grandmother's: a slim bodice, high collar, and a dress that presumably descended to within a scant whisk of the floor. She even had a knitted ivory shawl wrapped round her shoulders. Her face was less lined than Great-Great-Grandmother's, and she appeared to be fully alive. Oh, she also lacked Great-Great-Grandmother's distinguishing wart. She sat at an imposing oaken desk that easily occupied three-quarters of the room's floor space. The desk was a stark contrast to the rest of the room, its uncluttered top occupied by a broad leather blotter, two neat piles of paper, and a large, well-worn wooden box full of small, neatly stacked cards.

She looked up as I appeared, peering over half-rimmed glasses that were secured to her neck by a thin gold chain. "May I help you, dear?" she asked, her voice absolutely neutral and devoid of interest or emotion.

"Yes," I answered hesitantly. "I'm here to be tested. *Tested,*" I amended, emphasizing the word the way Great-Great-Grand-mother had.

Her eyebrows rose. She opened her mouth to say something but was interrupted by the *ding* of a bell. She immediately swiveled her chair around to face the wall as a small wooden panel slid upward, revealing a nook of some kind. She reached in and pulled something out, and then swiveled back to me. "Lunchtime," she said with a tight smile, setting her burden down on her immense wooden desk. "Be just a tic."

The panel behind her slid closed. I looked down at her desk, and saw a large china bowl filled with broth and what appeared to be some kind of cooked shellfish. Incongruously balanced atop it all was a cheeseburger. I *loved* cheeseburgers, although I hadn't had one since Mother had been taken away. The house's pantry didn't ordinarily stock ground meat. The woman smiled at me and said, "Meal selection number two." She licked her lips, revealing teeth that were perfectly white and straight. "My favorite. Just a quick bite and I'll be with you, dear." With that, she wrapped her hands around the cheeseburger, and the shellfish immediately started moving about in their broth. As she lifted the sandwich clear, I saw that several of the shellfish had clamped their shells to the bottom bun, as if in a race to see whether they could devour the burger faster than the woman could. The other shellfish were snapping their shells and attempting to jump clear of the broth and get their own hold on the burger.

The woman took a small, tidy bite of the burger and, closing her eyes, chewed slowly. "Mmmm." Her voice at last betrayed some kind of emotion. Swallowing, she opened her eyes, replaced the burger and its attendant shellfish in the bowl, and once again leveled her gaze at me. "What's your name, dear?" she asked, her voice again flat. One hand poised over the wooden box and it's little cards.

"Daniel Scratch." Not my real surname, of course; my family's True name was so old, so infamous, and so powerful, Great-Great-Grandmother said I must never use it with outsiders. I had faith that whatever arcane mechanisms witchkind used for keeping track of each other would be fine with the alias, though.

Never taking her eyes off me, the woman nimbly flipped through the stack of cards as if her fingers had a mind of their own. She stopped suddenly on a particular card and, without breaking eye contact recited, "Mother Beatrice and father Neville." Her eyebrows rose again. "Both deceased. No guardian of record listed." *Interesting,* I thought. Not that Great-Great-Grandmother would permit herself to be *listed* as anything so mundane. "There's a fee, dear."

My own eyebrows rose, as Great-Great-Grandmother hadn't mentioned anything of the sort. Then again... I dipped my hand into my coat-pocket, and found two coins lying there. I pulled them out and held them out over the woman's desk. She presented her hand—*never place your coin anywhere but in the hand you mean to have it,* Great-Great-Grandmother always insisted—and I dropped the coins gently into her palm. Not once breaking eye contact with me, she laid the coins on her desk, letting them *clink* softly, one atop the other.

"A meal is included, of course," she said. She tapped a small button that was embedded into her desk-top. "Another number two, I should think." Within seconds, the bell dinged again, and the woman swiveled around to retrieve another burger-and-shellfish lunch from the nook behind her. She laid it gently on her desk, in front of her own meal. "Join me?" she asked, once again reaching for her cheeseburger.

Don't eat the food, Father's words echoed in my mind. "No thank you," I said as graciously as possible. I hardly needed Father's warning to avoid this particular dish.

The woman froze, her eyebrows beetling down and almost meeting in the middle of her brow. She abandoned her cheeseburger, picked up the plate that had been intended for me, and unceremoniously dumped it in a bin next to her chair. I listened carefully, but didn't ever hear it hit bottom. "The kitchen isn't pleased," she said, voice still flat and void of emotion. "You've failed their test." She leaned back a bit in her chair, folded her hands on her lap, and stared at me. "You may go."

Shopkeepers had tried to dismiss me on past errands, and I knew to hold my ground. My family's coin couldn't be accepted without obligation, Great-Great-Grandmother had taught me. "I've paid for the Test," I reminded her, once again emphasizing the last word.

She lowered one hand to her desk, covering the two coins that still sat there. She made to push them toward me, but they wouldn't budge from their position. Looking confused, she finally broke eye contact with me and looked down at her hand. She once again attempted to push the coins, and they once again remained stubbornly in place. She lifted her hand and, for the first time, looked closely at the coins. Her eyebrows climbed nearly to her hairline, and her head snapped up as she skewered me with a a sharp gaze. "I see," she said carefully, her voice no longer flat but instead tinged with a mix of curiosity and respect. "Then the Test you shall have, young Mr. Scratch."

Once again holding my gaze, she reached down and opened a desk drawer. From it, she plucked a thin piece of ash-colored wood, perhaps the size of a playing card. "Take this." She gripped it by one corner and held it out to me.

I reached for the small piece of wood, but as soon as my fingers touched it, it began to blacken and dissolve. Within moments, it had transformed into a fine dust, joining the rest of the office's ample supply. The woman had never released it and now held, pinched between her fingers, what looked like a slim glass rod, no more than two inches long. With a twitch of her fingers, the rod flipped upright, pointing toward the office's moldy ceiling. She leaned forward, extending the rod closer to me. "Blow gently across it," she instructed, her voice growing soft. "Like blowing out a candle."

I bent down slightly until my lips were just a few inches from the rod's tip, and blew gently. The rod-end immediately erupted into an inch-long hot blue flame that blew away from me and toward the woman. I pulled back instinctively, but the flame continued to burn, flickering away from me as if I were still blowing on it. Tilting her head slightly, the woman stared at it for a moment, and then dipped the flaming end of the rod into her broth. The shellfish immediately started tossing themselves furiously around, only the weight of the cheeseburger keeping them in the bowl. Within seconds, the broth itself was boiling, and within a few more seconds, the shellfish had stopped moving. *Finally cooked,* I thought to myself.

"Well." She released the end of the rod she'd been holding and stared forlornly at the sandwich. "Number two, as I said." She pushed the entire bowl off the side of her desk and into her trash-bin. Like the one meant for me, this dish seemed to fall endlessly, never striking the bottom.

Then, in what seemed like a single sudden movement, she swiveled ninety degrees to her right and stood, reaching for one of the many boxes on the office's walls. The box she pulled down was a lacquered black cube, perhaps four inches to a side, with a key-hole occupying almost the entirety of one side. She withdrew a large bronze key from her dress-pocket, inserted it into the key-hole, and twisted. With a *click,* the box's lid snapped open. Releasing the key, she withdrew a small, irregularly shaped glass medallion that was suspended on a length of green ribbon. She flicked her wrist and the box-lid snapped shut again. She replaced the box on its shelf, extracted the key, and dropped the key back into her pocket. Then she turned to me.

"Lean forward," she instructed. I did so. She draped the ribbon over my head, sliding it so that the glass medallion hung over my sternum, then stepped back and resumed her place in her chair. "I shall tell my sisters of this strange and eventful day," she said, stepping back and resuming her place in her chair.

I looked down at the medallion, and saw the green ribbon slowly turning to black before my eyes. Small threads frayed away at the edges, but once the entire ribbon was a dark, glossy black, the change seemed to stop. The medallion itself changed next, turning from a crystal-clear, irregularly shaped shard into a flat diamond shape swirled throughout with deep red.

I looked up at her, and she made a flicking motion toward me with her fingers. I felt a rushing wind, and found myself back in the alley.

* * *

I knew enough to head directly to Great-Great-Grandmother's attic when I got home—there was no way she'd send me to be Tested and then take no interest in the results. Once again, I trudged up the four flights and stood on the landing as the attic door swung open. She drifted forward out of her darkness, and I saw her eyes immediately widen. She sniffed at the air—a short, sharp inhalation first, followed by a longer, deeper draught. Never taking her eyes from me, she nodded slowly. "Finally," she whispered in her rough, grating voice.

Her hand stretched out to me, but rather than extending a finger toward my forehead, this time her bony claws clutched a thick book by one corner. She held it out to me, spine down, the book never protruding past the doorframe. It looked to be quite heavy, but her old arm didn't waver.

I stepped forward hesitantly: Great-Great-Grandmother had never handed me anything tangible before. The book was easily three inches thick, bound in sturdy covers whose cloth was faded, but not frayed. I held a hand out, palm up, extending it almost past the doorframe and into the attic—the furthest any part of me had ever ventured into her domain. She dropped the book into my hand, her mouth quirking in—a smile? Impossible. I caught it, my arm drooping slightly from its heft. It felt like a box of rocks, and I couldn't understand how Great-Great Grandmother had held it so easily.

Suddenly, the house vanished from around me.

I WAS on a small rocky prominence, surrounded by fog, as if I stood on the top of a narrow, lonely peak that was just pushing through the clouds. A fierce wind roared all around me, pulling at my coat and hair. I still held the book in one hand, its spine resting in my palm and my fingers holding it closed. It seemed almost weightless compared to just a split second earlier, and the wind seemed to flow more gently around the book, barely fluttering my sleeve. It was as if the air itself was helping to support the massive tome.

A horrendous screech from above drew my attention. My head snapped up, and I saw an immense red dragon hurtling toward me out of the sky. I made to step back, but there was nowhere to go—only the rock-tip I was perched on and, as far as I could see, bottomless fog. The dragon pulled up short not thirty yards before me and hovered in place, its wings battering the air.

It was a massive beast, dozens of times my size. The howling wind didn't seem to bother it at all as its enormous wings stroked up and down, holding it in place. Its chest was broader than four doors placed side by side, its long, sinuous neck more than double my height. Four powerful-looking legs hung easily, each ending in a wicked-looking set of claws.

Suddenly, its head reared back, its mouth opened, and it lunged forward as a stream of black fire spewed between its jaws.

I closed my eyes as the fire washed over me. I screamed, the pain immense and all-consuming. My immolation lasted for perhaps two seconds, but it felt like an eternity, searing my skin, boiling my blood, and melting my hair and clothes. When it ended, I was somehow still alive. I opened my eyes, expecting to see little more than a charred husk, but to my disbelief I was fine. My clothes were intact. *I* was intact.

I looked at the book, which had also somehow withstood the dragon's fire. My arm was beginning to shake, the book's weight slowly returning, and my weakening grip allowed the covers to fall open. The pages it revealed were covered in deeply colored illustrations of fire, surrounded by magical runes rendered in thick, black ink. I moved it a bit closer to my chest, looking for any characters I could recognize and read. Both Mother and Father had taught me some of the more elementary runes that even a child could use, like the one that would cast a dim light in the darkness, or the one that would sound a great alarm if you were in trouble. But these runes looked nothing like those: these were twisty and intertwined, runes that only an accomplished witch might understand and use.

Another roar tore my attention from the book. Still hovering before me, the dragon drew its head back again, preparing to bathe me in more black fire. Without thinking, I held my free hand in front of me, palm out as if to somehow shield myself from another round of searing pain, and clutched the book to my chest. I looked away and again clamped my eyes closed in fear.

And the fire came. But this time, though I felt the heat, it was nothing more uncomfortable than the coal stove in my own kitchen. I cracked one eye open, and saw the fire flowing around me, as if I were encased in a bubble of magic. I relaxed slightly, letting the book settle into the crook of my arm.

The wind fluttered at the book, turning the page. This new page's runes were all sharp angles and spikes, centered around an illustration that was clearly meant to be a human hand. Almost of its own accord, my free hand clenched into a fist like the one depicted in the book, my index finger extended and pointing toward the dragon. The dragon started to ease itself backwards, its mouth slowly closing, no longer threatening me with fire.

Then, with a sudden sharp *crack*, a hole appeared in the dragon's mighty chest. I blinked in surprise, and I think the dragon must have done so too, for I could clearly see the sky and clouds behind it. I looked with amazement at my own finger, which had briefly become a sharp, elongated black spike, like a lance of pure ebony. The spike was now withdrawing, turning back into the finger I'd always known. In the blink of an eye, it had stretched from my finger to impale the dragon. When I looked back up, the dragon was already falling out of the sky, its wings twisting around it as it plunged into the clouds and vanished.

And I was back on the attic landing. Great-Great-Grandmother's mouth twitched approvingly, withdrawing into her darkness and closing the attic door before me without another word.

A Visitor

THE SUN HAD JUST TIPPED past noon, the afternoon light trying gamely to push its way through the house's dusty windows, when I made it back downstairs. Abbygail was in the kitchen with three others of her kind, happily scrubbing the kitchen's sturdy tile floor for what must have been the fourth time that month. Her eyes opened wide when she caught sight of me, and without a word, she waved one arm, directing me to the small nook-table, where she'd already set out a cold sandwich and a mug of warm tea. I nodded acknowledgement, and felt all four of the brownies' eyes on me as I sat down, placing Great-Great-Grandmother's book carefully on the table next to my sandwich.

It wasn't a cheeseburger, but at least there were no shellfish.

I ate slowly, the morning's odd events rolling around in my mind. Neither Mother nor Father had, in my short memory, ever worn a medallion like the one I'd been given. Great-Great-Grandmother didn't wear one, either—at least, not that I had ever been able to see. Chewing a mouthful of thinly sliced bread and savory, salty ham, I again looked down at the medallion, lifting it away from my chest to get a better view. The whorls of deep red seemed to move and flow as it caught the weary sunlight that managed to push through the kitchen windows. Letting it go, I hooked my fingers under the now-black ribbon and tried to pull it off over my head.

It didn't budge. It's not so much that it resisted me, in the way my coins had resisted the testing-woman's attempts to push them back. It was more as if my fingers simply... *slid* off the ribbon every time I tried to lift it. I appeared to be stuck with it, and found myself wondering if it would be damaged when I took my next bath. Doubtful. Father had often spoken of Artifacts—had, in fact, been obsessed with them—and how unnaturally durable they could be. This medallion was clearly an Artifact, or at least similar to one.

I wondered what it did.

I noticed that all but Abbygail had quietly left the kitchen, and as I looked up, she gave me an odd stare. I saw her tiny, silvery eyes briefly fall to the medallion before she shook her head and scurried out of the room.

I resolved to spend some time searching through the family's books that afternoon for an answer. This time, I would ignore the adventures that I normally preferred, and instead try to find one of Father's books on Artifacts. Perhaps something in one of those volumes could tell me what the medallion was, or even what it did. I sat up a little straighter, and at a little faster in anticipation. I loved little more than browsing through books, and it promised to be a satisfying afternoon.

My reverie—and my lunch—was interrupted by the door-bell. It was so loud and sudden that I almost jumped out of my skin. Even the brownies were startled—the bell hadn't been rung since my parents had died, and even when they'd been alive, visitors to our remote home were rare. Should I even answer the door? I looked at Abbygail for guidance, but she simply shrugged and went back to her floor-scrubbing.

I waited another moment, and the bell rang again. There were no sounds from the attic, though. I suspected—or at least hoped—that Great-Great-Grandmother would be giving some kind of indication if I *wasn't* to open the door. I took her silence as assent, stood up from the table, and moved to the front foyer.

Our house had been built for a large family of witchkind, back when witchkind *had* large families. It had also been built to entertain and impress, as befitted what was once one of witchkind's wealthiest families in this part of the world. Ironically, as far as I knew our family had always been somewhat small, and I'd never known my parents to entertain at all.

A dozen ample bedrooms were spread across the second floor, and between the smaller rooms in basement and on the third floor, easily a score servants could have been accommodated. The kitchen occupied more than half of the back of the house, leading to narrow corridors that bracketed a formal dining room capable of seating a dozen or more. The dining room opened to a larger hallway leading to the drawing room and study, each stationed in one of the ground floor's opposing wings. In front of them was the main foyer, with its coat-racks and hat-stands, curio cabinets and occasional tables, and the grand, double doors that led to the front porch.

Though the doors' heavy leaded glass, I could see the shadow of a single figure but could make out no details. I glanced to the side of the doors, where the security runes had been etched into the richly colored wood of the door-frame. A single stroke of those runes, Mother had told me, would seal the house and summon help. Where that help would come from *these* days was hard to imagine, but the runes' presence offered me some comfort.

I opened the left door. "Hello?"

That the man on the porch was witchkind went without saying: no human would have seen anything but an empty field on our property, and even if they'd been of a mind to wander in it, the old magic of the land would have gently guided them back to the road, not to my doorstep. He was in almost all other ways utterly unremarkable: his face was lean, but not too thin; his clothes were plain, like mine, and of neither too good, nor too poor, a quality. His black leather briefcase was, to all appearances, perfectly ordinary. He was the type of man you could pass on the street without acknowledging and almost immediately forget you had even seen.

"Good day," he said, his voice neither high nor low but somewhere firmly in between. "I am Alistair Nash. I am a solicitor-witch, and I have a letter for you. I presume you are Daniel Scratch, son of Beatrice and Neville? Grandson to Constance?"

I nodded. In thirteen years, I had never heard my grandmother's given name spoken aloud, although I knew it from the family tree, written in a thin ledger that sat on a table in the study. Simply hearing the name made me nervous. Grandmother had been almost as intimidating as Great-Great-Grandmother.

"Excellent," he said, offering a watery smile. Then he frowned, and swallowed heavily. "And, ah, I see you've been Tested. Very... very prompt." I realized he was staring at the medallion around my neck. He reached into his jacket-pocket, withdrawing a cream-colored envelope that he then handed to me. "You'll, ah... you'll want to read this." He seemed enraptured by the medallion. I hesitated for a moment, and then reached to accept the envelope. It was very high quality, made from heavy linen paper. The front had my name engraved in elegant script; on the back, its flap was sealed shut with a thick wax seal. I peered at the seal more closely. It contained a single rune that I couldn't identify. "I should warn you," he said sternly, drawing my attention back to him, "that if you are not the Daniel I have described, you would do well not to break that seal." He lifted his eyes slightly to meet mine for a moment, before flicking them back down at the medallion.

I looked back at the envelope. Placing a thumb on either side of the seal, I gently bent it until, without fanfare, it cracked. I opened the envelope's flap, and withdrew the single sheet of heavy, pure-white linen paper that was neatly folded inside. Unfolding it, I read the gently flowing script:

Daniel,

I am sure this will come as a great surprise to you, and at a terrible time, for our solicitor has been instructed to deliver this only upon our deaths. This means that we have passed before we could see you grow into a young adult, and for that we are deeply sorry.

Mr. Nash, or another member of his firm, has been given instructions and funds regarding your education and introduction to the broad society of witchkind. They will ensure that you are able to take up a trade that suits you, and grow into the wonderful man we know you will become.

With all of our love,

Mother and Father

I looked up at Mr. Nash, the question obvious in my eyes.

"Yes, well." He seemed somewhat nervous, pulling slightly at his collar. "It seems that the... unusual circumstances around your parents' passings caused us to, um... lose track of you, so to speak."

"For several years."

"It seems, yes," he admitted. "You sort of just popped back onto the radar today. The Test, I presume," he said, nodding his head toward my medallion. "Once we knew where to find you, I set out immediately to deliver this. They just ah... they didn't mention. You know." He tilted his head at my chest again.

"What does it mean?" I asked, looking back at the short note.

"The... what does what mean?" he asked nervously. I rustled the letter. "Ah. Of course. My firm was retained to ensure you were given a proper education. We were to act as your legal guardians while you completed your education, and ensure you are able to move successfully into a trade. I, ah..." he paused, and looked up at the house. "Have you lived here all alone, all this time?"

"There are brownies," I said, "and a kobold will drop in now and again. Also... Great-Great Grandmother is in the attic." I'd never been *told* not to discuss her presence, but I didn't want to say too much either.

"Great-Great..." he started, and trailed off. "Powers that be," he muttered. "Well. Ah, if I might come in, we could discuss our next steps?" His voice regained a measure of confidence. "That," he added, lifting one hand to point at the medallion, "will necessitate a somewhat... hmm, less usual approach."

"Oh?"

"That ridiculous woman told you nothing, I assume? When you were Tested?"

I shook my head.

"Public servants." The disdain in his voice couldn't have been clearer. "Well, nothing for it, and I suppose on the bright side, I'll be able to give you all the information you need. *Correctly.*" He gestured inside. "May I?"

I looked back at the letter. The front of the house faced due west, and the sun was just now cresting toward the horizon. As I looked at the page, the light caught it at a bit of an angle, and I saw an odd discoloration on the page, just below Father and Mother's signature. I peered more closely, tilting the page a bit, until I saw what had caught my eye: there was an impression of sorts in the paper. Not deep enough to be called an embossing, but definitely a deliberate marring of the otherwise-perfect surface. It was a single rune: the rune to bring a dim light into a dark place.

Yesssss, the house seemed to whisper, the cloying scent of butterscotch briefly wrapping around my nostrils.

I looked up at Mr. Nash. "Yes, please. Come in." I stood aside to let him enter.

"Ah, thank you," Mr. Nash said as Abbygail handed him a steaming cup of tea. His eyebrows immediately flew up, and he quickly stared at me and added, "–Daniel, for your hospitality." He offered a weak smile. I saw Abbygail roll her eyes as she stalked away; the prohibition on thanking brownies didn't apply to houseguests, but the lawyer must not have known that. He blew on his tea to cool it, and continued, "Do you understand how witchkind are educated, Daniel?"

I shook my head.

He leaned back in the rickety old chair—I'd led him to the kitchen out of habit, as I still couldn't picture myself in the cavernous, dimly lit dining room no matter the circumstances —and sighed. "Most of witchkind, and I include myself in this, receive our education in one of three Great Schools spread across the world. Your parents, for example, attended Disemstoke's, just a few villages from here. I believe your grandparents did as well." They had: I'd seen Great-Great-Grandmother's diploma hanging on the wall in what had once been her workshop, out on the back of the property. "Your parents assumed you would as well, and I have instructions to enroll you, should your Test have directed you there. But that," he said slowly, again pointing to the medallion around my neck, "changes things."

"Changes things how?"

"Our schools are intended to teach your average run-of-the-mill student. All of us have approximately the same abilities, and the same level of power, and so even though we all choose our own specialties, schooling starts the same for us all. And witchkind's schools presume a basic level of education, either from a private preparatory school, through home schooling, or something else. I assume you haven't had much education in the last few years?"

I shook my head again.

He heaved another sigh. "So you'd be woefully underprepared for Disemstoke's, even if it wasn't for the medallion."

I fingered the chunk of warm glass, suspended from its inky ribbon. "But I do have the medallion," I said softly. And I still didn't know what it meant.

"You do," Mr. Nash said heavily. "And so that will necessitate a different approach."

I waited for a moment to see if he'd continue, but he simply stared at me. "Different how?" I finally asked.

He sipped his tea before he answered. "The medallion indicates that you are of a different order of witchkind, Daniel. Above ordinary individuals like myself as much as I am, in terms of power and ability, above a human. Disemstoke's wouldn't know what to do with you, and frankly you'd be a danger to your teachers and to your fellow students. Witchkind's schools are forbidden from enrolling students who wear a medallion."

"I can't take it off."

"No, you can't. You're to be apprenticed to a Master, another more experienced practitioner, for personal education. When your Master deems you ready, he or she will remove the medallion."

"So I'll still be educated?"

"Well." He paused. "I mean, you have to be educated, of course. The problem is... well." He took a moment to gather himself. "If ordinary witchkind consists of generalists who choose to focus in a particular magical topic, those who receive medallions are born with a specialization, so to speak." I found myself growing nervous. I also got the distinct impression he wasn't telling me everything.

"They are *not* generalists," he continued. They are born into one of five Axes of Power, and the medallion bestowed at their Testing identifies which Axis. Once a medallion is laid upon a child, all of witchkind are bound to deliver them to a Master of the corresponding Axis. Unless they're a public servant, apparently," he added with a mutter. "And so that is what I must do. That is what I *will* do," he finished with a nod. He seemed to be trying to convince himself. "We should leave *now*," he added.

"Now... right now?" I stammered.

"Yes. Now that you are of age, your powers are at risk of manifesting without control. It is essential we—I—deliver you to a Master who can protect us—I mean, you—and teach you." He paused. "*Essential.*" I noticed beads of sweat beginning to form on his forehead. He seemed just as agitated as I was becoming.

I clamped my jaw shut. "Excuse me," I said between my

teeth, trying to remember my manners. I left the kitchen, dashing up the four flights to Great-Great-Grandmother's attic. This time, I didn't wait quietly on the landing as her door swung open: I stepped forward and rapped sharply on the door. "Grandmother!" I called loudly. "Grandmother, I need to speak with you! There's a man–"

The door swung open sharply, catching me off-guard and almost sending me tripped backwards into the stairs. Great-Great-Grandmother was there, her wrinkled skin tight around her eyes and mouth. "Foretold," she croaked, shaking her head ever so softly. "Predestined." Her eyes widened slightly, and her withered breast expanded as she inhaled deeply and intoned:

Sky and Earth, Flame and Sea
Cast adrift, their center lost
Until a Sixth might come to be
To join them all, or pay the cost

This complete, her eyes seemed to sink further into her ancient skull, and her shoulders drooped. "Go," she whispered roughly. "Go and never return." She stepped back into her never-ending darkness, muttering softly. The attic door swung shut. A fog seemed to settle over my mind. I needed to go with Mr. Nash, I realized, and I needed to go immediately. She'd placed a directive on me, her magic pushing away my trepidation. Honestly, I'm glad she did it. I suspect I would have dithered for as long as possible rather than leaving the only home I'd ever known.

I turned and made my way down the stairs in a magically powered daze. I stopped briefly on the third floor and whispered, "Goodbye, Father." I listened for a moment, but didn't hear any of the scratching-in-the-wall that presaged his attention. I sighed and continued my descent.

I stepped back into the kitchen, and saw that Mr. Nash had

risen to his feet. Next to him stood Abbygail, a quizzical look on her little face.

"Are you all right?" Mr. Nash asked. "You look a bit ashen, my boy."

I nodded, my head still spinning. "Abbygail," I said, "would you please pack a case for me? I'll be gone for... for some time. I..." I stopped and swallowed heavily. "I may not be coming back."

She gave me a sad smile, a tear rolling down her face. She made a gesture, and two other brownies—both ones that had been with me for some time, although they'd never shared their names—dragged a satchel in from the opposite hallway. "We knew you'd be leaving us some day, Master Daniel," she said softly, her small voice filled with emotion.

"Yes." This all felt... perfunctory. Normal, even. Why did this seem normal? Some small part of my mind wanted to object, but then I'd been a child living in a massive house by myself for three years. What *was* normal? I tugged the satchel open and slid Great-Great-Grandmother's book into it. Whatever magic she'd cast over me wasn't letting me leave the book behind. Mr. Nash cocked his head slightly at the book but said nothing as I re-cinched the bag shut. "Goodbye, Abbygail."

She looked deep into my eyes then, and her voice took on a heavy new layer of meaning. "It will be lonely here without you."

I blinked. Of course. I'd been so caught up in my own bewildering day that I hadn't even thought about it. If I left, she and the other brownies would be here with nothing but Great-Great-Grandmother's spirit to care for—and spirits didn't require the kind of care a brownie could offer. That wasn't fair. I looked into the others' dark, brown eyes, and then looked back to Abbygail. "Abbygail," I said firmly, "I thank you, and your friends, for your service."

She gave me another small smile, and clasped her hands in front of her. A wisp of wind rolled through the kitchen, and they were gone.

"That was well done, Daniel," Mr. Nash offered quietly. "Well done indeed." He motioned toward the kitchen exit. "Shall we?"

Silently, I shouldered the satchel and led the way to the front door. I opened it, allowing Mr. Nash to step through, and then joined him on the porch. I pulled the door shut behind me. We descended the short flight of stone stairs to the front path, where I stopped and turned to look back. I had never known a home other than this one, which had been in my family for generations. It seemed a shame to leave it here on its own, with nobody to care for it. As I looked at it, the house itself seemed to exhale softly, a breeze picking up a few dry leaves from the ground and flipping them 'round and 'round in the air. I tilted my head to the side for a moment, and then, very softly, said, "And thank you for your service as well."

"Daniel?" Mr. Nash called.

I looked over my shoulder and saw that he'd made it to the front gate. I followed him through it and turned to close the gate behind me— more out of habit, I admit, than any concern about trespassers. As I did so, another soft gust of wind rolled around me. I looked up at the house.

The house was gone. My hand, which had been resting on the gate, was now hovering over empty air.

The Tower of Endings

BEFORE FATHER HAD DIED, and before Mother lost her mind and was taken from me, they'd had occasion to take me out of the house a handful of times. None of those trips were, in retrospect, especially momentous, although for a young boy they'd been grand events. We'd taken a picnic in a country field, or a short trip into the village, or off to see a distant relative in their home. What stood out to me on all of those trips is how quickly the traveling itself passed. Although as a powerless child I'd always taken the hour-long walk into the nearby village, adults of witchkind traveled much more efficiently.

Mr. Nash was no exception. He took my hand in a somewhat firmer grip than I thought would have been necessary, and we stepped along the same dirt lane I'd walked before. But now each of our steps seemed to carry us leagues, the scenery blurring gently as we rushed along. A handful of steps took us to the village, and a few more took us clear to the coast—a journey I knew would have taken me many days. I remember thinking how powerful a magic it was, although of course that was simply because, at the time, I knew so little of what ordinary witchkind could do with such little effort.

At one point I clearly remember "walking" over the sea, Mr. Nash never once slowing or faltering in his miles-eating strides. When we came to a halt, it was sudden enough to take my breath away.

He'd brought me to a small, rocky islet, well off the coast. Far enough away, in fact, that I couldn't see anything on the horizon but the choppy gray sea. The water crashed indifferently into the islet's rocky shore, *hissing* down the sides of boulders that were black with age. The islet itself was little more than a hard mound rounding itself out of the water. There were no trees, and no life at all that I could see. Instead, the entire landscape seemed to consist solely of tall, sharp, jagged spires of rock that jutted up from the ground and thrust angrily toward the islet's one feature: a soaring, dark Tower positioned precisely at the land's tablet rise, in the dead middle of the isle. I thought it odd that the spires all tilted *toward* the Tower, as if they were meant to keep something *in* it, rather than keeping enemies *out.* Those spires even continued out into the sea, pushing out of the ocean and toward the Tower like bony, grasping fingers.

Mr. Nash and I stood at the foot of a smooth earthen path that started at the shore and gently wound its way through the crags to the base of the Tower. From where we stood, the Tower appeared to have been carved directly from a column of native rock: its base blended easily into the ground, and at this distance I couldn't make out the individual blocks of stone that *must* have formed the structure.

The Tower was capped by two small turrets. About halfway down from their caps, a third, somewhat larger turret was affixed to the side of the Tower, as if it had grown up and latched on like some parasitic fungus on the bark of a tree.

There were a few small windows that I could see, although none of them displayed any sign of light or life.

"This is where my Master lives? This is where I'm to be apprenticed?"

"I'm so sorry, Daniel," Mr. Nash said quietly. "But the Law is the Law, and... well. I'm sorry." I turned to ask him a question, but with a small gust of wind, he'd stepped off and away.

I was alone.

* * *

You may think it odd that I was taking all the day's events with such aplomb. Obviously, looking back over such a span as I am now robs some of the urgency and emotion from that day. I also strongly suspect that Great-Great-Grandmother had done something to soften and ease my mind. Then too, so much had already happened to me so young: my Father's death, my Mother's incarceration, discovering Great-Great-Grandmother in her attic—it is possible that, even at such a young age, I simply wasn't easily shaken.

Being left alone on a strange, forbidding island was certainly stretching things a bit, though. But at that point, there seemed little to do other than walk the path to the Tower. Mr. Nash had mentioned a Master; surely this was what he'd meant. I had expected an introduction of sorts, but perhaps this was how these things were done. The fog around my mind had started to fade at that point, and I *was* growing a bit concerned about basic necessities like food and shelter. So I hoisted my satchel and began trudging toward the Tower.

I kept my eyes on the path for a while. Although it was smooth and firm, the islet had an inexplicable feeling of *age* about it, and I didn't want to step into a pot-hole or something and turn an ankle. After several minutes though, I looked up to gauge my progress. I was startled. The Tower didn't seem much closer than when I'd stepped off the shore. I looked back over my shoulder, and saw that I'd only taken a few steps. Odd. I returned my gaze to the Tower, and took another step. I *felt* my legs moving under me. I *felt* my feet press against the ground and push me forward. Yet the rocky spikes around me seem to *slide*, leaving me in exactly the same place.

I frowned. I might not have had the formal education a witchkind school would expect, but I'd spent years in the house with little to do except read. I'd picked up a *few* things. Father had maintained an excellent library in his study, and although I tended to ignore the more technical books on Craft, I'd read plenty of the adventures and fictions I'd found. This seemed like a classical test of some kind, something that I, as a presumptive apprentice, would need to solve.

I set my jaw, and stepped forward more firmly, keeping the Tower firmly in my sight and *willing* it to grow closer. I felt a kind of liquid resistance pushing against me, as if the air had grown thick. My medallion suddenly flashed hot against my chest, and I smelled a pungent, burning, sulfurous stench. It cleared as quickly as it had come, though, and I'd taken an *actual* step forward.

Encouraged, I tried it again. This time, the smell and flash of heat were accompanied by a pop of light, momentarily blinding me. When my vision cleared, I'd not take a step—I'd taken *all* of the steps. I was a nose-length away from the tower's only door, a sturdy-looking wooden slab banded and bound in black iron straps. I blinked, took a step back, and—having nothing to lose—reached out to knock on the door.

My small knuckles made a quiet tapping noise, no more. But a moment later, they seemed to echo inside the Tower. The echo repeated and grew, until it was the sound of a battering ram against an iron door, clanging and pounding. I dropped my satchel, and made to cover my ears with my hands, when the racket abruptly ended. I slowly lowered my hands, stooping over slightly to reclaim my satchel, and the door swung open.

The inside was dark, the only light that which streamed hesitatingly through the open door. Whatever room was past that door was empty of any furniture I could see, the walls barren stone, the floor devoid of carpet or ornamentation. It appeared, from my limited vantage, to be completely empty. It felt both sinister and... somehow, welcoming. A place where few belonged, except...

Except that I was one of those few.

I stepped inside, and it swung shut behind me.

* * *

It was pitch-black inside, so dark I couldn't even see the hand that I raised in front of my face. I stood quietly for a moment, listening carefully, but heard nothing—even the noise of the sea-winds was completely cut off.

"Lengvas," I intoned, naming the rune Mother had taught me, picturing the rune in my mind as she'd told me to do, the same rune that had been on the letter Mr. Nash had given me. A soft yellow glow appeared around me. I could now see the stone floor I stood upon—eerily smooth and seamless—but little else. Outside the small circle of light I'd cast, there was still nothing but impenetrable darkness.

I stepped forward, and my circle of light followed me. I could, I supposed, walk forward until I found a wall, or a door, or even a chair or something. Perhaps—

"Ho," a voice said. It was a woman's voice, deep and husky. It didn't so much *echo* as it did *flow* around me. That single syllable seemed to have substance of some kind, and I turned quickly to one side, hoping to catch sight of the speaker. "What have we," the voice said, seemingly from behind me, causing me to quickly pivot toward it. "a boy-child with a toy rune to bring–" the voice continued, once again from behind me. I whirled again just as the voice cut off.

"Ah," it purred. I could almost feel the speaker's lips brushing against one ear, and I twitched away from it. "I wondered if I'd be the one," it said quietly in my other ear. This time I held my ground. "Here I'd thought the defenses were finally failing." It was farther away this time, perhaps a handful of steps, and it no longer seemed to be moving around me. "But you're meant to be here, aren't you, boy?"

"I was brought here." My voice sounded flat to me, without the slightest trace of echo. "I was Tested this morning."

"And disposed of as quickly as possible," the voice said, now seeming to carry a note of humor. "Must have given your Tester a right start. Did they feed you?"

As if on cue, my stomach growled. "Father said not to eat the food."

A sense of wry approval wafted over me. "What's your name, boy?" the voice asked, its tone kinder now.

"Daniel Scratch."

There was a long moment of silence, and I could feel the voice's owner regarding me carefully. "That's a lie," it said at last. "Though I begin to suspect why you'd tell it. I'll ask once more, boy: *What is your name?*"

I swallowed. I'd been cautioned for as long as I remembered that our name was not to be said aloud. But this was clearly not a situation my parents, or even Great-Great-Grandmother, had foreseen. Well, perhaps Great-Great-Grandmother had. I swallowed again, and inhaled deeply. "Daniel Teisejas," I whispered, still afraid to give my full voice to my true name. "Daniel Drake Teisejas."

My dim little circle of light faded then, but a moment later the entire room was bathed in light. I blinked furiously at the abrupt change, and as my watery eyes cleared, I saw that I was in a round ante-room of sorts, perhaps thirty feet across. A door—the one I'd entered through, I thought from its size—was to my left, and another, smaller door stood exactly opposite it on the far wall. Torches were set into the wall every few feet, blazing with steady blue-orange flames. And *she* was standing directly in front of me.

Her long, straight, gray-and-black hair was gathered into a loose tail, and draped forward over one shoulder. I could not have put an age to her: her face was weathered and hard, but her ebony-colored skin had no wrinkles save for a fine set of webs around her brown eyes. She wore a simple shirt and trousers made of gray homespun, the trousers disappearing into sturdy black boots. Over it all, she wore a heavy cloak of the deepest red. In fact, it reminded me of the red swirls in my medallion. My left hand dropped my satchel on the stone floor as my right hand absently touched the medallion.

She crossed her arms in front of herself. "You'll do well to forget that name for a time," she said. "Here we shall simply call you Daniel. It has been an age and more since anyone needed to name *me*, but for now I think 'Kirmin' will do." She paused and looked me over for a moment.

"An *age*," she repeated softly, "but here we are now. Welcome to the Tower of Endings, Daniel."

* * *

"That contains clothes?" Kirmin asked, pointing at my satchel.

"And my book."

"Book?" She tilted her head curiously. "Show me."

I bent over, tugged the satchel open, and withdrew the immense book Great-Great-Grandmother had given me. Standing, I saw her eyes grow wide. She took a step forward, her arms uncrossing. "Sacred vows," she whispered. She looked like she was ready to rush over to me, but she pulled herself up short and pointed at the book. "That is impossible. How do you have it?"

I glanced down at the book, taking in its sturdy cover. "Grandmother gave it to me."

"Your grandmother?" she echoed.

"Technically my great-great grandmother," I clarified. "She–"

"Don't say anything more," Kirmin interrupted quickly. "That– well. At least it's *here*, where it can do no harm and not *be* harmed." She crossed her arms again, one finger tapping the opposite elbow. "Leave the satchel," she said at last. "You won't need anything in it. The Book, though." She paused, considering. "Put it in your coat-pocket."

I blinked. The book would barely be covered if I wrapped my entire coat around it. "I don't think–"

"I know," she interrupted again. "That's why you're here. So *don't* think. Just *do*. Put the Book in your pocket."

I stared at her, uncomprehending.

"*Now!*" she ordered, lunging toward me and reaching for me with both arms.

I backpedaled, almost falling to the ground, then tucked one corner of the massive book into my coat-pocket and pushed. If this crazy woman wanted me to rip my pocket open, so be it. But all at once, my hands were free of the book's weight. I looked down, and saw a tiny, slim version of the book nestled easily in my coat pocket. My coat hung crookedly on my shoulders though, the book's full weight was dragging down at one side despite its diminutive size.

"Good," she said, stepping back and re-crossing her arms. "It should be happy there until we're ready for it. Don't," she continued, looking intently at me, "even think about removing it until I've given you leave, do you understand?"

I nodded rapidly. "What is it?"

"It's a book, obviously."

"Well yes, but–"

"But why am I so agitated about it?" I nodded. "It's *our* Book. Or supposed to be. It should have been here in the Tower, but it was lost. Ages ago." She frowned. "Or taken. I can't remember, and that alone makes me suspicious. But it's meant to hold our lore, our magic. Everything we've learned about the Axis. Not that we should need a book to hold our memories." She shook her head a bit, as if to clear it. "But it's here now, and you'll keep it in that pocket until I say otherwise."

"I understand."

"Good. Now, do you know why you're here?"

My mouth gaped open for a moment, and I must have looked like a dead fish. The question seemed a bit silly, given all that had happened today. "I was Tested, and given this medallion." I reached up to finger the piece of glass at my chest.

"Mmm, yes, but that's not the entire story. Technically, you were Chosen. The Test merely identifies the Choice. And the Sixth Axis rarely Chooses without a good reason."

"Like... what?"

"Usually a great need. Something it feels is urgent. And you showing up with that book... well. Suffice to say it's probably a *very* great need, although the Axis's sense of urgency isn't always the same as ours."

"What do you mean?" This woman was becoming more confusing by the moment.

"The Axes are eternal. For them, 'urgent' could be something on the order of millennia. Or it could be something you need to take care of tomorrow. It's hard to tell."

"What was I Chosen for, then?"

She chuckled, and shook her head at my naïveté. "*That* will take some time to find out. But if it's something you need to do tomorrow, it won't get done. You'll be here for years, learning your way with the Axis and taking your place as its adherent in the world."

"Years?"

"You're thirteen, right?"

"Yes."

"Then yes, years. You'd have spent at least five at any of the Great Schools, and you should expect to spend just as long here. Hopefully the Axis took that into account when it Chose you."

"Five years?"

"You're catching on."

My stomach growled.

She laughed, a rolling, happy sound. "We can probably start by getting you something to eat, if you're hungry."

My stomach growled again in agreement.

"Kitchen usually catches on fast." Turning, she made her way to the smaller interior door. I followed warily.

"Everything else will take a few hours," she added, although I had no idea what she was talking about. "Fresh clothes will likely have to wait until morning, as the driežai won't all venture back until nightfall. Should be a pallet or something somewhere that's not too rotted." She seemed to be talking more to herself than to me now. "No rodents or insects at least, more's the praise for that. Come, boy!" she called, her voice growing louder as she opened the door and stepped through. "Let's get you fed and see what new age is upon us."

I followed her through the door.

* * *

She led me down a flight of spiraling stone stairs, and we emerged into a small, cheerfully lit kitchen. A massive hearth occupied most of one wall, a small fire banked to one side. A heavy wooden table took up much of the middle of the room. On one end of that table sat a steaming bowl of stew. A single chair was pushed under the table. At Kirmin's gesture, I pulled the chair out and sat down.

The stew smelled fantastic. Abbygail had often made a rich, herb-scented meal that was one of my favorites, and this smelled almost exactly like it. My mouth began watering in anticipation, and my stomach gave a low growl of demand. "Do you have brownies, too?" I asked.

"No, the Tower... well, I guess you could say that brownies wouldn't feel very welcome here. It takes care of itself. You'll see. Tuck in." She perched on the side of the table and twisted to look at me. "You're going to be full of questions as we always are, and so I'll be doing the answers I suppose."

A simple wooden spoon was already in the bowl, and so I scooped out a first bite. It was wonderful, some kind of well-cooked game in a thick brown broth, accompanied by chunks of orange and white root vegetables.

"So. How much do you know?" Kirmin asked as I ate.

I swallowed before answering. "I'm to be apprenticed to a Master. That's what Mr. Nash told me. He brought me here."

"And your medallion?"

"It means I'm not normal witchkind."

Normal. There was scorn in her voice. "Shortsighted cowards, that's 'normal' witchkind. You're no different from any of them, save that you've been granted extra gifts by the universe. Gifts or burdens, you decide. That's why they push us away, make us live apart, just as they all keep their distance from humans. Afraid the humans will burn 'em at the stake, afraid we'll subjugate them or something. So much fear," she finished, shaking her head sadly. "Let me tell you a story," she offered.

* * *

When the world was young, *she began,* its energies flowed randomly, without order. The world was still figuring out what it was, you see, and what it wanted to be. Eventually, some of those energies were attached to some of the animals of the world. They grew used to each other, over the centuries. Those animals learned how to use those energies, and the energies learned how those animals could keep them both fresh and alive. That was the beginning of witchkind.

Some of the world's other animals were far more numerous but also far less interested in the energies around them. Instead, they spent their time breeding more of themselves, chasing down other animals to eat, and planting things in the ground. They lived harder, shorter lives, but they were *much* better at the breeding part, so they slowly spread to cover most of the world. Those were the humans.

Humans and witchkind lived side by side in those days. The gentler energies that witchkind had become companions with could heal a broken leg, bring a gentle rain to a field of crops, or even predict when the weather was about to turn bitter and cold. Witchkind and humans protected each other. They provided for each other.

But some of the world's greatest energies never did settle down. They remained wild, untamed. They weren't interested in lighting a home, or heating a meal, or diverting a storm. They wanted to fly, to dive through the seas, and to crunch their way through the earth. They flitted around the companion-energies of witchkind but never tied themselves to them. There were six of those wilder energies, back then. Four of them were behind the mighty forces of nature, bringing earthquakes, volcanos, the great storms, and the tsunamis of the sea. A fifth was one of the oldest of them, carrying the spark of life itself, but that one had always been elusive, as beginnings often are. That one interacted constantly with humans, and to a lesser degree with witchkind, but only on its own terms. The sixth great energy was its opposite, and just as old: an energy of endings and completions. Death, some would come to call it.

Witchkind could influence those greater energies to some degree or another but could never tame them. And all the world suffered for it, as those wild energies went on random rampages. Even the power of life and creation was a mystery to witchkind, sometimes generous with its gifts, and other times denying them.

At last, one of the greatest of witchkind convinced his brethren to do something about it. They would pool their own smaller energies, he said, and bring the greater, wild energies to heel. They would capture them, imprison them in physical form, and gain command over them. His compatriots agreed, and they created the most powerful magics ever seen before or since: the *suvienijimas*.

It took more than a decade of preparation, and more than half of witchkind died in the attempt, sacrificing their lives to bind those greater, wilder energies to their will. Sadly, almost half of the humans also died in the backlash, forever making them enemies of witchkind. In a way, the *suvienijimas* became the *triuškinantis*, a word that means shattering or sundering. From that time, humans have ever been the enemies of witchkind, seeking to destroy us for daring to tamper with the world's energies. Seeking revenge for our hubris.

But the *suvienijimas* succeeded, after a fashion. The great energies were drawn into physical forms, at least. But not all of witchkind would be able to command them, for the wily, wild energies remained too powerful. And so six of witchkind's greatest, the six who stood at the center of the great working, took some of the wild power into themselves. They bound their minds and sacrificed their bodies, becoming the *šešios ašys,* the Six Axes: One Axis for each of the world's great powers.

By merging their minds and bodies with the greater energies, those six ensured that *some* of witchkind would be able to control the wild powers of the world. Every one of witchkind now carries the *potential* to reach out to their spiritual counterparts. Seeds, if you will, with the promise of communing with them. Directing them. Perhaps not *controlling* them, but influencing them more than witchkind ever could.

But those six seeds, all of that hope and promise, were scattered throughout witchkind, with no way to track where they landed. And so witchkind now Tests its children. Tests them, to see if any of those seeds has taken root, through time and space, and sprouted. In any generation, at least *one* of witchkind would bond with each of the world's greatest magics. And the Tests do more: they help determine which of the Great Schools any child of witchkind might be destined for. But make no mistake: the Tests were first made to find *us.*

The First Axis holds the power of the Sea. It was bound by Jura Sea-Father, forced into the body of the great kraken that roam the deeps. Its shape is the teardrop, its color the green of the deepest oceans.

The Second Axis bonds the power of Flame. It was captured by Liepsna Flame-Mother and forced into the form of the great dragons. Its shape is the triangle, representing flame, and its color the bright orange of fire.

The Third Axis captured the power of Earth. It was brought to heel by Zeme Rock-Brother, embodied as the great

Wyrms who can survive the hottest magma. Its shape is a square, and its color the deep gray of bedrock.

The Fourth Axis harnessed the power of the Sky. It was tamed by Vejas Wind-Sister and given physical form as the Wraith. Its shape is the circle, its color the brightest blue.

Gyvenima Life-Bringer sought to tame the power of Creation and Beginnings, but she failed. That great power, white and hot, was older and more wily than the others, and it refused to be captured. Instead, it dispersed itself through every living creature on the world. It gave up its existence as a greater power, and became millions of small, tiny lights within each of us. To be truthful, it had already left much of its power in us, and some suspect that it was merely bowing to the inevitable. So the Fifth Axis never came to be.

Galas End-Watcher *did* manage to capture the great, wild power of Endings and Completion. But that great, wild power refused to be completely constrained. In the end, Galas bound it only to his own spirit, giving the power more free reign to act in the world as it saw fit. It was connected, but not harnessed. Bound, but not conquered. His sacrifice ensured that witchkind could still direct that power, and he gave the Sixth Axis its shape and color: the diamond shot through with deep red. Unlike its brethren, the Sixth Axis scattered its seeds further, and wider. Many a generation has come and gone with no-one bearing its seed, no-one able to commune with it or direct it. In that way, the world's last great power remained largely wild and free. Humans and witchkind alike came to fear it, and to distrust it. And when its seed does take root, whether by whim or accident, those of witchkind who bear it also bear that fear and distrust.

* * *

"And that is why," Kirmin said, "we of the Sixth Axis have always been bound to this islet. Kept and caged, in the belief that doing so will also keep and cage Death itself, and prevent it from running amok."

I blinked. "So... I'm trapped here?" I asked. I'd recognized the reference to the medallion I wore, and I knew I must be one of the ones who'd somehow wound up with some kind of vague connection to Death.

"Oh, of course not," she said with a small laugh. "Not in the long term, at least. Not any more than the idea of death itself can be bound into a single place. No, the old stories get a lot of it wrong, and people, being people, tend to believe them. They thought... well, they thought that by trapping *us* here, they'd trap death as well, somehow. Or Endings. But no, you're only trapped here until... until you complete your training and decide you don't *want* to be trapped here anymore."

"So... I'll be able to leave eventually?" I ventured.

"Of course. The isle can only hold those who haven't reach their End, yet."

"My End?" I asked. I didn't quite understand the significance, back then.

"All things End, you know. Seasons. Meals. Arguments. Wars. Lives. The Sixth Axis is the power of Endings and Conclusions. That's scary for some people. But Endings, especially ones that are justified and well-planned, aren't anything to be afraid of. The isle can only hold you here until your End. And once your training ends, you'll decide if you want it to hold you here still.

She smiled. "This is probably a good time to get some sleep."

* * *

Kirmin had, in fact, found a bedroom with a proper—if tiny—mattress elevated off the stone floor on a proper metal frame. The beds in my family's house had been huge, easily capable of sleeping three adults. I still had fond memories of crawling into my parents' bed in cold nights, snuggling between them. It hadn't been until Father's last year that they'd begun insisting I slept in my own bed. Mother used to joke that it was my restless kicking during the night that gave her bruises along her ribs.

The room was on the same level as the kitchen, just one flight down from the main entry to the Tower. From the kitchen, she'd led me down a short hallway with four bedrooms and a spacious, shared washing-room at the end. She'd assured me that appropriate clothing would be available in the morning, but that I was to keep my coat—my Book still in its pocket—with me at all times. I'd taken her seriously, folding the coat under my pillow before falling asleep. I laid the rest of my clothing on the bare stone floor.

The room was windowless, and the lighting was... interesting. It was lit by one of the torches that seemed to line every wall of the Tower. I'd tried extinguishing it before climbing into bed, but it had stubbornly resisted my huffing and puffing. But as I'd pulled the covers over myself, defeated, it had dimmed, flickered, and eventually died. I'd briefly wondered if I'd sleep forever, with no sign of the sun to rouse me, but my exhaustion had claimed me.

I slept deeply but uneasily, if that makes any sense. I don't remember waking at all during the night, but I had the most vivid and unusual dreams. I don't even know if I can describe them: their intensity, and the urgency of them, remains with me to this day. But at the time they seemed unformed and vague. I remember feeling anxious—I was, after all, trapped here on an island with a strange woman who would be teaching me to become one of the most powerful of witchkind. I also remember feeling curious, for her stories had sparked some of the same feelings that my old adventure-stories had. And oddly, I remember feeling comfortable, somehow. I felt that I belonged here, even more than I ever belonged in my own family's house. There I had felt overlooked, forgotten. Lying here in the Tower, tossing in my small bed, I had the feeling that my life before now had been nothing but a placeholder, a period of waiting for my real life to begin.

Morning

AS MORNING BROKE, the room was lit by some other magic. Although the torch remained unlit, the light in the room had grown brighter and brighter as I'd blinked my way to wakefulness. Even now, it was getting brighter and whiter, as if the sun had finally crested the horizon. Yet I could still see no openings, not even a slit, though which sunlight might be admitted. It was as if the sunlight were somehow being collected elsewhere and then simply *appearing* in my room. For all I knew, that's exactly what was happening.

I wasn't entirely surprised, when I awoke, to see that my clothes had been replaced by neatly-folded articles of the same gray homespun she'd wore. I dressed myself quickly and made good use of the washroom, which had gained clean, simple gray towels at some point during the evening. I found it odd that neither of the two water-basins featured a looking-glass, though. I shrugged, ran my fingers through my short hair and figured that was sufficient. My morning ablutions complete, I made my way back to the kitchen.

Breakfast had been laid at the end of the table, the same

chair pushed under and awaiting me. Kirmin was there as well, perched cross-legged in the middle of the table just a few feet from the meal. "Good morning!" she offered brightly, indicating the plate of food with a nod. "How did you sleep?"

"Really good," I said, stifling a yawn. "It feels like I slept for a week!"

"That would just be silly, sleeping for a week." She grinned, and pointed at the food again. "Dig in!"

The plate contained mostly recognizable breakfast foods: a thick chunk of bread, a couple of slices of meat, and a generous pat of butter. But it also contained some things I hadn't seen before. Things that looked suspiciously familiar after my encounter with the Tester. I eyed the plate warily for a moment, an then glanced at Kirmin.

"What?"

"Are these safe to eat?" I picked up my fork and nudged the odd-looking shellfish.

She frowned. "What do you mean? Of course they're safe. They're austrių. Why wouldn't they be safe?"

I hesitated for a moment, not wanting to offend her. "They look like... it's just... when I was Tested, she had a bowl of–" I stopped as Kirmin's face broke into a wide smile. "What's funny?"

"Testers." Her voice was full of mirth. "I'm guessing those were druskos moliuskai. The humans call them 'salt clams.' They're popular, but in witchkind eating them live can temporarily suppress magic. Just a little, but many of the women who become Testers are phenomenally overpowered for the job. They eat those to help take the edge off, so they're not buzzing with power all the time."

"She offered me a bowl." I felt my lip curl slightly, remembering the smell of them.

"Nobody said Testers don't have senses of humor." She

chuckled, shaking her head. "Seriously, these are fine. You'll love them."

She was right. The austrių were delicious, adding a light, briny note to the meal. A tall glass of cool water helped wash everything down as I ate in my usual fashion of small, neat bites. Kirmin said nothing further while I ate, satisfying herself with gazing curiously at me.

"Interesting hairstyle," she commented wryly.

"There's no looking-glass," I mumbled through a mouthful of food.

Her tone grew dark. "You won't be so eager to see yourself after a few decades here. But," she continued, her voice lightening again, "I'm sure you know a rune or two to create one, even temporarily. No?"

I shook my head.

"How is that?"

I swallowed "My mother didn't know very much magic."

"And your father?"

"He didn't come out of the basement much."

"Ah." She fell silent, watching me continue to eat.

Just as another forkful was on its way to my mouth, I started upright, my head snapping toward the hearth. The fire had been built up a bit since last night, and was now crackling merrily in the hearth. A shadow thrown by that fire must have flickered in the corner of my eye, I thought as I turned back to my meal.

But just then another flick of movement caught my attention, this time from the opposite side of the kitchen where the sinks and cutting-boards sat. I blinked to clear my eyes, and saw —again, just in the corner of my vision—another movement.

Kirmin chuckled. "That would be the driežai. You asked about brownies, yesterday."

"One named Abbygail took care of me after my parents

died," I said. "And we always had a few more besides, to help out."

"Driežai are the Tower's brownies. They're shadow-creatures, of a sort."

Of a sort? "You mean spirits?" *Shadow-creatures* was always a euphemism for dark spirits in the adventures I'd read.

"Not in the way you mean, no. They were once living creatures, but they're past their End. Now they're literally formed of shadows given solid form. They're not spirits, and they don't have much of a mind of their own. They..." she paused, thinking for a moment. "They're more like your own arms and hands. Your hands don't think for themselves, they just respond to the will of your mind. In this case, the driežai respond to the will of the Tower itself. You're meant to be here, and the Tower's meant to see to your needs, and the driežai are its hands in doing so."

I ignored another *flick* of movement and resumed my meal. "Do they always flicker around like that?"

"They'll seem more solid at night," she assured me. "Right now I think the Tower's probably just curious about you. Once it gets to know you, they'll settle down. They did for me."

"But they don't need to care for *you* anymore, do they?" I asked, keeping my tone respectful.

"No," she said with a sad smile. "No, they don't. I'm long past needing their care."

I swallowed a bit harder than was necessary, and said, "So you're dead?"

"Not exactly. I am past my End, to be sure, and for most people that would be close enough to dead as to make no difference. For adherents of the Sixth Axis, it's different."

"My great-great grandmother was dead," I told her, "but she still lived in the attic and helped take care of me. Father was dead too," I added, sorrow coloring my voice, "but he'd sometime speak to me from behind the walls of the house."

"They would have been spirits. UnEnded spirits, but past life. Your grandmother and father would have been truly dead, just not at rest. Not able to let themselves go, for whatever reason. It's a bit different for me. For us."

"How so?"

She thought for a moment. "Not every End is the last word in the story. A season can End, but it brings another season behind it. A married couple can divorce, Ending their relationship, but perhaps a new and different relationship—for good or ill—comes afterwards. Death is a kind of Ending, but it doesn't mean nothing follows it. Like your grandmother. Her life may have Ended, but her spirit clearly felt it had more work to do."

"I think Great-Great-Grandmother felt responsible for me," I said softly.

"May well have. Likely your father did as well," she added kindly.

I shook my head, disagreeing, but said nothing. She merely tilted her head to one side, watching me finish my breakfast. When I'd swallowed the last bite and pushed my plate back a bit, she sat up straighter.

"Each of the Axes—as far as we know, since the Fifth Axis never came to be—has certain powers in the world, above and beyond those of normal witchkind. Seven powers apiece, to be specific, which we call the Seven Forms."

She paused, and I prepared to memorize what I sensed would be a list.

"They are," she continued, "Communication, Travel, Mind, Defense, Attack, Essence, and Calling. Each of those typically has some variants. There are a few kinds of Defense, for example."

"And my Book lists them all?" I asked.

"*Your* Book? It's no more *your* Book than it is *my* Book. But yes," she allowed, "*the* Book contains them all. But you won't need it. You've got me."

"How did Great-Great-Grandmother get it?"

"I honestly don't know. Once I passed my own Ending... well, it's a bit different for us. Adherents of the Sixth Axis don't need documentation and journals and the like. The Sixth Axis... it takes care of those things for us, in its way." She paused and chewed her lower lip, looking at me. "I suppose I lost track of it," she said at last. "It's not that the Book doesn't have its uses. You'll find them. It's just that after you've used it for a while, you don't need *it* as much anymore."

"So you'll teach me the seven Forms?"

"And more. It will take... time." Her eyes seemed to unfocus then, as if she were looking at something far away. "It's odd that the Archons never thought to tame Time, but I suppose it was never wild and dangerous to begin with."

"The Archons?" She'd never used that word before.

"The ones who sacrificed themselves to tame the great energies and form the Six Axes," she clarified, her eyes refocusing. "Jura, Galas, Vejas, all the rest. They founded the Axes, and we call them the Archons."

"So," I said, nodding slowly. "Where do we begin?"

She held up a finger. "Not just yet. You need to understand something first.

"This is a major undertaking. It will require *years* of your life. It may not... it may not *conclude* the way you want. This isn't just learning some runes and words of power. You have to come to understand the *essence* of the Axis. You have to come to understand *why* the Axes exist. They are the lines our world revolves upon, their shared Origin the place where our world began. The Forms? Pfft. Ordinary witchkind can communicate at great distances, travel at great speeds, cast magics for offense or defense. When *we* do so, we are not just drawing upon the power in ourselves or the latent power that lies dormant in the world, waiting to be tapped. We are commanding some of the most fundamental forces of the world, *directing* them toward beneficial outcomes. The world turns on the Axes, and those Axes bend to our direction.

"We tamper with the basic foundations of our world, and we do so at great risk to ourselves, to all of witchkind, and to the humans that surround us. It's not a journey to be undertaken lightly."

I thought about it for a long moment. "Do I have a choice?"

"Everyone has choices, Daniel. I could End you. End your journey—your life—at this time and place. It might be better and easier than living out your days alone on this isle."

"That seems a little drastic. Can't I just leave?"

"No. Witchkind will not allow an untrained adherent to wander the world, particularly one of the Sixth Axis. You were trapped on the island the moment your man brought you here. I can End you here, but the only way you can leave is to complete your journey."

Again, I thought for several moments before replying. "I have nothing off this isle anyway. No family. No house. So I may as well take this journey and see what comes of it."

She gave me a soft smile, her dark eyes sparkling. "Nothing to lose. I like that attitude. If you can hold on to that, I believe it will serve you well." She swung herself off the table and held out a hand to me. "We begin."

First Lesson

"FIRST, tell me what you know about how witchkind are governed," Kirmin said.

She'd led me back up the flight of stairs to the Tower's main level. Just off the gray circular entryway was a room she called the "public workroom." It too was circular, and maybe thirty feet across, just like the tower's entry foyer. It made me wonder if all the floors on this level were built that way. It would certainly explain the odd-shaped hallway that contained the spiral stone staircase leading down. Idly, I wondered how one reached the upper levels.

We sat on opposite sides of a dust-covered, heavy stone table that dominated the center of the room. A small slit in one wall admitted sunlight—a frankly remarkable amount of it, given the narrowness of the slit itself—revealing complex runes carved into the circular wall, ceiling, floor, and even the door we'd entered through. Small, simple sets of shelves dotted the wall, containing jars whose contents were unknown to me. We occupied the only two chairs in the room, and both were simple, sturdy wooden affairs with no cushions.

"Not much," I admitted. "Mother and Father kept mainly to the house. They told me some of our family history, but not much else."

"I know... or, that is to say, I've done some research on your family. There's not much to know, or at least not much I can remem– I mean, find. No more powerful than any of ordinary witchkind. Unremarkable. Wealthy, which implies powerful connections, but never part of government. It's unclear where the money came from, as I can't find any mention of a specific trade. Most wealthy families are known for shipping, or farming, or something, but not yours. Not known for lavish spending. They'd attend the right social gatherings, but never host one. It's as if the family wanted to be... secure, in some fashion, but otherwise left alone. Some of your ancestors were nearly hermits. And you seem to be the last of them."

As far as I knew from the family tree, I was. I said as much.

"And that's a thing. That 'family tree,' you call it. Most of witchkind maintain books or journals, but they don't use them for genealogy. They're more like family grimoires, their own versions of the... well, more powerful, *true* grimoires, like the Book in your pocket. Anyway, witchkind is governed by a council. A main Council, the Taryba, for the entire world, and subsidiary councils in each major region where witchkind lives. From there, you might have a senior family whose head holds consensual authority over a village or town or something."

"Seems simple."

"It's meant to be. Witchkind tries to stay out of sight of humans, and these days the councils seem mainly preoccupied with ensuring that."

"What about the... the adherents?" I asked, trying to remember the word she'd used over breakfast.

"Adherents," she confirmed. "We who received medallions at our Testing. Who showed an affinity for one of the Axes. We aren't governed by the Council, or by any council, for that matter. We cooperate with them, of course. If a region is short on rainfall, and they don't have the power to do anything about it, then they'll send a delegate to the nearest adherents of Sea and Sky and apply for an intervention. Otherwise we keep to ourselves in one way or another."

"Do all the Axes have isles like this one?"

"Hah! Hardly. Most adherents live in luxury, smack in the middle of a large town, or in a manor on a huge estate, or whatever they like. The Sixth Axis isn't as... welcome, I suppose you could say, as the other four."

"Because people don't like death?"

"The Sixth Axis isn't *death,* Daniel," she said firmly. "Oh, it's *attracted* to death, because the Sixth Axis is a wild force built around endings. Death is an ending of course, but there are many kinds of End. Without an End, nothing new can begin or continue. Without an End, why try to accomplish anything?" She sighed. "Yes, as a wild force, before the Archons, what became the Sixth Axis was most destructive, bringing about destructive ends. Entire settlements, usually, if it couldn't manage more. But that's because it was unguided, and it gorged itself on what it loved. That's no different than a child gorging themselves on sweets, though. The child's happy at first, but sick to its stomach later. That's how the wild forces were: as children, lacking guidance, and harming themselves and others. The Sixth Axis would destroy an entire village, savor the Endings it had brought about, and then sleep it off for years." She paused. "It's more nuanced now. More subtle."

"Because we—you, that is—control it?"

"No," she said, even more firmly. "Never *control.* Understand that any of witchkind, or even humans for that matter, can cause death. We're no different in that regard. Where we differ is that we *guide* the Sixth Axis. The great Endings it can create can be useful, beneficial even. Endings *must* be a part of the world. We ensure that they can *help* the world, move it to better places. We use our judgement so that instead of creating great, destructive Endings on a whim every decade or so, the Axis creates smaller, more precise Endings whenever our world needs them. Do you understand what I'm saying?"

"I think so."

"It will become clearer as we go on." A grin stole over her dark features. "But that's enough background for now. We focus today on the First Form, that of Communication."

I listened dutifully, ready to learn whatever she would teach me. I had spent the last years alone, my only tutors the books in my family's house. I found that I was eager to learn from a living, breathing teacher.

"Every Axis's Forms reflect its basic essence," Kirmin began. "Adherents of the First Axis communicate by sending songs through the sea, typically only between their fellow adherents of the First. The Second Axis's adherents communicate through wisps of fire, usually only across short distances, I'm given to understand. Those of the Third Axis communicate through rumblings in the earth, again only amongst themselves. Adherents of the Fourth Axis arrange clouds into messages that their fellows can interpret. But we of the Sixth Axis are unique in that our Form lets us communicate between *any* of witchkind, adherents or no. Our First Form is called *šnabždesys* in the True Language: the Whisper.

"I like to think," she said after a moment's pause, "that its power reflects the whispers of those who have gone beyond their End. The whispers our ancestors place in our hearts. The whispers that a restless spirit murmurs into its family's ears." She closed her eyes. *:It sounds like this.:* her voice sounded gently in my ear.

I jumped up, and my chair clattered to the floor behind me.

She opened her eyes and grinned. "This is its rune." She traced a simple rune in the dust on the stone table's top.

"Picture that in your mind, held over the image of the one you wish to speak to. Or a group even, once you've become strong enough. It's said," Kirmin added, a gleam in her eye, "that Galas addressed all of witchkind with a single Whisper, once he'd tamed his wild force and created his Axis."

I closed my eyes. I held the rune in my head, its gentle curves and rounded ends superimposed over Kirmin's dark features and black-gray hair. *:Like this?:* I thought, concentrating fiercely.

"It's called the Whisper," she laughed, and I opened my eyes to see her smiling. "Not the Scream. But yes, like that." *:You don't have to concentrate so hard, especially when you're close by and especially when it's me. The Axis already binds us.:* Her voice flowed gently into my mind, her lips remaining still.

:Okay.: I thought to her, focusing on being quieter.

:Better.: "Let's try it when I'm not right in front of you," she suggested.

She vanished.

I inhaled sharply, although it wasn't the oddest thing I'd seen these past few days. I righted my chair and sat down, closing my eyes. Once again, I held the image of the rune in my mind, superimposed over her face. *:Can you hear me?:* I sent.

She replied at once. *:If I could* hear *you, you'd be doing it wrong. Let's try a bit further.:*

We continued for some time, and I could tell that she was moving around the isle, further and further from the Tower and close to the shore. As the distance grew, I could feel more energy being spent to reach her. Not *my* energy; I never felt tired or even the slightest bit exerted. But I could sense energy coming from someplace and being directed to the effort. I said as much.

"That's the Axis," she said aloud and she reappeared in the room. "Ordinary witchkind gather their energy from the world around them, but they can only *spend* the energy they've gathered into themselves and made their own. They're limited, although some have learned to gather and hold tremendous amounts. Adherents are different. Even when we work the minor magics of ordinary witchkind, we never spend our own energy to do so. The Axes *are* our energy. Even a minor illusion rune, something most of witchkind could maintain for a few hours at a time, costs us nothing. We could maintain an illusion for all of time and feel none the worse for it, provided we could stay awake."

"I'm not sure I understand."

"Hmm. Think of it this way, maybe. Ordinary witchkind are like sponges. You've seen sponges?"

"Abbygail used them in the kitchen."

"Good. Ordinary witchkind are like sponges, then. They soak up magic from the world around them, but can only hold so much. They squeeze themselves to use that magic, and when they're dry, they're out of power. But we aren't like sponges. We don't have our own personal power. Instead, we ask our Axis to act on our behalf. And the Axis *is* power, so it never runs dry, no matter how hard we squeeze. But that squeezing takes effort, and if we're not strong enough, or if we're too tired, then we can't command the Axis until we recover."

"So we have no limits?" I asked.

"Oh, we've limits. They're just much further out for us, and our powers work a bit differently. For example, take the Whisper: any of witchkind could cast a similar runes to speak to someone, and most can do so and respectable distances, say across their village or town.

"You'll be able to cast that magic clear across the world, with practice. And here at the Tower, you can operate the magic in reverse, bringing others' words *to* you without their knowledge."

My eyes widened. "How is that possible?" I asked, awe in my voice.

"It's just a side effect of the prison the isle was built to be. Those stone spires point inward, and they contain you, trapping you here. Were you to attempt to Travel from here, the points of those spires would spear you. They might even kill you, but they'd keep you here regardless. But they also work to funnel energy *in.* They can bring us the words others whisper aloud, whether in conversation or not."

"From what you've told me, I'm surprised the rest of witchkind permits it."

She grinned. "They can't prevent it. As I said, it's a side effect of how the island was built. To do any less would give you the chance of escape, and they'd rather have you spying on them than walking amongst them. Besides, most of them don't know it's a thing. In a way, it fits part of the fundamental essence of the Sixth Axis. Can you tell me how?"

I thought for a moment and then shook my head.

"It's odd.... Your family's last name—don't say it," she cautioned, "do you know what it means?"

Another shake of my head.

"In the True Language, it means *judge.* That's why I find it so odd that your family has never held position or privilege, beyond their wealth. It's almost as if..." Her voice trailed off.

"As if what?" I prompted.

She shook her head. "Never mind. It was just an idle thought. But judging is part of the Sixth Axis's true essence. As a wild energy, it created undisciplined destruction. Bound to the Axis, paired with its adherents, Endings can be put to the greater good. But that means *we* must have the knowledge needed to direct it well. We gain that knowledge in part by listening, rather than speaking. That's why the Tower has always been more than our prison. It has been our base, our center. Here, we gain the knowledge we need to judge when and where our Endings are best applied."

She slapped the table and stood. "And that is enough for today's lesson. You must be hungry," she said, and smiled at my stomach's answering rumble, "and so I will send you to lunch. The rest of the day is your own. Explore the Tower—it will not grant you access to anywhere you shouldn't be."

"Will I see you tomorrow?" I asked.

"You will see me for your next lesson."

And with that, she was gone.

* * *

I used the Whisper to call out to Kirmin several times, but to no avail. She'd either vanished or was hiding someplace and ignoring me. And while she didn't seem the type to play such tricks, the end result was the same: I was alone.

It's worth pointing out that even before Mother and Father passed, I had always been a lonely child. As I've mentioned, my parents rarely took me from the house. Father himself almost never left, engrossed as he was by his experiments in his base-ment workroom. Since a very young age, I'd been quiet and self-sufficient, happy to have a book to read. I realize now how neglected my education was: as Mr. Nash had explained, most parents of witchkind would have enrolled me in a preparatory school or home-schooled me, but Father ignored me when he could and Mother taught me only a scant few runes.

I decided to explore.

The little isle that the Tower sat on seemed the most appeal-ing, and so I walked outside. The sun was bright overhead, the sky clear, and the smell of the sea fresh and crisp. But I quickly discovered that there wasn't much to explore. The same path led back to the little beach where I'd arrived, although at least this time the Tower didn't try to prevent me from walking up to it as it had yesterday.

But I hadn't noticed how tightly spaced the rocky spikes were. They surrounded the Tower on all sides for as far as I could make out, and they left no more than a hands-breadth at most between each other. They jutted out from a hard, rocky foundation that was itself littered with sharp granite shards in the few thin spaces that the spikes left bare.

The small beach, no more than a ten foot by five foot patch of finely ground rock, was the only clear area on the shoreline that I could see. The four foot wide path leading from the shore to the Tower's entrance, also covered in an inch of the same powdery rock, was the only part of the island free of the huge spikes. The rocky base of the Tower itself merged seamlessly with the spikes in a sheer, cliff-like mass, making it impossible to edge myself more than an arm's length around the structure.

And so I contented myself with sitting cross-legged on my little beach, staring out at the waves that chopped their way along the surface of the sea. I saw no birds, none of the legendary leviathans my adventure books had told tales of, and no ships that might bring company to the island. I remained alone with my thoughts, wondering what Kirmin would teach me next.

About the time the sun was starting to set in earnest, a thought occurred to me. Kirmin had said that the Whisper could work in reverse too, bringing others' voices to me here on the island.

I decided to try it.

I closed my eyes and tried to quiet my mind, unsure of what to expect. I didn't know the rune to bring conversations to me, so I simply held the Whisper rune in my mind, feeling the Axis's energy trickle into it. My keeping my mind blank, I hoped that the Axis would know I was trying to *hear* rather than to *speak,* but nothing happened.

I tried again, this time picturing Mr. Nash's tired, dour face. I held myself absolutely still and silent, not wanting to accidentally *send* him anything, and instead concentrated on simply listening.

:*No, I'm afraid not.*: His voice rang in my mind, clear as if I had been sitting next to him. :*Well, to begin with, there was no will, and so it would be entirely out of order for me to simply start giving away their possessions. And the boy is the only heir, so anything remaining would be his by law.*:

There was a pause, and I realized that I could only hear Mr. Nash's voice.

:*Well, it's all moot regardless. The house is gone.*:

Another pause.

:*Into thin air, yes. You know how they were.*:

A longer pause.

:*I haven't the slightest idea, and I'm hardly in a position to ask the boy at this point. Nobody is.*:

A short pause.

:*The Tower of Endings.*:

There was nothing more for several long moments, and I opened my eyes, breaking the connection.

He'd been speaking about *me*. But to whom? And why? Who would have wanted anything in the family house? One of Father's relations perhaps, although I'd always understood that he'd renounced them in order to marry Mother. Did I have family somewhere else?

I stood, brushing the fine grains of rock from my pants. While there was nothing I could do now, perhaps I could ask Kirmin about it, or send a message to Mr. Nash.

For now, my stomach was reminding me that I'd sat on the little beach through lunchtime. I trudged back up the walk to the Tower and down into the dining room, where I found a meal already waiting. As I ate, my thoughts churned with the notion of a family I'd never met, and those thoughts stayed with me in my dreams all night.

Exploring the Tower

I AWOKE THE NEXT MORNING—INCREDIBLY well-rested, I should mention—to find a hot breakfast waiting for me, but no Kirmin. Given that the isle had proven so uninteresting, I decided to explore the inside of the Tower. Mr. Nash's words from the day before were still rolling around in my mind, but they simply had nowhere to go. I tried casting the Whisper again with Mr. Nash's image in my mind, but nothing happened. Perhaps he simply wasn't speaking to anyone right then.

A little exploration, I hoped, would prove distraction enough until Kirmin returned.

* * *

The Tower's two lower levels were open to me: the kitchen, a small cupboard containing plates and bowls and the like, and the four bedrooms. Mine, or at least the one I assumed was permanently assigned to me, was the only one to feature a complete bed or any other furniture. The other three had worn but serviceable bed frames, but no mattresses. At the end of that hallway was the washing-room.

The level below that, accessed via a narrow staircase hidden behind a tiny closet door next to my bedroom door, was a vast and empty room that had the feel of a workroom. Broken up only by the pillars that supported the levels above, it was cold, windowless, and stark. It was illuminated by the same magic that lit my bedroom, a diffuse, warm light that seemed to come from nowhere yet lit the entire room evenly. The smooth stone floor showed where furniture had once sat—mainly a quantity of tables, from what I could tell—and one corner featured an alarmingly large scorch-mark that apparently even the driežai had not been able to scrub clean.

The main level was, as I'd suspected, comprised of four large, circular rooms. Kirmin's public workroom and the entry foyer were of course the two I'd already seen. Next was—to my great delight— a library. I was so thrilled to discover it, lined floor-to-ceiling with books of all manner, that I almost closed its door behind me and never emerged. Several comfortably upholstered chairs were scattered throughout the library, along with a few reading pedestals that could hold the larger, heavier books. A finely made table occupied the center of the room, empty save for a fine layer of dust. It would be a comfortable enough place to read, and the light was clear and bright inside. I knew I'd be returning soon, if given half the chance.

The fourth room was... hard to describe. It was full of oddly shaped machines and contraptions that I couldn't make sense of. One section of the floor was odd as well, as if the stone had been pulled up and replaced with a flat substance of some kind. My memories of Father's machines made me hesitant to touch any of these, and I assumed Kirmin would explain their purpose in due time.

I walked outside the Tower and stood for a bit to gain a

clearer idea of the path of the sun during the day. By doing so, I determined that standing outside and facing the Tower was to face as close to north as I could figure. Walking north into the Tower was, of course, the entry foyer. Straight on was the staircase room, and straight on from that was the library. To the west was the oddly equipped room, and to the east was Kirmin's public workroom.

Here is the floorplan of the Tower's main level: draw a large circle on a piece of paper. Within the circle, draw four more circles, all of roughly equal size. Each of these smaller circles touches the larger one, and its two adjacent circles. In the middle of them there will be a large blank space: this is where the main stairs leading down to the kitchen were located, and where doors provided access to each of the four rooms. Only the foyer had a second door, leading to the outside.

This central space has the look of a star of sorts, although the stone walls had filled in the most extreme parts of the "points," so that the staircase room featured pleasantly rounded edges. But even accounting for the thick lower walls of the Tower, you will notice an immense amount of missing space: four roughly triangle-shaped areas, to which I could locate no access. Now it could be that they were simply solid stone, designed to buttress the walls to support the upper floors. It could be that they were just storage spaces, although again I could find no way to access them. It could be that, for whatever arcane reasons the Tower's original builders might have had, they were left empty.

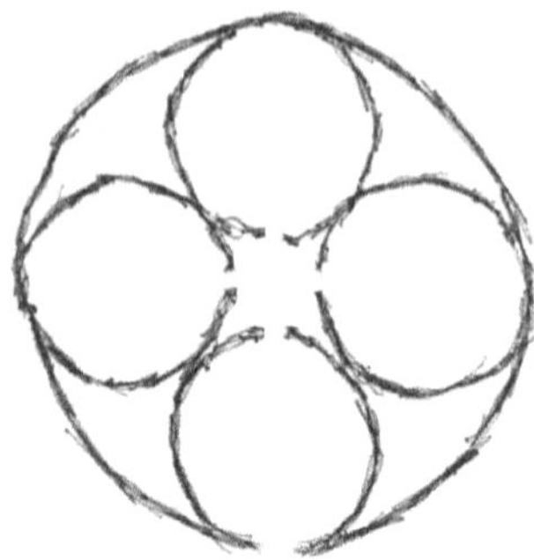

The Tower's upper levels were apparently off-limits to me as yet, because I could find no stairs leading upward. I assumed that some means of ascending would make itself known once I was ready or Kirmin deemed it allowable.

Kirmin, as it turned out, did not return for almost two weeks, and so the library became my home within the Tower. I left only to eat and sleep, spending all day and much of the night amongst its many books.

I quickly determined that the library lacked the sort of adventure stories that I'd so enjoyed in my family's home. The library's northern wall focused mostly on scholarly pieces, discoursing on advanced magical techniques that were far beyond my understanding. The western wall consisted mostly of the record-books I mentioned earlier: genealogies, lists of towns and villages, and the like. The eastern wall contained what seemed to be various textbooks of runes and magic. The southern wall, through which one entered, contained histories. Or at least I presumed them to be histories; if what was inside them was true, then that is what they were. They also could have been fabulously dull stories, versions of my adventure-books written by stale and crusty old men and women who had lost their passion for life.

At first, I found myself thoroughly enjoying the process of flipping through book after book to get a feel for what they contained. But after a two weeks of inventorying the library's offerings, I sighed and decided to read one of the books in earnest. I walked to the wall containing textbooks, and began looking for one suitable to my sadly neglected education.

"Perhaps later," Kirmin's voice said from behind me, startling me quite badly. I whirled, my back to the book shelves, my heart pounding. She offered an impish grin. "Shall we continue with your lessons?"

Second Lesson

"ANY OF WITCHKIND can travel from place to place faster than a human," Kirmin started. We had moved to her workroom, and once again sat opposite each other around the heavy table. "Your Mr. Nash used a magic called *dideliais laipteliais,* roughly translated as 'mighty steps.' For most of witchkind, it's a popular way to travel, and you can learn to use it as well.

"Adherents of the First Axis can travel through and under the water with great speed—far faster than ordinary witchkind could with any magic. The Second Axis is probably the fastest for moving physically from place to place, as its adherents can travel on fiery rays of sunlight—but only during the day. The fire of the moon is too cold for them to move at night. The Third Axis can tunnel through the earth. I don't know exactly how that works," she admitted with a frown, "for they seem to simply sink into the earth in one place and emerge some time later in another. The Fourth Axis adherents fly, of course. We of the Sixth do things a bit differently."

I was getting used to that being the case, as the Sixth Axis seemed to have a unique twist on any concept you could throw at it.

"Our Travel Form is *aplankyti,* the Visitation."

"It lets us leave the island?" I asked.

She smiled. "No, and if you tried, the spires of the isle would catch you on their tips and hold you here. Initially, you'll be able to send your spirit, not your body, and only for a limited time. As you grow stronger and more used to it, that time will grow longer and longer, but your body will remain here."

"Forever?" I asked softly, disappointed.

"No, not forever. There will come a time when you surpass the isle's ability to hold you here, and then the Visitation will become physical, if you wish it. But for now, it will be traveling in spirit only." She sketched a rune in the dust on the table.

I noticed that the dust had evenly redistributed itself since our last lesson. I memorized the rune. "You'll picture the place you want to visit, and lay the rune over that in your mind. As you begin, I recommend you remain seated," she said with a small grin. "I fell over flat on my face the first time I tried it. You tend to lose track of your body while your spirit is away. Why don't you start by going just outside the Tower, at the entrance?"

I closed my eyes. I'd seen the Tower's entrance enough to picture it clearly in my mind and to superimpose the rune over it. I felt a sensation of sudden movement, and found myself standing outside. It was another dismal gray day, and the wind was blowing strongly enough to lift droplets of sea-mist this far. Neither they nor the wind seemed to touch me, though: they passed through me, and I didn't feel the wet or the chill.

:Release it from your mind to return,: Kirmin sent to me. I relaxed, and opened my eyes in the workroom.

"It works with people as well as places, so long as you have a strong enough connection to them. Why don't you come find me?" And with that, she vanished.

I closed my eyes again and held her image in my mind, laying the new rune over it. With another rush of wind, I was standing outside with her amongst the jagged spires that angled toward the Tower. She smiled, and vanished. Almost immediately, the wind swept me up and I was again standing in front of her. She cocked her head to one side, and smiled approvingly.

I chased her for an hour or so, and was delighted to learn I could come to rest in places where my physical body couldn't: on the tip of one of the spires, on the roof of the Tower's lower turret, and even right at the shore, where Mr. Nash had left me here.

At last, I opened my eyes back in the workroom, tired but pleased.

"Good. Would you like to try leaving the isle?"

My eyes widened, and I nodded slowly. I closed my eyes and pictured Great-Great-Grandmother's ancient features in my mind, overlaid the rune and—nothing happened. Frowning, I tried again, with Father's face, although I had difficulty filling in all the details of his severe, hard face. Again, nothing. Both times, I felt a sense of... emptiness.

Well, both were dead, so perhaps they were beyond my ability. I tried again, this time picturing the prim woman from the Testing center in the village near my home. I imagined her in her crowded little office, flipping through her card file, and felt a rush of wind. I was *there*. And she was exactly as I'd pictured her, although I'd clearly come at lunchtime again, because she had another odd dish on the desk in front of her. She paused for a moment, and then her head swiveled unerringly to look at me. "Scat," she ordered, flicking her fingers at me. I felt a jolt, and my eyes popped open back in the workroom.

"And?" Kirmin asked.

"I did it. But I couldn't find Great-Great-Grandmother or Father."

"I would expect not."

"But I did go to the Testing center in the village."

"Ah," Kirmin said encouragingly. "And?"

"I got there, just by picturing the woman."

"Excellent. The Tower enhances our ability. When you're here, it can help you use the Visitation on someone you barely know, or even someone you don't know at all. It can usually find them even from a sketch you've seen of them."

"I think she kicked me out."

"She'd be familiar with apparitions, and any well-educated amongst witchkind can end the Visitation if they've a mind to, and if we aren't forcing it. With enough concentration, you could probably have chosen to stay, if you'd wanted. In fact, you can choose to remain unseen when you use the magic, although the most sensitive of witchkind will still be able to tell you're there. "

I thought about that for a moment, and asked, "Could I try once more?"

"Of course."

I closed my eyes and pictured little Abbygail. *Unseen,* I

thought intently as a rush of power swept me up. I opened my eyes and there she was.

I was in a kitchen much nicer and more modern than the one in the old house, and Abbygail was standing atop the stove, humming cheerfully to herself as she stirred a steaming pot. I caught sight of another brownie just leaving the room, carrying a tall stack of clean plates. Abbygail reached into her apron and withdrew a handful of bright green herbs, which she sprinkled into the pot as she continued stirring with her other hand.

She was in her element. She looked *happy*. I found myself smiling when she suddenly get very still.

I held my breath—pointlessly, of course, as I wasn't truly there. Her small head turned slowly toward me. Her eyes were unfocused, and I realized that she couldn't actually see me, but she must have sensed a presence of some kind.

"Daniel?" she whispered, so quietly I almost didn't hear.

"Abbygail," I whispered back.

She slowly shook her head, her eyes darting to and fro. "You can't be here," she said softly. She smiled every so slightly. "We were thanked for our service," she said, her voice kind. "We're serving others now."

"I miss you," I breathed.

"And I you. But our time together is done. You thanked us," she repeated. "Go. Go have your adventures, now." Her expression was kind, but firm.

I felt a sudden wrenching in my heart. Abbygail had been like family to me, but of course she *wasn't* family. Or if she was, she was family to whomever owned this bright, sparkling kitchen, and who needed the help her kind offered. *My* family was... gone. Long dead, even Great-Great-Grandmother faded and vanished.

I released the Axis' magic and opened my eyes in the Tower.

"Find what you were looking for?" Kirmin asked, her voice soft.

I nodded, but said nothing for several long moments. She waited patiently until I asked, "Do adherents talk to ordinary witchkind? Or even humans?"

Kirmin tilted her head at the change in subject. "Sometimes. More rarely for us, more often for the others, I suppose.

"I'll tell you a story."

* * *

This happened quite some time ago, *she said,* and involved a small fishing village named Harbsmouth. It was a human village, as most are, but it had a good-sized contingent of witchkind who preferred the seaside life, or who had chosen to specialize in aquatic magic. The village survived on the efforts of its fleet of small fishing boats, and exported a good amount of seafood to the larger inland towns.

Now as it happened, this particular village's fishermen weren't too careful with their husbandry of the sea-life they hunted. Prices for bottom-dwelling flat-fish had risen in recent months, and so the fisherman sought to bring in as many of those as they could. They hung great nets from their boats, and weighted them down with chains so that they would drag along the ocean floor. This captured more fish, and more of the bottom-dwelling fish that the inlanders sought, but the heavy chains also devastated the seabed. All manner of fish and crustaceans were hauled into the fisherman's nets, and all the unwanted ones were simply dumped, lifeless and broken, back into the sea. Within weeks, the fishing boats were coming back less and less full, as they overfished the local populations.

The witchkind in the village did what they could to stop, or at least slow down, the humans' witless greed. They cast runes to inflict minor damage on the fishing boats, keeping them in their docks for repairs. They cast passing sicknesses on the fishermen, keeping them in their beds. But these were little more than delaying actions, and eventually the village council sent word to two adherents of the First Axis, begging for help.

The two adherents lived nowhere near one another, as they —like most adherents of an Axis—preferred solitude for their studies and works. But as it happened, both answered the council's call, arriving at the village on the same day and at near the same time. Both had understood the severity of the humans' actions, and so both traveled swiftly under the sea, stepping onto the shore and seeking out the council.

After coming to understand the emergency, the two conferred. They swam under the sea to inspect the damage, and they looked carefully at the humans' fishing boats and chain-weighted nets. After a day and a night of examining and discussing, they came back to the council with a sad decision: the village would not be saved. The damage was too great, the humans' fishing range too extensive. This area would need to be shut down, left in peace, and allowed to recover. If the village was destroyed, they reasoned, the humans would disperse and leave. They promised to investigate other nearby fishing villages to determine if the same atrocities were being committed, and to resolve whatever ones they could.

The witchkind who lived in and near the village were devastated, and asked the adherents if there was any other way. The two again conferred and offered a compromise: the village would need to be destroyed, they said, or the humans would simply continue destroying the sea as they had been doing. But certain of the homes could be preserved, giving the older, retired humans a place to live in peace, if they desired. That would also give witchkind a way to remain, provided they agreed to be on the watch for more greedy fisherman and to notify the adherents should they find any.

The council agreed, and so it was that on the next day a great wave crashed onto the village, destroying the waterfront harbors, the fishing boats, and most of the village's store-houses and homes—not to mention the majority of the village's human residents. A few homes were spared, seemingly as much by luck as intention, and these homes were all ones that sheltered older, retired humans, or those of witchkind who'd wanted to remain. The fine, sturdy road leading into the village was washed away, reduced to a rubble-filled track through which few humans would bother trudging. The village became a quiet place. Those of witchkind who remained focused on rehabilitating the sea, and creating a peaceful, restful estate for themselves. The area became known for its healing waters, and attracted humans and others of witchkind who were less interested in fishing and more interested in living out their days at peace.

* * *

"So adherents *do* work with ordinary witchkind," I said. My heart was still aching with loneliness, but I wasn't in the mood to discuss it. If the Axis was going to be my future, perhaps it was best to focus on that and just... let the past go.

"It's one of our biggest charges, actually. We're free to do what we like with our time, but when we're called upon to help, we do. Well, not always, but we'll get to that in due course."

"Did you know the two adherents?"

"I did. And that's the interesting part of the story."

* * *

There was no question, *she continued,* that the village needed to be destroyed. But humans would simply have rebuilt it. The fishermen needed to go as well. Both of those adherents had taken it upon themselves to ensure that most of the fishermen died in that great wave. Their theory was that the remaining humans—the children and the women—would abandon the village once their men and income was gone. And some did, of course. The decision to kill the fishermen was certainly within the adherents' domain: the wild forces of the sea had long claimed humans and witchkind as victims, and they were directing it with good intent.

But some amongst the village's witchkind objected to the taking of human lives, no matter the intent, and they called upon the Sixth Axis—myself—to judge whether the death and destruction had been justified. I responded; adjudicating for local councils, and the Council, is one of the primary functions of the Sixth Axis. We determine when an End is warranted, and when it is not.

In this case, I judged that the adherents of the First Axis had been justified. The humans of the village were doing their best, even unknowingly, to bring an End not only to the sea life off their shores but to their own way of life. That kind of self-destructiveness can rarely be fixed through education or pleading. No, it was better to End them, or at least some of them. Better to End the greater destruction. It wasn't merely to appease the First Axis adherents, although they were certainly pleased by the outcome. It was simply the *right* thing to do. I should note that we never stand in blind solidarity with the other Axes. We are independent, and we need neither love nor approval from any of them.

Death doesn't *need* to be the End, *she said more quietly,* and an End doesn't need to result in death. But the First Axis's actions brought both to that village, and the End was justified.

* * *

"So any of witchkind can summon us?"

"Yes and no. In the old days, yes. These days it's usually a council, if not *the* Council. But in theory any of witchkind can still issue the Summons. It's a simple enough piece of magic, and while I doubt it's taught routinely anymore, it would be easy enough to look up. But nobody can *command* our presence or attention. It's up to us—it will be up to *you*—to decide whether to respond or not. It's something you'll learn more about as we go."

I thought for a moment. "You mentioned two adherents of the First Axis," I said at last. "Do all the Axes have multiple adherents?"

"The others can, but not ours. It's... complicated." She fell silent. Then after a while said, "Sometimes, not even that."

"There isn't... isn't always someone here?" I asked quietly.

"No. I mentioned it earlier, I think. The Axis... hmm. I guess it's more accurate to say that there isn't always someone the Axis would accept. Or maybe that it needed. So even during some dark times, when a judge was sorely needed, there wasn't one."

"Why?" I asked, even more quietly. I could sense her mood growing sober.

"Perhaps I was asleep," she said, and I had the impression she was almost talking to herself. Then her voice grew cold. "Perhaps they didn't deserve it." She looked deep into my eyes and vanished.

* * *

Kirmin was gone for longer this time. A *lot* longer, it felt like, although I couldn't say exactly how long. I quickly returned to my usual routine, the days and weeks blending seamlessly into one another as I began making my way through the library's offerings. On the few occasions I ventured outside, the sky was almost always a featureless, even gray, the sea a darker gray. Time passed on the isle, but it didn't pass in seasons or even in the stark contrast of night and day. Gray days faded into black nights, and the library's warm, even lighting remained the same throughout.

It was easy to lose track of time, so was I surprised one evening by a small yet sumptuous feast laid out in the kitchen: a joint of roast meat, a large platter of roasted root vegetables, fresh bread with butter, and more. There was even a mug of spiced wine, which is what tipped me off: it must be Midwinter, and the driežai had prepared a traditional Midwinter Feast. I teared up a bit. Abbygail hadn't had the supplies needed for a proper Midwinter Feast, and so the last one I'd enjoyed had been before my parents died. The little brownie had done her best, though. I remembered plenty of dried vegetables, some salted meat, all combined into a rich, thick stew. She'd made a small loaf of fresh bread, and—as had been our tradition since my parents passed—she and the other brownies joined me for the meal. It was one of the few times I could pretend I still had family.

I sniffed a bit, shook myself a bit, and sat down to enjoy the meal.

If only the driežai had been able to enjoy it with me. Without even the brownies to join me...

I thought I'd been a boy who was naturally accepting of solitude. Given my family, my parents' death, and everything else, I'd *always* been alone. Or so I'd thought: there'd always been Great-Great-Grandmother, for whatever small comfort she was. There'd been the brownies. There'd even been the occasional errand to run in the village, where I'd at least *seen* other people.

I had none of that here.

It was especially lonely that evening.

* * *

After my solitary Midwinter Feast, I decided to experiment with the two Forms I'd already learned. I returned to my little beach near sunset and settled myself into the warm sand. I closed my eyes and invoked the Whisper. This time, I focused on nothing specific, and tried instead to focus on the entire world, holding all of witchkind in my mind.

I felt the Axis's magic pulse dangerously, and then my mind was filled with chaos. Every voice, every utterance, slammed into me with the ferocity of a hurricane.

Too much! I screamed, struggling to hear even my own thoughts above the din.

The noise instantly abated, dying to a dull, rumbling roar that at least left me with room to perceive my own thoughts. I sensed a... curiousness, hovering just on the edge of my perception. I'd seen a human walking a small dog one time, in the village near my family's house. The man had been distracted by another passerby, and had stopped to converse. The dog, anchored to the main by a length of rope, had sat down and looked curiously at its master, waiting for some signal that they'd be on the move again. But it didn't wait patiently: I'd watched for several moments as it shifted its weight from side to side, looking around at the other people bustling past. *Tell me where to go!* it had seemed to be saying.

That's what I was sensing now. An eagerness to do *something*, anything, if only I would decide *what* and *where*.

But I didn't know anybody. *You decide,* I thought loudly. *What's interesting?*

The rumbling noise in my mind seemed to pause for a

moment. For a brief second, maybe less, it became a low, pure tone that thrummed through my body, resonating in my bones. Then it seemed to rush away, growing louder but less chaotic. Within a couple of heartbeats, I was listening to a woman and man arguing.

I don't understand why we can't just corral them. It'd be faster.

I've told you, Shura, that's bound to attract far too much attention. And the idea isn't to kill them, just to drain off a little and let them go.

Still seems like a waste of time, Loran. And there are witchkind in the village, we're putting all of them at risk as well.

We're not. The runes won't target witchkind, only humans.

We already know that's not true.

That wasn't one of ours, Shura. He was a rogue. He renounced us.

So we just let this go on forever?

It won't be forever.

It'll seem like it.

The clan has been on this path for a century, Shura. This is the endgame. It's worth years, a decade or more, to do it right. This is how we take our place.

How a puppet takes a place, you mean.

The first one is set up, Shura. All you need do is monitor it. And protect it. She's the key.

Clever of you to have figured that out. Would her brat have been able to do it too?

Possibly. Maybe. We'll never know. Dorian could never find him, once they'd taken her. Family always had damn peculiar magic.

Pity.

Focus on the now. Focus on the future. We have her, she's the key to the rune, and your job is to begin the task.

As you say, Loran.

The power spun away from me then, and the voices faded away.

What had I just heard? What did it mean? Surely it was the Axis itself that had taken me to that conversation, but why? Was this the 'urgent need' that Kirmin had told me about, the need that had cause the Axis to Choose me?

Shaking, I stood and brushed the sand from my clothes. Dinner would be waiting, and I had much to consider.

* * *

When I awoke next morning, I felt so rested and refreshed that the strangeness and urgency of the conversation I'd overheard had diminished somewhat in my mind. That is, it still *felt* urgent to me, but I sensed that urgency coming from somewhere other than myself. The Axis, I assumed, pressing me to accomplish whatever it had in mind. But there was nothing I could do. As Kirmin had said, I was only thirteen, and it would be years—at least five, apparently—before I was equipped to wield the Axis to any real purpose.

Besides, this morning I had my own mission in mind.

After breakfast, I sat at the large table in the workroom, picturing the rune for the Visitation. But I'd never seen the place that I now wanted to go, and so I didn't have a firm image to hold in my mind. Instead, I concentrated on what I thought it must be like: cold and damp. Dark and lonely. Solemn and distant. I knew it was near Witchhold, and I knew—and this I held most firmly in my mind—that it contained the only person I'd ever truly loved, and who I knew had truly loved me.

For a long moment, I felt the magic... *searching*. It was questing about my mind, looking for hints and clues of what I was after. It was darting out into the world and back again, flicking here and there for clues. Then, suddenly, I felt it latch on to something dark, and cold, and solid.

With a quick sensation of movement, I found myself in what I hoped was the mausoleum of witchkind where my mother's body had been laid down.

I immediately saw that a ceremony was in process, a small crowd of mourners standing in a loose circle around a black-garbed officiant.

I felt tendrils of the Axis's magic drift into that circle of people, curling around two of them in particular. I stepped closer to the opposite side of the ring, peering between the mourners so that I could see the two that the Axis was touching.

The first was an older man with pure white hair and dark, deeply lined skin. His mouth was set in a straight line, and his jaw was clenched. He looked more angry than mournful, and I wondered how he'd been related to whomever had died.

The second was a younger woman, with skin just as dark as the man's, but with dark black hair to match. Her face was devoid of emotion, almost bored-looking, as if she'd been forced to attend.

Both of them were dressed in the gray mourning clothes of witchkind, but they were the only two who looked so... emotionless. The other dozen or so mourners looked sad, as you might expect. Some were crying, others clearly holding back their tears.

All of them wore bronze-colored medallions, suspended from their necks on matte black ribbons. The medallions were engraved with a rune:

I had no idea what the rune meant, or what significance the medallions played in the ceremony. I took a step closer to the circle, hoping to get a more detailed look at one of the medallions so that I could describe it to Kirmin, when the older man's eyes locked onto mine. His lips suddenly moved, and I could tell he was saying something under his breath. His eyes never left mine, and now they burned with anger.

A moment later he finished whatever he was saying and a bright red light filled my vision and blasted me backwards, disrupting my own magic. Back in my body, I blinked furiously to clear my eyes, tears suddenly rolling down my cheeks.

Fair enough. I suppose barging in on someone else's funeral ceremony wasn't exactly the height of good manners.

I also supposed I wouldn't tell Kirmin about this.

* * *

I spent the rest of the morning in the library, giving the ceremony time to complete, and then returned to the workroom to try again. The return was easier: having seen the place, the magic latched on almost instantly and carried me directly there. This time, the mausoleum was empty, and I took a moment to look around.

I'd read descriptions of witchkind's burial chambers before, and this one corresponded almost exactly with what I'd read. It was a deep warren of dark caverns, lit by torches that flickered with ancient versions of light-magic. That was traditional, I'd read, and preferred over the newer, steadier light-magic that most households would use today. The walls were packed tightly with large plaques, each one covering the burial place of a single person. The bodies were stored with no rhyme or reason, and left for not less than fifty years for remembrances. After that time, unless the person's family paid for additional decades, the crypt was emptied and reused.

"Beatrice Scratch," I whispered.

Just as my books had suggested, a trail of dim blue light appeared in the air, winding off into another cavern. I followed it through several twists and turns, passing through three more burial caverns, before I saw it curving into one of the plaques set low on the wall, just a couple of feet above the smooth, rocky floor.

I approached, and saw Mother's name engraved into the plaque. There were no other words, as I saw there were on some of the surrounding markers. No claims of how beloved she'd been, who she'd left behind, or even the dates of her birth and death. As a prisoner of Witchhold, she rated a proper burial but no more.

"Mother," I whispered, and even that soft word seemed to echo in the high-ceilinged cavern.

I had so few firm memories of her. The two of us laughing in the grass behind the house, an afternoon picnic spoiled by a sudden, warm spring shower. Her bending over me to kiss me goodnight as I lay in bed. The smell of her hair as she held me tightly, protecting me from one of Father's shouting episodes.

I had far more, and clearer, memories of *those*. Father's obsession with his machines had made him single-minded, and whenever he encountered difficulties with them, he would rant and rave for hours. I was to never interrupt him, even to bring him a sandwich or a drink. Even Abbygail politely refused to descend into the basement workshop.

It had slowly driven Mother mad.

She'd become paranoid in the last couple of years before they'd finally taken her. And in her paranoia she'd also become prone to lashing out with random magics. One time, she'd come to me in tears, apologizing for the brightness of the sun and promising to protect my rare, pale white skin from its ravages. The next morning, I'd awoken to find every window in the house covered in a thin layer of grime that no amount of scrubbing could remove.

I knew from her offhand comments that she'd had a few encounters in the village as well. She'd become obsessed with fresh food toward the end, and spent as much of her time as possible in the village to avoid Father. She took me with her sometimes, and more than once I'd seen her cast magic to ascertain the freshness of a piece of fruit. She believed herself to be surreptitious about it, but on several occasions others of witchkind had quietly come up and scolded her for her public displays. When Father... when he died, the Proctors had come, and Mother had raved and threatened them, her mind finally shattered.

"I miss you."

But there was no point in my being here. I'd survived without her for years, and now had my own path. If I wanted to be alone someplace that was isolated and made of rock, I had a perfectly good island to return to.

But it still bothered me that the doctors at Witchhold had never discovered the cause of her ailment. Witchkind simply didn't go mad, according to everything I'd read—and after her death I'd made a point of finding every book I could on the topic from the house's vast library. Humans went mad all the time apparently, and my family had collected several books on the subject. Humans even differentiated between maladies of the body and of the mind. But witchkind? We rarely got sick, and we never lost our minds.

Mother had lost her mind.

I decided then and there that I wanted to learn more.

* * *

I'd read several adventure stories featuring Witchhold, the famous—or infamous, depending on your perspective—prison for witchkind. More than a few of those stories had included drawings of the place, and I hoped they were accurate. Holding the most vivid of them in my mind, I re-cast Visitation, and felt the sudden, quick rush of motion that signaled the magic was working.

But unlike my previous trips, this one felt... *thick.* It felt like I was struggling through a series of closely spaced curtains, flailing to push them aside and becoming wound up in them. This lasted for... well, for several moments at least, before the resistance vanished and the magic completed the journey.

I found myself standing at the edge of a dense forest, on a narrow path of packed dirt. That path led out of the forest and up a tall, wide hill. Atop that hill was the imposing stone structure of Witchhold.

According to the stories, the building was said to be almost as old as the world itself. It was the first structure witchkind had ever built for themselves, and had originally housed some of the earliest tribes of witchkind as they came together and formed a society. Originally, it had been intended as the centerpiece in a shining new city. But shortly after its construction, the witchkind who moved in found their access to magic inexplicably reduced. Runes refused to work the way they were meant to, and even trying to empower a rune could tire out all but the strongest of the new tenants. After struggling to find workarounds to the problem, they eventually gave up and moved several miles east, starting over with the foundations for what became Evermore. When that new society found themselves with their first criminals, it occurred to them that a place of weakened magic might be a perfect place to sequester those malcontents, and Witchhold's life as a prison began.

Witchhold was awesome to behold. It looked as if its four outer walls had thrust directly from the earth, and given the legendary magic of old witchkind, that might well have been the case. Those walls were formed from gray granite, and even from this distance I could see how they'd once been sharp-edged and craggy. All these centuries later, of course, many of the sharp edges had been worn down by the elements, but the building still looked forbidding. It offered few windows, the mostly featureless walls having been conceived more for defense than for aesthetics. In the stories, witchkind had huddled inside this fortress while human Hunters tried to push their way in. Today, the fortress was intended to keep people *in*, not out.

I tried to use the Visitation magic to carry myself to the front door, but the resistance I'd felt earlier renewed itself, and if anything was even more powerful. So I sighed, and trudged my way up the narrow path toward the fortress. Almost an hour must have passed when I found myself at the doorstep, staring at the heavy stone slab that served as the main entrance. A weathered bell-rope hung next to it. Frowning in irritation, I waved my hand through the rope—I couldn't affect anything physical in this form. Then it occurred to me: if I couldn't affect physical things, then perhaps they couldn't affect me either.

Unseen, I thought loudly.

I faced the door, closed my eyes, and stepped forward.

I felt only the faintest sensation when I passed through the heavy wooden door, something like a soft piece of linen brushing against my skin. When I opened my eyes, I was inside a wide, shallow foyer. The ceiling was quite low—I could imagine a taller adult brushing their hair on the stone above—and was made of the same featureless gray stone as the walls and floor. Directly opposite me was another less stout-looking door, flanked by two worn old desks. The desk on the left was unoccupied, but the one on the right was staffed by a younger woman who was focused intently on whatever document she was writing.

I took a step forward, and a candle on the corner of her desk flared to life.

Her head snapped up and her eyes locked onto mine. "Oh," she said, blinking once or twice in confusion. "Can I... that is, how can I help you?"

"I wanted to talk to someone about a woman who died here, around four years ago." I tried to keep my tone even and calm, but I could hear the tension in my voice. I could accept that she'd seen me, of course, but why didn't she seem more alarmed by it?

"You have to have an appointment." I watched the confusion leave her face, replaced by a firm resolve. She was probably used to brushing people off.

"How do you know I don't?"

"Because you aren't in the appointment book. We have no appointments for today. And..." She fell silent, and blinked at me a few more times.

"What?"

"Well, you can't be here without an appointment."

"I just wanted—"

"No," she said, her tone conveying a bit of panic, "you can't *be* here without an appointment. It's impossible. The entire building is warded against travel magics." Her eyes narrowed. "You're very young. Are you from Duocastella's?"

"I just wanted to talk to someone about my mother," I said quietly. "Please."

Her expression softened. "Your mother... you said she died here?"

"Beatrice Scratch. My name is Daniel."

She bit her lip for a moment, clearly weighing my request. I did my best to look lonely and pitiful. Finally, she sighed and gave a quick nod. "I'll see if I can get the file. Wait here?"

"Okay."

She stood and bustled through the door to her left, closing it carefully and quietly behind her. I took a couple more steps to close the distance between myself and her desk, and stood patiently. I tried counting to myself to measure the time, and it must have been ten minutes before she returned, once again carefully clicking the door shut before resuming her seat.

"Sorry," she said, placing a thin leather folio on her desk and quickly unwrapping the braided thong that held it shut. "We can't use any of the magical retrieval systems here, of course, and so you have to find everything yourself." She finished unwinding the binding and flipped the folio open. "Beatrice Scratch. Yes, I see. Hmm." Her eyes darted back and forth as she read the first page. "She wasn't here very long. They— oh." Her eyes darted up to mind. "I'm so sorry about her passing."

"Thank you."

"But I'm afraid there's nothing to tell. She passed unexpectedly, it says. She died in her sleep."

"She... she had a condition."

"Yes, I see that here." Her eyes dipped back to the paper and scanned a few more lines. "Her... her mind was 'uneasy,' it says here. But there's nothing more listed about her health." She flipped the folio shut. "I'm sorry. And you really mustn't be here. I'm so sorry about you mother."

Something about the woman's demeanor seemed off, but I didn't know what else to say. "Thank you... I'm sorry, I didn't catch your name."

"Emma," she offered with a quick smile. "Emma Emerald. I'm sorry I couldn't be of more help. Now *really*," she added, her voice dropping to a whisper. "Danna will be back from her break anytime, and you *mustn't* be here when she returns!"

"Thank you, Emma." I released the Visitation magic from my mind, and found myself back in the Tower.

Third Lesson

I REMAINED lazy about tracking the passing of days, but I reckoned it had already been six or seven weeks since Kirmin had vanished and left me to fend for myself.

I was depressed by the memories of Mother and the lack of information from Witchhold, but something in my mind simply wouldn't let her go. I suppose it could have been my own loneliness that kept me grasping at the one relationship I'd ever had that felt... unresolved.

I decided to try visiting the house again. It had to be *somewhere;* an entire house couldn't simply vanish. I mean, it clearly had done exactly that, but it still had to exist *somewhere,* didn't it?

For half the day, I sat in the workroom, picturing the house, and invoking the Visitation magic. Again and again, nothing happened.

Well... not *nothing.* Not exactly. After several repetitions, I began to be a bit more sensitive to the subtle nuances of the magic. For comparison, I sent my spirit back to the village a few times. Traveling to the village was straightforward: the magic would stretch out, and I could feel it connect itself to whatever I was picturing. It would then wrap itself around me, and sort of *snap* me to my destination. It was as if the magic was a long, stretchy piece of string: I could send it out with my mind, and it would knot itself around whatever I'd visualized. It would then wrap its other end around me, and release me from the anchor of my body. The tension in the string would haul my spirit to wherever I'd knotted its end.

Trying to travel the house was noticeably different.

When I'd sought out my mother's grave, the magic had taken a while to find something to knot to. I'd never been there before, of course, and so I couldn't picture the destination. It seemed to have searched for the memory of my mother, and connected itself to that. With the house, I felt a similar sense of searching: the magic would flicker about, trying to find what it was I was visualizing so clearly in my mind. The search took only a scant moment, but instead of knotting against my destination, the magic just... fell apart. It's like the string began to fray not the end, the magic losing its direction until it unraveled completely. In fact, the more I tried to reach the house, the faster the magic would almost seem to find it before inevitably unwinding, leaving me back in the Tower.

It was frustrating.

I gave up on the spell for the rest of the day, instead poking aimlessly around the library looking for something that would occupy my mind.

I returned to the magical primers I'd found before my lesson in the Axis's Form of Travel, and found a primer by Albert Disemstoke—the founder of the school I would likely be in right now, had my Test not ended with the medallion being placed around my neck. The book seemed quite entry-level, and it began with the light-bringing rune that Mother had taught me. I worked through it quickly, practicing the runes and words in Kirmin's workroom. I discovered that her great, dusty table was designed to be that way: I could write any rune I wanted in its surface and it would have no effect, and once I turned away, the even layer of dust would return as if I'd never touched anything. I would later discover that the extensive runes on the workroom's walls, floor, and ceiling were designed to protect me. A bit of magic cast slightly wrong could have explosive effects, but the workroom would simply absorb them, keeping me safe.

Over the span of a few more days (weeks? The Tower seemed to make it hard to tell), I taught myself a variety of useful tricks: how to summon a nearby bird (which I tried, but it didn't seem to be able to reach far enough to actually find any), how to levitate small objects, and how to cut a piece of cloth in a straight line. I even found a rune construct that compensated for the weight of the shrunk-down Book in my coat pocket, finally allowing my coat to hang normally. I'd grown so accustomed to holding the garment in place that it felt odd to no longer have to do so.

But it was the final rune in that first primer that turned out to be my prize: creating a looking-glass over a stone wall. I'd been without one in my washing-room since I'd arrived, and when I first cast my new find, I was shocked at my appearance. My dark hair had grown shaggy, and the fuzz that had begun growing on my chin looked ridiculous. I scoured the Tower— the parts I could access, at least—but could find neither scissors nor razor. I wasn't quite bad-looking enough to risk the cloth-cutting rune on my face or hair, but I immediately found Disemstoke's second-level primer and started looking for hair-cutting runes.

I also began reading some of the many history books in the library, and some of the tales were so familiar that it made me wonder if all of the adventures I'd taken as fiction had been based on real life. Looking around the library, I realized I would have ample time to find out, if Kirmin stayed away for long.

In the records section of the library, I found a handwritten tome whose title, printed in bold black letters on its spine, proclaimed it to be a list of all of the past adherents of the Sixth Axis. I pulled it from its shelf with great excitement, and lugged it to one of the book podiums. Opening the cover, I was disappointed to find it written in a script I couldn't understand—the only book I'd ever run across that wasn't written in the letters Mother had taught me, and that every other book I'd ever seen had been written in. It was obvious enough that it was a list of names, each accompanied by a few words, but that was all I could gather. I flipped through several pages before giving up. I did, however, discover that the book wasn't finished: easily a third of its pages remained blank, waiting to be filled in.

I wondered when someone would write *my* name in it.

I left the book on the podium, vowing to return to it when I could read it, or when it was perhaps time to add my own name to it.

* * *

One morning, I decided that I needed to get out again. Not to try and find the house, or even to visit my old village—I had no desire to experience the frustration of the house again, and the village was no longer interesting. Instead, I sent my spirit to Twynsits, a city I'd read of—and, most importantly, seen drawings of—in one of the library's many books. It was a sprawling metropolis, in my mind, straddling a mighty river. The book had described it as a "center of trade, and second only to Evermore in its community of witchkind." It sounded like a wonderful distraction.

I chose to remain unseen for most of my visits. I would

duck into a shop and observe the patrons, slip into a tavern to see what people did there, and even sneak into the resident's homes to compare them against each other. The city was densely built, and almost all of witchkind lived and worked in spaces that were hidden from the humans: a knickknack shop was accessible through a mouse-hole in the outside of a farrier's workshop, a tavern could be entered through the mail-slot next to the door of a small bank, and so on. For most of the businesses and public places, simply drawing near to the entrance would suck me in and deposit me inside. For people's homes, I found that I needed to stand very near to them when they activated whatever magic triggered the entrance. Incorporeal as I was, I couldn't actually touch the small runes scratched into the sides of buildings that provided access to these private spaces.

Over the course of many visits, I started to become less interested in the *places* and more interested in the *people.* And not just the people of witchkind, but also the far more numerous humans who populated the place.

I will tell you this: what I saw tore at my young soul.

I had read books for almost as long as I could hold them, and I knew, intellectually, about families, and relationships, and love. I knew that my own situation had been... unusual, to say the least, and that orphans were more often taken in by distant family or by some well-meaning (or not) shelter or other enterprise.

But to *see* it...

Everywhere I looked, people spoke to other people. They laughed, and sometimes they cried. They clapped each other on the back and called one another "friend." They hugged each other and cried together. They sat and ate and drank, they walked, they ran down the streets.

They *touched* each other.

Young men bashfully presented flowers and tokens to

young women, who would smile and encourage their atten-
tions. Older women would playfully bat their husbands away,
but their eyelashes would flutter at the welcome attention of
someone they'd clearly known and loved for years. Even the
oldest of them, walking alone down the avenue, seemed to have
a satisfied *weight* about them, the heaviness of a life that, if not
well lived, had at least been lived *with* someone.

I had none of that.

Trapped as I apparently now was in the Tower, I *would* have
none of that.

I was no older than the youngest of the boys just trying
their first hand at courtship, and I'd never play that game.

Something inside of me began to shift then. Slowly, but
deliberately. I *wanted* a life. I wanted the lives I saw, any of
them. I wanted to *touch*. I wanted to *be touched*.

Phantom tears welling up in my eyes, I ended the most
recent of my visits to Twynsits, returning to my Tower. I curled
up in my bedroom, water streaming from my eyes.

I missed Mother so very much.

* * *

Years and years later, I learned that some magic of the Tower
made it difficult for strong feelings to linger long. All I knew at
the time was that my feelings of loneliness and emptiness
seemed to settle in to stay, but that they became less immediate,
less biting. I spent a few days moping about the place, poking
desultorily at my meals and flipping aimlessly through books
that scarcely registered in my mind. If I had to guess, I'd say that
within a week the sharp sting of my loneliness dulled, and I
found myself merely bored.

Tired of the feelings that were still prowling in my mind, I
decided to focus instead on my body. "A strong day's work," I'd

once read, "is more than cure for what ails the soul." Fine. I'd try that.

At first, I simply ran from the Tower to the shore and back, over and over and over. *That* became more tedious than simply being bored, and gave me far too much time to *think,* so I started exploring the fourth major room on the Tower's main level.

It turns out the room was an exercising room! By means of trial and error, I slowly discovered what the various odd pieces of equipment did. One section of the floor, which I'd taken to be nothing more than a dark rug woven from some rough, sturdy material, turned out to be a way of walking or running endlessly. Once you stood in the middle of it, you could step in any direction and it would kind of slide under you, keeping you in place even while your legs moved. The first time I used it, I immediately became worried I'd be trapped on it forever, until I tumbled—quite literally, as I tripped over my own feet—to the solution of simply jumping off of it. It wasn't much more interesting than running to the shore and back, but I did use it when the weather outside turned especially poor.

The room contained a pair of metal balls, complete with metal handles atop them. On the side of each ball was a knob that, when turned, made the ball lighter or heavier. It may seem the very height of boredom to simply pick up a heavy ball and then set it back down again, but it got my blood moving, and the physical effort greatly improved my mental outlook.

Another item in the room seemed specifically designed to increase strength. It was a small square of differently textured stone on the floor, perhaps three feet to a side, with a complex rune carved into it. I stood in the middle and pictured the rune in my mind to invoke it. Immediately, it became harder to move, as if I were standing in a thick paste of some kind. Breathing remained easy, but moving any of my limbs in any direction was significantly more difficult. The effect continued so long as I held the rune in my mind: once I dropped it, my movement returned to normal. It seemed to adjust itself, so that I always had approximately the same level of difficulty, even though I could feel myself slowly growing stronger and stronger as the weeks rolled by.

Between my magical primers and my exercise, I kept myself well-occupied, even if my days did start to blur one into the other. But I did have one other activity to keep me occupied, and it was the one I knew Kirmin would have approved of: practicing.

* * *

I guessed that it had now been at least four months since I'd last seen Kirmin, and in that time my mood settled even further, and I began to think more about Kirmin's lessons and my place in the Tower. My interest in Shura and Loran returned, probably reinforced—if not prodded—by the Axis's own interest in them.

I began to spend at least two hours per day practicing the Visitation rune. I held off on further visits to Twynsits for the time, having no desire to bring on another wave of sadness for my solitary condition. So I instead tended to experiment, and to focus my efforts on the village I'd been Tested in. Mother had taken me into the village on several occasions, and I'd run many errands for Great-Great-Grandmother, so I had plenty of familiar sights that the Visitation magic could latch onto. I would take myself to the edge of the village and walk in from there, directing the Axis to leave me unseen. I noticed that moving around in my spirit-form was easier than physically walking, and discovered that I could almost drift effortlessly in whatever direction I wanted. Over time, I explored the meadows and abandoned farmlands along the lane, but for a long time I resisted going all the way to the where the house had been. Eventually, of course, I gave in, and was unsurprised to see that the house was still gone. And not only gone: There was no sign of it whatsoever, although I was sure I'd gone far enough—and even a bit further, just to be sure. The gate, the path leading from the road to the gate, even the small outbuildings that had been out back—all were gone, without so much as a flattened patch of earth to indicate they'd ever existed. A house that had been there for centuries, that had housed more than ten generations of my family—all gone. I made several attempts to Visit the house, and each time found the magic flailing and unravelling almost immediately—even when I was already standing in the exact spot where I was certain the house itself had once sat.

After that final attempt to reconnect with my old home, I tended to restrict my Visitations to the village proper. On the few trips I'd taken in person, I'd become accustomed to being ignored by the villagers, all busy with their own lives and concerns. But in this spirit form, I confirmed that *none* of the humans could see me. It wasn't that they were ignoring me as they had; at one point I stood directly in front of a man and he walked *through* me as if I wasn't there. Since I knew that at least some of witchkind would be similarly blind, I crept into the small places where I knew witchkind would be found—a small tavern inside the walls of the village pub, the council chamber in the belfry of the village's courthouse, and so on—and found that even very few of witchkind could sense me when I didn't want to be seen. I never put myself directly in the path of another of witchkind though, fearing that either I or they would come to some harm.

I did try to find Shura and Loran. Knowing their names apparently wasn't enough for the Visitation magic though, and I had obviously never seen them. I tried to use the Whisper, gently suggesting that the Axis reconnect me to them and concentrating on the sounds of their voices, but that also produced no results. I did genuinely worry what they were up to, but I saw nothing I could do about it at this stage in my training. I considered bringing it up with Kirmin when she eventually returned but... I don't know. Something made me want to keep it to myself. Perhaps it was the Axis, perhaps it was something else. Besides, I told myself, what could Kirmin do? And what could I do, even with her advice, until I learned more?

But my skill with the Visitation magic improved nonetheless. One day I decided to see how high I could allow my spirit to drift while using the magic. My half-formed thought was that, if I could rise high enough, I would be able to see another village, giving me more variety in my practices. It turned out that I could only float about as high as I could leap, perhaps a couple of feet off the ground. I could, however, jump from place to place. I discovered that I could appear in the village at street level, quickly memorize a location higher off the ground—the second floor of the post office, for example—and then switch myself to that new location in an instant.

I used the technique to travel down the lane leading out of the village—in the opposite direction the house had been— more quickly. I would stand in one place, look as far down the lane as possible, and then quickly shift to that location. It worked well for the longer, straighter stretches of road, but became quite tedious on the more common, curvier sections that wound through the forest outside the village. I grew bored before arriving at anyplace new, and returned my consciousness to the Tower and opened my eyes.

"Very nice," Kirmin's voice said, startling me. "Are you ready for your next lesson?"

* * *

"How have you been occupying yourself?" Kirmin asked. We'd returned to her workroom, seated in our usual positions across the table from each other. "Other than practicing, which I'm glad to see you doing."

"Exercising. Reading. I've found some primers on basic magic."

She nodded approvingly. "That's good. I'm very pleased to see you taking responsibility for that. Anything else?"

"Exploring what I can. There's not much more to look at."

She groaned. "That's my fault, and I must apologize. There's no need for you to be restricted to only these levels of the Tower, now. Each of the upper levels corresponds to one of your lessons, and after today I'll unlock the first three for you. The rest will come as you advance." My eyes must have lit up, because she chuckled. "Forgetful of me, I know. But after today you'll have three new floors to explore."

"Which takes us to your lesson. Today we will learn the third Form of the Axis, the Form of Mind. This is an unusual Form, in that the other Axes all have the same basic version of it, while ours, once again, has the capability to be much different.

"The other Axes' Form of Mind focuses on control: The First Axis induces calmness in others, the Second incites anger, the Third enforces surety and confidence, and the Fourth brings forgetfulness. All with variations, of course, depending on the skill and strength of the adherent. These powers are effective against both humans and witchkind, and can even be used to affect large numbers of people—more so with humans than with witchkind.

"I will be clear," she said, looking at me level and a note of warning in her voice. "I regard all of those as abominations. Our own Axis would let us induce fear, for example, and I will have none of it, and neither shall you. To control the mind of another being is an evil, evil work. I focus only on the unique power of our Axis, which in the True language is *išsiaiškinti.* Loosely translated, it means 'to know.' This is its rune." She used her finger to sketch it on the table's dusty surface.

I quickly committed it to memory: an elegant if unexpectedly simple character. "Hold that over the image of a person who is in your presence, and you will know their truths from their lies."

"Like reading their mind?" I asked. That seemed little less invasive than compelling them to fear.

"No, not reading their mind. They will still need to *speak* their mind to you. You will simply know, beyond a doubt, whether they intend their words as truths, as lies, or as something in between. In our role as judges for witchkind, this is a crucial power, and it is what makes the Sixth Axis the ultimate judge. When on our guard, we cannot be deceived."

I understood. "You said I would know whether they *intend* their words as truths or lies."

She smiled. "You're paying close attention." I flushed under her praise. "That's good. Yes: we *can* hear mistruths and take them as truth, if the person speaking the words *believes* that they are telling the truth. For example, if they have been lied to by another, and accepted those lies as truths, then we will hear them repeated as truths. That is one reason you should rarely base your actions on what one person says another has said or done. We take our evidence from the source, or we risk being led astray."

"Okay." That made sense to me.

"Let me offer you a story."

* * *

I was Summoned to adjudicate a suspected murder, *she said*. At this time, I was... well, suffice to say I did not answer Summons often. But in this case, my attention was caught: a man had been killed and a woman in the same community stood accused of his death. She had had both means and opportunity to commit the crime, and while she claimed she was innocent, she seemed resigned to her fate.

Now, you must understand that most councils hear evidence and adjudicate crimes on their own. The Sixth Axis isn't some kind of itinerant judge, wandering from town to town hearing cases. We are a court of last resort, if you will. But in this case, the man and the woman were both highly placed in the society of witchkind: he had *been* a councillor, and one much beloved by the community. She was the head of the village's wealthiest family, one that had been through several arguments with the council over property rights and other issues. The council felt predisposed against her and in favor of their murdered colleague. But they were at least aware of their bias, and so they called upon me to ascertain the truth.

Even though the woman seemed ready to accept their sentence for the crime, the councillors were justifiably concerned about making an error. Murder amongst witchkind is exceedingly rare, and is grounds for death, you see. That is not a sentence one undertakes lightly.

I Traveled to the village, and immediately questioned the woman. "Did you kill him? Or cause him to be killed?" I asked simply. I find that the simplest questions, with simple answers, work best.

"No," she told me. I had already invoked the rune to Know, and immediately knew she was telling the truth.

"She is not guilty of the crime," I said. You will note that I am always deliberate with my wording, especially in these matters. I could not broadly declare her *innocent,* because I knew nothing about the rest of her life. But of *this* crime, I knew she was not guilty.

"Who, then?" the council head demanded. She was the one who had Summoned me, and although I was not responsible for investigating the crime, she knew I could more easily obtain a truthful answer, if an answer existed.

The woman paused, and looked hard at me before she answered, "I do not *know.*" She placed an odd emphasis on the word 'know.'

It was a lie, and yet it was not a lie. It was an odd sensation, one that I have never felt before or since. I stared back at her for several moments, before it occurred to me that she was being as deliberate as I with her words. She did not *know.* That is, she did not have personal, irrefutable knowledge or evidence. But she *suspected.* She may have even suspected with some certainty, short of full confidence, and that's what created the odd feeling I'd perceived in her answer.

I felt certain she was protecting someone. She lived alone with her two children, her husband having died in his sleep some years back. I wondered if perhaps one of her children had committed the crime, perhaps without ill intent, perhaps even in an accident. The council would be lenient in that case, I knew. I opened my mouth to ask her another question, to force her into a corner where careful words would not protect her.

But then I stopped.

As I said, it is our place, when called upon, to Judge. The Sixth Axis's Form of Mind gives us the ability to separate truth from fiction, although as you have seen in this story the two can be entangled and hard to pull apart. But it is *not* our role to investigate. It is not our role to ferret out wrongdoers. We ascertain truth. We Judge. We bring an End to matters, when we deem it necessary. But we do not involve ourselves in those matters.

"She is telling the truth," I told the council. "She does not *know.*" I repeated her emphasis on the word, giving the council the only subtle, sly clue that I was willing to offer.

I left the village that evening, and was never recalled. To this day, I do not know if they found whomever killed the man, nor do I know what befell that woman after I left.

* * *

My heart was hammering in my chest as she ended her story. Some of my panic must have shown on my face, for she tilted her head and quietly asked, "What's wrong, Daniel?"

I shook my head, saying nothing.

Her eyes showed a mix of concern and curiosity. "There's something about that story that upset you, isn't there? What is it?"

Again, I shrugged, not trusting myself to speak.

"I should tell you," she said calmly, "that I cannot use the Form of Mind with you, nor can you use it with me. We are both too tightly bound to the Axis now, and it will not differentiate between us in that way. It is one reason," she added, "that our Axis only ever has one adherent." She paused. "So you can tell me whatever you like." Her voice was kind then, inviting me to open up to her.

Still, I remained silent. "Very well," she sighed. "Let's get you practicing the Form. I'm going to show you a sketch of a man, who lives in a village far from here. He is expecting you today. You're to use Visitation to go to him, and then ask him what he had for lunch. You're then to return here and tell me what he had. Understand?"

I nodded, and she pulled a rolled-up piece of parchment from inside her cloak. She unrolled it on the tabletop, holding the edges flat so I could see. It was an excellent sketch, full of detail and closer to a portrait than the word 'sketch' implied. I studied it carefully for several moments, closed my eyes, and invoked the Visitation rune.

The man gave a start as I appeared before him. "I'll never get used to that," he said with a grin. His voice was friendly. I looked around, and we seemed to be in an office of sorts. It was a sparse room, with little more than the table he sat at, the chair he sat in, and a couple of small paintings hanging on the wall. A plate, empty but for a few breadcrumbs, sat in front of him.

I pictured the rune in my mind, holding it in my vision as I looked evenly at him. "What did you have for lunch?" I asked.

"A salad," he answered promptly. A feeling pulsed through me. It felt... comfortable. Warm. Friendly. I felt safe. I interpreted that as truth, but it didn't line up with the bread crumbs on his plate. Had he *also* had a salad? Were the breadcrumbs a diversion? I was mindful of Kirmin's line between Judging and investigating, but in this case I wasn't actually adjudicating anything was I?

"Did you have anything else?"

He smiled. "I had a sandwich." I felt another pulse of warmth and comfort.

"Anything else?"

"No." This time, the feeling was the exact opposite: cold, uncomfortable, and anxious. A lie.

"What was everything you had other than the salad and sandwich?"

His smile grew. "I also had a bowl of grapes." Warmth and comfort. "That's it." Warmth and comfort.

"Thank you," I said, bowing slightly and dropping the Visitation magic. I opened my eyes in the workroom. "Sandwich, salad, bowl of grapes," I told her.

Kirmin smiled. "Catch him in a lie?"

"One."

"Excellent. Now, if you will excuse me, we have a visitor."

An Interruption

"STAY HERE," Kirmin instructed before she vanished.

I chewed my lip for a second, and then closed my eyes. I pictured her now-familiar face in my mind, overlaid the rune for Visitation, and felt the rush of wind that carried me to her. I stayed well back: my experiments suggested that while some of witchkind could see me in this spirit form, many could not, and anyone I was not explicitly trying to visit would be very unlikely to see me.

Kirmin was at the shoreline, on the lone path that led from the Tower to the water. Her back was to the Tower, and her formidable form was blocking my view of whomever she was talking to. I saw her head twitch to the right as I arrived: she'd sensed me. She said nothing, though, and so I crept to one side of the path to see who the visitor was.

It was Mr. Nash.

"I hope the boy is well," Mr. Nash was saying.

"Well enough," Kirmin replied.

"Is he... can I see him?"

"No," Kirmin said flatly. "You know how this works."

He frowned. "Yes, but... it's just that his family *did* charge me with his well-being, and of course–"

Kirmin held up a hand and his voice trailed off. "That isn't how this works," she repeated. "He was Tested. He was given a medallion. From that point, he belonged only to the Axis. He belonged *here*. To me."

Mr. Nash said nothing for a moment. Kirmin waited patiently. "There's a bit more to his story than you may know," he finally offered.

She tilted her head a bit. "I know there's more, but... he's not chosen to share."

"I'm..." Mr. Nash began. He stopped and looked away for a moment. "There's reason to be concerned for his safety," he finished.

"He belongs to the Axis," she repeated. "None of what we do is especially *safe,* but there's no reason to think he's in any special danger, is there?"

Mr. Nash took a small step toward her. "You don't *know,*" he said, his voice low.

"Know *what?*" Kirmin's voice was beginning to show irritation. I felt my own heart slow and grow cold. He *couldn't* know.

Mr. Nash sighed. "Daniel's mother was Beatrice and his father was Neville. When they married, they took *her* family name, not his. Scratch is... an alias, of sorts. It's a family tradition."

"I know that," Kirmin said. I could tell she was growing impatient. "And I know his True family name."

"You don't find it ironic?"

"Of course I do," she snapped. "But irony isn't my business. What of his family?"

"Beatrice's mother was Constance. And *her* mother was Patience." He paused, as if to let that sink in.

I could almost feel Kirmin's sudden confusion. "Patience..." she mused. "Not...?"

"Yes, the one and the same."

"The family? *The* family? Patience, daughter of Pranasa?" That was Great-Great Grandmother's name. "How could I have missed that?"

"What do you mean?"

Kirmin waved a hand. "I... did some cursory research on the boy's family. The Tower has an extensive memory. Library, I mean."

"They were very careful to keep a lot of... hmm, private details out of the official publications," Mr. Nash said. "And many publications don't list the correct lineage, because they insisted on keeping the women's names, not their husbands."

Kirmin thought about that for a moment. "They were hiding something."

"Yes. Neville always resented it. He resented losing his name, but that was the family's tradition. He resented the restrictions the family put on them. One child only, he was told, and Constance took steps to ensure it. I wouldn't put it past her to have ensured the child was male, the first male offspring in six generations. And even after she died, Pranasa was never... *Ended*, you know." Kirmin simply nodded, offering no commentary. "Neville... he found solace in his own works. Experiments. He built a lot of machines, and tried to imbue them with some very specific magics. Nobody's sure what his aim was. He grew... obsessed, I'm told. Reclusive. Quick to anger."

My chest was clenching more tightly about my heart, my limbs growing colder.

"He... beat them. Especially Beatrice."

I imagined I could hear Kirmin's teeth clenching and

grinding together. "And she finally lashed out?" she said through her teeth.

Mr. Nash shook his head very, very slowly. "No."

My mind exploded.

* * *

Mother stumbled up the stairs from Father's basement workroom, one hand covering the side of her face.

"Mother?" I asked quietly. I knew not to be loud in the house.

"It's fine," she said, looking away from me. But she had to turn back to close the door—gently, so gently—and I saw. There had been bruises before. Cuts, even. But her whole face was bloody, thick red oozing between her fingers, staining the delicate white lace of her sleeve. "I'm fine," she repeated, attempting a smile that was ruined by the blood pooling over her upper lip. She gave one sharp bob of her head and quickly moved toward the kitchen.

My brain felt like it had caught fire.

I opened the basement door—carefully, so carefully—and stepped slowly but evenly down the stairs. He'd hit me before, but he usually took it out on her. I wondered what slight she'd committed this time, to earn his wrath. An offer of dinner? An interest in how his day was going? I'd never heard her raise her voice or use anything but a gentling tone, and yet his hand flew so often.

Father was standing at one of his workbenches, hunched over his latest contraption. Sloppily made runes covered the walls, and the floor space was jammed with the odd metal creations he constantly made, railed at, and then abandoned. My foot must have scuffed the packed-earth floor, because he stood and whirled to me in a single motion, his hand moving up to strike a taller person. Surprised, he looked down at me. "What do *you* want?" he snarled.

I truthfully do not remember what came next. My next memory is in the sitting room, where mother sat on our worn old chaise lounge. I lay next to her, my head in her lap as she stroked my hair and told me that everything was going to be fine.

* * *

My eyes cleared as I heard Kirmin say, "The boy killed his father?"

Mr. Nash nodded. "Not officially, of course. It was impossible, after all. The man was fully grown, and the boy not even in his teens. Un-Tested and untaught. But my firm was made to know the truth. Poor Beatrice apparently went quite mad afterwards. The boy knew nothing of magic—I suspect that was a deliberate decision on their part, for some reason—and shouldn't, *couldn't* have had the power to take out a full-grown man hardly past his prime. And yet. It wasn't long before the authorities came for her. She was found incompetent to stand trial and incarcerated in Witchhold. Of course," he added softly, "it wasn't a case deemed worthy of Judgement."

I remembered the white-jacketed Proctors, remembered them wrapping the iron chains around Mother to suppress her magic. Remembered her alternating between shrill laughs and angry screams. Abbygail had ushered me back into the kitchen, then.

Kirmin was quiet for a moment. "No. I suppose I wouldn't have come if they'd Summoned me."

"There were always rumors that Beatrice was innocent, but there was no better explanation. So you see, when he was given the medallion—*that* medallion—I and the others of my firm, we..."

"You wondered if I'd Judge him now," Kirmin said flatly. "I wouldn't have, then. And even now, I will not. He is *of* the Sixth Axis. None of you know what that means, but he will not be Judged. I'm not even sure he *can* be Judged," she said a bit more quietly. "It would be... a contradiction. At best."

"I've also some concerns that Neville's former clan will... desire the boy."

"Desire?"

"There were some... *inquiries,* when Beatrice died. Someone was looking for the boy."

"And they never found him?"

"My own firm failed to find him. That house of theirs prevented it."

"They'll hardly be able to come here," Kirmin pointed out with a smile. "And once he's free of the island, he'll be more than capable of taking care of himself."

Mr. Nash was quiet for a long moment, and then said, "Well. I suppose I must leave it with you, then." He turned to leave.

"I've a question for you, though," Kirmin stopped him. "Daniel's father. What kind of... what kind of man was he?"

Mr. Nash sighed. "Not a good one," he admitted. "He beat his wife, if not the boy. He didn't fit into the family. They were remote, isolated, and they forbade him contact with his former clan. He spent much of his time in the basement with his machines."

Kirmin's head twitched back toward me for a moment. "Machines."

"No idea what their purpose was."

Kirmin spoke slowly. "I see. Well, thank you."

"I'll see myself off."

He turned and *stepped* off the isle, vanishing in an eyeblink. Kirmin turned and looked unerringly toward where she'd known I was watching. She inclined her head slightly in acknowledgement, her face calm and solemn, and then she too vanished.

* * *

I spent the rest of the day and much of the evening in the library. I tried to find something, *anything,* that would tell me more about my family.

Anything to take my mind off of Father.

I scoured the genealogical books that were on the shelves in the section of records, all covering the greatest families of witchkind, but found nothing. Although according to Mother my family had been one of the great families of witchkind, we apparently hadn't been great enough to warrant inclusion in these books. The best I found was a copy of *Occam's Register,* a listing of all the major families of witchkind, providing little more than the names of the current family heads, and the locations where the families were centered. Flipping to the *S* section, I found *Scratch. Pranasa,* it said, *matriarch and head. Only child, Patience. Estate not disclosed.* Other books would only hint at my family—mention a name, usually a man's, or list a birth—but offered no details.

I closed the last book. I sat for more than an hour, staring blankly at the shelves of books that surrounded me. Eventually I gave up and trudged down the spiral staircase for my dinner.

Passing the Time

AT FIRST I was glad of Kirmin's absence. After her discussion with Mr. Nash, I wasn't eager to talk to her. At least not right away—the memories he'd rekindled were ones I'd thought safely suppressed. Although I had the upper levels of the Tower to explore... something kept me from it when I awoke the next morning. Call it hollowness in my heart, an empty space that my family should have filled.

I needed to see people.

I decided to return to Twynsits.

I took myself to Kirmin's workroom, made myself comfortable, and cast the Visitation rune. The seasons had changed since I'd last been in the city: it was now cold and blustery, the sky gray and dull. None of that stopped the city's teeming population from scurrying about their day, and I once again set in to watch them.

A young couple of witchkind captured my attention. They couldn't have been more than a few years older than me, and I followed them for most of the morning. They stopped at a small cafe, where the young man bought them both a hot beverage. They huddled together on a small table just outside the shop, hunched over their drinks, chatting softly with each other. The girl was stunningly attractive, her eyes bright violet and her hair—escaping in merry wisps from her knit cap—a dark, reddish-brown. Her deep, dark skin was flushed with the cold. Every time she smiled—which was often—her bright white teeth caught what little sunlight was filtering through the clouds, lighting up the square.

I was enraptured.

I imagined myself sitting with her, imagined her giggling at whatever jokes and stories I was telling. I could clearly feel the warmth of her breath as she spoke, and almost feel the soft skin of her ear as I whispered into it.

It was maddening.

They frittered away the morning in each other's company, stopping at small shops now and then. I could dimly sense the magic they were using to stay warm, and felt that the boy was powering most of that. It gave them an excuse to stay even closer together as they walked, sharing the small area that he could empower with his magic. When they stopped in a human-owned pub for lunch, I drifted in after them, carelessly sliding through several humans as I did so. They found a small table in a corner and once again sat close to one another, sharing a sandwich and picking at a large bowl of greens.

I found myself growing inexcusably jealous of the boy. How could she have noticed him, and not me? What did he have, that I didn't? I was to be the adherent of one of the most powerful forces in the world, and this boy struggled to warm an area just a few inches larger than his own body!

Another human walked through me, snapping me back to myself. This wasn't helping me feel less alone, it was making me... insane. I shook my head, took one last look at the happy couple, and allowed my magic to dissipate. I sat in Kirmin's workshop for most of an hour, missing my own lunch time, steeping in my own abject misery.

Eventually, the lure of the Tower's upper levels finally overcame my dejection, and I stood and walked out. When I left Kirmin's workroom, I discovered a major change: the spiral stone staircase that led down to the kitchens also now led *up*. I was still too shaken by reliving Father's death to explore that first day, but after several days had passed and I'd regained a sense of composure, I ventured up to the first level.

Kirmin had said that the levels somehow "corresponded" with my levels of advancement in the Sixth Axis's Forms, and I immediately discovered that she'd meant that quite literally, at least with the first level. It was another library, but this time it was filled with journals. Each was bound in an identical blue leather cover, labeled in silver with a month and a year. Some were quite slim, while others were much thicker. I pulled a thinner one off its shelf at random, and opened it.

It took me some time to understand what I was looking at, but once I did I was awestruck. Apparently, use of the Axis's Form of Communication was recorded in these journals, and this library was a literal record of every discussion the adherents had ever had using the Whisper. I replaced the journal, and looked around with a sense of wonder.

Near the center of the room, next to the staircase, was a heavily built book-podium. It was not unlike the simpler ones in the library below, but this one had a sort of impression in its top, obviously meant to hold a large, heavy book in place. Intrigued, I took one of the larger journals and carried it to the podium. But when I laid it down, it seemed to slip right off, and I barely managed to catch it before it tumbled to the floor. I tried again, and it once again slid right off. Whatever the podium was meant for, it wasn't for reading these journals. I quickly returned the journal to its shelf.

Then a thought occurred to me. "I wonder," I said aloud, "if there's already a journal for me."

I turned slowly, trying to guess where the current month's journal would be. A shadow flickered at the edge of my vision, and my head snapped around. It wasn't one of the driežai this time. Instead, it was a clearer, more solid-looking shadow that resembled a person. Its features weren't clear, but it was definitely a person. It glided over to the far wall, floated a few feet into the air, and reached out and removed a thin journal from a high shelf. It descended back to floor level and began gliding to me. When it reached me, it held the journal out. I took it, marveling at this shadow-librarian. It retreated into the shadows by the stairs, and I opened the journal.

It was mine. Here, I could see the repetitive and dull phrases I'd recited to Kirmin, along with her replies, as I practiced the Whisper in our first lesson together. It was amazing. I walked to the section where the book had come from, but realized I couldn't reach the proper shelf. "Excuse me," I said aloud, "but I'm done with this and I can't–"

I hadn't even finished before the shadow-librarian slid out from the shadows and glided over to me. It accepted the journal from me, rose to replace it on its shelf, and then glided back into the shadows.

I was still shaking my head in amazement as I made my way to the stairs and up to the second level.

* * *

The second level was just as clearly aligned to the Form of Travel as the first level was to Communication. Most of the round room was empty, but one side contained an enormous semicircular table whose top was a map. As I approached it, I could see that it was a map of the very isle on which the Tower stood, surrounded by featureless gray sea. I looked at it for several moments, but didn't see much point in such a large map of such a small place. The detail was amazing, though. I leaned in to look more closely, running my fingers across the finely made image.

As I did so, the map shifted.

I pulled my hand back suddenly, but nothing further happened. I touched the map again, more slowly this time, and slowly dragged my finger across. The point directly under my finger *stayed* under my finger, the rest of the map dragging along with it. *That* was the point of it, then—not to show this small isle, but to presumably show anywhere in the world!

I eventually moved the map far enough to find the shore of the mainland, and was amazed at how far away the Tower actually was. The depiction of the mainland was even more fascinating, with every little village picked out in fine detail.

A flicker out of the corner of my eye made me start, my head once again snapping around. Another shadow-creature, similar in shape and size to the shadow-librarian, stood respectfully at the edge of the map, no longer moving. Maybe it was the same shadow as the one below—I couldn't tell. Beside it, I saw, was another sturdy book-podium, identical to the one on the level below. I looked around, but saw no books elsewhere in the room.

I looked back to the shadow and said, "Can you show me where my house is? Was?"

It held still for a moment as if thinking, and then placed a single shadowy hand on the map. The image moved so quickly that it almost made my head spin, but it stopped just as quickly. I leaned in, and could see the small village where I'd been Tested. I followed the road out of the village, looking for any sign of the house, but there was nothing. Just as there'd been when I Visited. I took this as final proof that the house was indeed gone forever.

"What about the nearest large town?" I asked.

Again, the shadow-figure touched the map, this time sliding it only a small amount. The nearest town—down the curving road that I'd briefly traveled before growing bored—wasn't all that far away. Peering at the map, I guessed it was maybe a full day's walk. "What is its name?" I asked.

In response, the shadow-being pointed at the town.

"Yes, that one," I confirmed. "What's it called?"

Again, it pointed, slowly and deliberately placing one shadow-finger nearly on the map, but not dragging it to move the image.

Ah. I reached out and touched the town, slowly and deliberately. *Carvendam* popped into my mind. With the name came more information: the town was known for its carved wooden dam, situated just upriver of the town's center. It had a population of around 2,000 humans and a few hundred of witchkind. The specific building I'd touched was a fishmonger's shop, and a clear image of the shopfront was fixed in my mind. It was *amazing*. With this information, I could travel to a place I'd never before seen. "Is there a way to make it bigger?" I asked the shadow.

It pointed to the map with both index fingers, hovering its shadowy fingertips just above the map's surface. It slowly moved the two fingers apart, paused, and then withdrew its hands.

I repeated the motion, actually touching the map with my two index fingers, and then slowly moving my fingertips apart. As I did so, the town grew larger. Less would fit on the map table now, but what was there was as clear and detailed as if I'd been hovering several hundred feet in the air above it. Repeating the finger-gesture, the town became large enough that I could make out individual people actually walking down its cobbled streets. I reversed the finger-motion, and the town grew smaller again.

My knowledge of the town, including the image of the fish-monger's shop, were already fuzzy and fading in my memory. A short-term effect, I realized, probably meant to ensure one's head didn't fill up with useless facts about faraway places. This would indeed be useful. But I wasn't in the mood to actually Travel right now.

I had one more level to explore: The spiral staircase ended on the third level. I presumed more stairs would appear when I completed future lessons and "unlocked" the upper levels, but for now this is where my explorations would end.

* * *

The third of the upper levels was supposedly meant to align to the Form of Mind, but at first glance I did not understand the connection.

The round room, like the two below, was accessed by the staircase that ran directly through its middle, like the hub of a wheel. This room had been divided into two halves. One half was yet another library, with rows and rows of bookshelves. I walked down one row and saw books of law, history, and more. One or two titles seemed to be the same as ones I'd seen in the main library below. I didn't touch any of the books, as I wasn't in the mood for reading right now.

The second half of the room was set up in a very particular fashion, making me believe it had some sort of formal, defined purpose. Against the Tower's curved exterior wall sat a high-backed, severe-looking chair, elevated from there rest of the room on a wide dais that followed the curvature of the wall. Another heavily built book-podium sat on the dais next to the chair, presumably to hold a book for reference purposes. This level's shadow-servant—I'd actively sought it out, this time, rather than waiting for it to surprise me—stood quietly on the opposite side of the dais. Two narrow tables stood a few feet apart in front of the chair, perhaps ten feet away from it. Behind the two tables, closer to me, were four rows of low benches for seating.

The purpose of the room eluded me. "What is this room for?" I asked, directing my question at the shadow-being. It didn't reply, or even so much as move. I shrugged, and looked around at the rest of the room. I made a mental note to ask Kirmin about this room's purpose, and stepped onto the staircase to head down.

* * *

I returned to the upper levels, particularly the map table, often over the next few weeks. But apart from the amazing map table on the second level, there wasn't actually much to do or see, and so much of my time remained occupied by the main library and by my ever-more-vigorous exercising.

I'd found a slim volume on physical health, and it contained recommendations for a number of exercises I could perform in the exercising-room. Some of the movements were difficult at first, but over the days and weeks I became more and more proficient. If nothing else, they gave me something with which to fill my time. Back home, I'd taken breaks from reading by wandering the estate, but here on this isle—with its single, lonely path to the sea—the exercising-room offered more variety.

I'd managed to complete levels two, three, and four of Disemstoke's primers, leaving only the level-five volume. My skills in ordinary witchkind magic had grown considerably, advancing from the simple, single-rune magics of a child to more complex, multi-rune constructs. I'd mastered the rune that would let me travel great distances with a single step, although it wasn't terribly useful on the isle. I'd taken a single step toward the shoreline, a single step back, and decided that rune would need to wait until I could leave. Assuming I even needed it; my Visitation magic was far more flexible and speedy.

I'd learned runes for warming food, preserving food, and even Mother's rune for summoning food. That one had been a bit more mundane than I'd expected: apparently, unless you were planning to steal something, you needed to have coin in hand when you cast the rune. Basically, the magic just swapped the food for the coin. Whatever magic kept the Tower's pantry full was far more convenient, to my thinking. I knew runes that could summon clothing from a closet—which briefly made me wonder where the driežai obtained my clean clothes every morning, and where the used clothing went—and a rune to clean clothing (which I immediately applied to my coat, as it had become more than a little dusty). There were runes for dispersing rodents and other pests, runes for casting light, and runes for speaking to a loved one across great distances. There was even a rune grandly named *nematomas*, or "invisible" in the True language. I'd eagerly memorized it before I read the accompanying text, and was disappointed to learn that it couldn't truly make something invisible. It simply changed your appearance to blend in with your surroundings, and had to be continually re-cast if you were moving around. I suppose, for a book of runes that was bring read by children, it was wise not to teach them to be invisible.

To my great delight, the fourth of Disemstoke's volumes included a rune construct for grooming, promising to finally tame my hair—which I'd taken to tying back in a tail not unlike Kirmin's, only with less gray—and smoothed away the increasingly rough stubble on my chin and cheeks. I cast the construct while looking into a summoned looking-glass in my washroom, and was pleased to see something of my old countenance return. *Something,* but not all. My cheeks had narrowed since I'd left the house, the skin of my face growing firmer and more taut. The gray eyes that looked back at me from the looking-glass were mine, and yet somehow they were not. I was growing up, and surely my time at the Tower was affecting me as well.

I ran a hand through my now-shorter hair, marveling at how light it felt compared to the unwieldy mop it had been. The grooming rune had even cleaned the shorn hair, saving me from having to use a cleaning charm I'd had ready for that purpose. As I lowered my hand, it caught my eye. I raised my other hand next to it. They too had grown—stronger, certainly, as I continued to gradually turn the dials on the weight-balls upstairs—but somewhat rougher as well. I looked back in the mirror. It was still *Daniel* who returned my gaze, but it wasn't the Daniel I remembered.

* * *

My days progressed in a familiar pattern that I'd settled into some time ago (although in the moment, I honestly couldn't have said how long, as the Tower offered no reliable ways to track the passing of time). I awoke in the morning and broke my fast. I spent an hour practicing my Whisper and Visitation, although I'd grown so proficient at both that neither presented an especial challenge. Visitation was certainly more interesting now, as I had the map-room in the upper levels to find new places to observe. Regardless, wandering around new towns and villages soon lost its appeal, and I mainly kept it up out of a sense of duty to Kirmin.

I made a special point of not following young couples around anymore.

I'd stopped myself, on several occasions, from using my Visitation to look in on Mr. Nash. I wanted to know what he knew about my family, about my Mother. About me. I didn't understand *how* he'd known about me—had Mother somehow managed to tell him, before she was taken? Did Great-Great-Grandmother communicate with him? Had Mother said something to the Proctors in Witchhold, before she'd died? His sudden appearance at my house, and his willingness to simply abandon me on a strange island in the middle of the sea all seemed to point to him *knowing* something, and I wanted to know what it was. Were there more mysteries of my family he could shed light on? How long had his firm known my family? My mind spun with questions. Each time I dwelled on him for too long, I began to picture him in my mind, but always stopped short of calling up the Traveling rune. What good could come of it? And what if he returned—the one person in the world, I suspected, who knew where I was—and told Kirmin? Would she be upset?

One afternoon, I decided I didn't care. I pictured Mr. Nash in my mind, cast the Visitation rune, and let the magic take me. *Unseen,* I ordered as it took me away.

I appeared in what I assumed was his office, standing behind him. He was hunched over a broad wooden desk. I stood between him and a wide window that was covered by heavy blue curtains. He started slightly when I arrived, and I held very still for a moment, worried that he'd sensed me. His posture relaxed almost immediately, and I drifted carefully to one side until I could see what he was working on.

Unintelligible legal paperwork, something to do with parties of a second part doing some kind of drayage work for a party of a first part. His desk was filled almost to overflowing with piles of paperwork, some rolled into tight scrolls and bound by twine, others laying in disorderly stacks, some even spilling over one side onto the floor.

I drifted to the front of the desk. *Let me be seen,* I commanded.

Nash noticed me instantly, pushing himself upright in his chair so quickly that it almost tipped over backwards. His eyes flew open, and I could see at once that he recognized me. His jaw fell open.

"Daniel," he said after taking a moment to collect himself. "What... I should say, *how* are you... that is–"

"It's part of the magic," I said, surprised to find my voice hard and flat.

"What... what, ah, what can I do for you?"

An unexpected rage filled me. "You abandoned me. You came with a letter from my mother, and you abandoned me. Alone, on that island. I'm still there, do you understand? I'm trapped there!"

"Ah." He seemed to deflate at that, his shoulders drooping. "There's no choice, you have to understand. You were Chosen."

"You didn't have to take me."

"No, but... Daniel, if I hadn't, others would have. The Proctors would have come next, assuming they could find you. They'd have been able to, even that house wouldn't have stopped them. The Inquisition, if the Proctors have failed. The other adherents, even." He shook his head sadly. "It's one of the highest, most immutable laws of witchkind, Daniel. When an adherent is Chosen, *especially* one of the Sixth, they're to be delivered immediately."

"Why didn't the woman who Tested me do it, then?"

"Those women have enough to worry about. They mark you, and from there you're known." He nodded toward my chest, and one of my hands went up almost of its own accord, brushing the medallion that I seldom even thought about anymore. "I'm sorry you're alone," he finished quietly.

"I think you're the only person I know who's alive," I whispered. My rage was abating, and his words were filtering through my brain. "What do you mean about the house stopping them?"

"That house," he growled. "Took me hours to get in. Your family always had... odd magic. The women, at least. I knew your grandmother. Did you know she could talk to animals? Commune with them, almost. She could draw magic from them, too. Kept a whole flock of sky-gulls around her at all times, said they were especially potent. The women's magic... I don't know. Either leaked into the house over the years, or maybe they did something to it. I wouldn't put it past your great-great-grandmother, that woman was a legend in her time. But the house... it had *opinions* about people. When the Proctors finally went for your mother it took them a week just to find the place, and two of them nearly drained themselves forcing their way in."

I hadn't known that. "It's gone, you know."

"The house? It's not gone, it's just hiding."

I perked up at that. "Hiding?"

"You'll never find it. Only the women in your family could order it about. And there are no more of them."

I thought about that for a moment and then switched gears. "How long did you know my mother?"

"Since she was born, the little angel. I handled the paperwork for her marriage to your father." He frowned. "Nasty business that, but it was your family's way. As soon as she and your father moved into the house, they cut him off from his family and your mother off from her hobby. Your grandmother lived in the place for another five or six years, until you'd been born. Then she passed, quite before her time, really."

I wasn't interested in my grandmother. "What was my mother's hobby?"

"She loved humans," he said with a sigh. "Pretended to be one of them, much to your grandmother's embarrassment. Always careful never to do magic around them of course, but she always seemed to be more comfortable around them, more energetic. The longer she was away from them, in that house, the more lethargic she seemed to become. I stopped meeting her there, in fact. We'd meet every month or so in the village for lunch."

My mind was spinning a bit. That all felt *terribly* important, but I couldn't piece together *why.*

Nash and I spoke for several minutes longer before I thanked him for his time and left. My initial, irrational rage was completely abated by then, my overpowering sense of loneliness dimmed by this new knowledge of my mother.

* * *

The next afternoon, I was curled up in one of the library's most comfortable chairs, reading a history of the laws of witchkind. Witchhold featured prominently in the book's accounts of witchkind's greatest criminals, and an entire chapter of the book covered the history of the prison. It provided far more detail—and likely accuracy—than the stories I'd read when I was younger.

That's when it occurred to me, springing into my brain so fully formed that I almost couldn't imagine why I hadn't thought of it sooner. I laid the book on a nearby podium and immediately used the Visitation magic to take me back to the imposing prison. As it resisted letting me in, I concentrated fiercely, pushing aside the veils and curtains that sought to push me out, forcing them to admit me.

I managed to appear within the lobby itself this time. Emma was at her desk. The other desk was empty again, and I had a moment of intense relief—I'd acted so quickly that I hadn't even considered what would happen if her coworker had been present. Once again, the candle on the corner of her desk flared to life.

She looked up sharply "Daniel." Her tone was wary, and I saw her eyes dart to her right as if ensuring her coworker was gone.

"Hello, Emma. I wanted to ask you one more question, please, and then I'll go."

She stared evenly into my eyes and said nothing.

"Did the file on my mother say *nothing* more than what you told me?" As I spoke, I cast *išsiaiškinti,* holding the rune steady in my mind, feeding magic into it.

"No," she said. "I told you—"

"You're lying," I interrupted gently as ice water trickled down my spine.

She froze, her mouth open. But she recovered quickly. "I'm not, Daniel. The—"

More ice water. "Please tell me the truth, Emma."

She looked at me quietly for a long moment. "What are you doing?"

"I'm not what you think I am, Emma. Please, tell me what happened to my mother."

She threw another glance to the empty desk to her left, then her gaze snapped back to mine and her expression softened.

"There was something odd in the file."

"Odd how?"

"The death certificate. It was signed by Warden Domonte himself."

"That's odd?"

She nodded. "Normally, the Head of Healing would have signed it."

"So what does that mean?"

Another furtive glance to her left. "I asked some of the guards. Most of them have been here for decades."

"And?"

"One of them, Gerald, said she hadn't even been taken to the Healing Hall."

"Hadn't—what do you mean?"

"He says they carried her away."

"Carried her... you mean, her body?"

"No, Daniel," Emma said, shaking her head vigorously. "He said she wasn't dead."

The warm feeling of the magic was still trickling down my back. She was telling the truth. Or at least, accurately relaying what the guard had told her.

"He said she looked... tired. Drained. But he says he saw her arms move of her own volition." She swallowed heavily. "I think the certificate may have been faked," Emma whispered.

I nodded, dumbstruck. I believe I may have mumbled a thanks before I let the Visitation end, snapping me back to the Tower. I sat for a moment, Emma's words replaying in my mind. One word in particular kept rolling around and around: *drained.*

I ran for the stairs.

"My journal," I shouted as I ran up the stairs and into the first upper level. The shadow-librarian, as if understanding my urgency, whisked itself up to the shelf where my communications journal sat, trapped the thin volume, and darted down to me.

I quickly flipped through the first pages, finding the passage I needed:

I don't understand why we can't just corral them. It'd be faster.

I've told you, Shura, that's bound to attract far too much attention. And the idea isn't to kill them, just to drain off a little and let them go.

Still seems like a waste of time, Loran. And there are witchkind in the village, we're putting all of them at risk as well.

We're not. The runes won't target witchkind, only humans.

We already know that's not true.

That wasn't one of ours, Shura. He was a rogue. He renounced us.

This. This had something to do with Mother. I just knew it. These people, this Shura and Loran, had done something to drain humans of... of *something*. And there was a concern about it harming witchkind—harm that they'd apparently already seen before. Harm caused by someone who'd renounced them.

My father had renounced his clan. He'd been forced to, in order to marry Mother.

He'd spent almost all his time in his basement workshop, tinkering with machines.

Numbly, I handed the journal back to the shadow-librarian, who returned it to its place. Almost without thinking, I slowly descended the stairs to the dining table. It was far too early for the evening meal, but I just sat there for hours, thinking. Eventually, the shadowy driežai flickered in, laying out my dinner. I stared at it for several minutes, simply watching the food cool, before I finally picked up a fork and began eating.

"Why so glum?"

My head snapped up. Kirmin was sitting cross-legged on the table, smiling. In her hands, she held a small, frosted cake.

"Happy birthday!"

Fourth Lesson

"SLEEP WELL?" Kirmin asked.

"I slept okay," I lied. I was half-surprised to find her still in the Tower, perched on the table in front of my breakfast. We'd engaged in small talk over my birthday dinner, forcing me to ruthlessly shove my recent discoveries aside in my mind, and she'd vanished when I retired to my bedroom. I'd laid awake most of the night though, trying to understand what I thought I'd pieced together, and struggling to think of something I could *do* about it. Eventually, fatigue had won, and I'd slept like the dead until the lights in the room brightened enough to wake me.

The fact that Kirmin was still here meant that this would be a lesson day.

"You seem distracted," she noted.

"You've been gone for a while, maybe this is how I always am, now."

"Ah." She paused for a moment, watching me eat. "Solitude getting to you?"

"Would it matter if it was?"

"I suppose not. But... you know, you *can* talk to me."

"I'd rather just get on with it."

"Okay," she said with a small frown. I realized at that moment how much I missed her when she was gone. The Tower *was* a lonely place, and I was starting to understand that being the adherent of the Sixth Axis was a very, *very* lonely occupation. I suspected Kirmin's long absences were meant to prepare me for that solitude, although I deeply resented it. "You sure there's nothing you want to talk about?"

"I'd love to know why there aren't any clocks or calendars here." I kept my tone light, but I wasn't really joking.

"Mmm. Do you know what the average lifespan is for one of witchkind?"

"A century and a half, maybe more," I replied promptly. I'd read as much.

"What about an adherent?"

I was stumped. I'd never even known about adherents until I came here.

"Adherents can live a long time, Daniel. Especially adherents of the Sixth. Some of our predecessors stuck around for *centuries.*"

"How could they tell, without any calendars?"

"Hah! Wisecracks before you've even finished breakfast. You're growing bolder. My point is that living that long can be trying. After a bit, you kind of *want* the days and weeks, and even months and years, to blend together a bit. It makes it all more tolerable. You kind of settle into whatever routine sustains you, until some major event happens to add some variety."

I thought about that for a few mouthfuls of food. "So that's why it feels like I've only been here a few months? Instead of a whole year?"

"Correct. But you're making good use of the time, yes?"

"I've finished most of the magic primers in the library."

"And you've been taking care of yourself physically, from the looks of it."

"Did you use the exercise room?"

"Me? A bit at first. Turns out this incredible body requires no maintenance," she joked. Then her expression grew more serious. "So aside from there not being a strong reason to keep track of the hours and days here, was there anything else you wanted to discuss?"

I knew what she meant. She hadn't been gone so long that I'd forgotten her brief conversation with Mr. Nash. "Not really."

"Not even your side project?"

I froze, a forkful of food halfway to my open mouth. "What do you mean?"

"You're welcome to use the magic for whatever you wish, you know. You don't have to tell me. But, if I can, I'm happy to help."

I slipped the food off the fork, chewed slowly, and swallowed before answering. "No thank you."

She nodded, her eyes a little sad. "This is about your Mr. Nash?"

That actually seemed like a safer direction for this conversation to go. "I thought about Visiting him."

"And did you?"

I shook my head, unable to voice the lie. She'd said she couldn't use the Form of Mind to tell if I was bring truthful, but I didn't trust my own voice not to crack and give me away.

"Why not?"

I shrugged.

"There probably isn't any point. At least, not until you can visit him in person and have a proper conversation. Difficult conversations are... well, no less easy, and certainly more difficult, when done by Visitation. When you practiced the Form of Mind that way, you had the Tower supporting you, but you'd have found it difficult to cast all that by yourself, still."

I didn't mention that I'd already done exactly that at Witchhold, and hadn't found it at all difficult. "Will I get stronger? I've been practicing a lot."

"That's good to hear. And yes, of course. You'll get stronger. But... it's different for us, as most things are. The other four Axes strengthen their adherents through practice, but the Sixth Axis isn't about the *doing,* remember. It's about the *Ending.*"

"What does that mean?"

She hesitated. "You understand that I'm not truly an adherent anymore, right?"

"You're past your Ending." I'd put that together weeks— months?—ago.

"Yes," she said, drawing the word out and looking away for a moment. "Yes, I am, but that's not what I mean. My time as adherent was done many, many years ago. There's no adherent now. Not until you're fully trained."

"So where is it you go when you're not here?" I'd assumed she was off doing... whatever it was she did.

"Nowhere. Much like I suspect your great-great-grandmother, and perhaps even your father. I'm not exactly dead, Daniel, but I'm certainly not alive. I'm here... well, for *you.* To pass on what I know and see you take up the mantle."

My mind struggled to piece it all together. "So if practicing doesn't make me stronger, what will? And why are you gone for so *long?*" I asked, coming back to the one point I thought I could comprehend.

"First, practicing makes you quicker. It lets you direct your power more readily. It's good to practice. But there are certain... barriers. Many imposed by the Tower itself, as part of its purpose to keep us here as much as possible. Daniel, the adherents of the Sixth Form weren't *meant* to leave the Tower. This was our base, our home, but also our prison. Once in the Tower, no living adherent of the Sixth Axis can leave. You've seen the third level?"

"Yes. I couldn't figure out what it's for, though."

"That's our court. Even as they sought to imprison us here, the rest of witchkind recognized our value. When we are called to adjudicate, we can summon the parties, their witnesses, everyone, right to that room. We hear their case, we Judge them, and then we send them home again. As for why I'm gone so long... I don't exactly experience the passing of time as you do. I... I'm here when I *need* to be here. I'm here when you're ready for me to be here. I can linger, but frankly I'm a poor companion."

She paused to let that all sink in. *I'm always deliberate with my words,* she'd said on more than one occasion. I felt my eyes widen as I finally made a connection. "You told me 'no living adherent of the Sixth Axis can leave.' Does that mean..." I let my sentence trail off. She'd implied something similar our first couple of days together. I was only now putting it together, realizing it was more than just... mysterious words.

"Ah, you've finally got it. What nobody realized when they created this place," she said quietly, "is that the Sixth Axis is all about *Endings.* That's how we circumvent the prison. That's how you take up the mantle, and come into your full power. You *End.*"

My breath caught in my throat. "But..."

"Not *die.*" She held up a hand to forestall me. "*End.* It's different. You know that there can be life... well, beyond life. Your great-great-grandmother. Me. We're different, but we've that in common, in a way. When you're no longer bound by

Endings, you will direct them." She paused. "Tell me about your father, Daniel."

I swallowed heavily. "He never seemed to love Mother." It hurt to say it out loud, and so I kept my voice soft. "Or me. Not that I ever knew. He was obsessed by his machines. The entire basement was full of them. He'd magic them to life, but I don't know what they did. He hated being interrupted, even for meals. He..." I stopped.

"He hit you. And her."

"One time—I was ten—he hit her too hard. She was bleeding, but she was still trying to pretend everything was fine. She..." I swallowed again. "I was angry. I *hated* him for it. I went downstairs and... I don't remember it." I closed my eyes. "I never saw his body. But they came, the Proctors. They took her away. She died at Witchhold. They never... I don't know why they left me." I swallowed again, holding back the tears I could feel at the back of my eyes.

"You've been around the edges of Endings your whole life, Daniel," she said, sadness tinging her voice. "I suspect your own guilt kept your father's spirit in the house, past his proper Ending. You may have even had something to do with those Proctors leaving you, although I doubt you could have realized it at the time. The Sixth Axis was coiling around you, just out of your reach, but you managed to touch a small portion of it. You and Endings are connected, and that probably attracted it."

"I... I did all that?"

"Yes. Probably. It's hard to tell, from here and now."

"But I wasn't even trained."

"I know. But that's why children with medallions are taken to an adherent as quickly as possible. It's the Axis's power we use, not our own. If the Axis is willing, you can direct it without any training. It's just that the results can be a little... unpredictable. Dangerous."

"And you say Father's spirit... that was me?"

"It could have been. Again, it's hard to say for certain. But witchkind are incredibly hard to End properly, Daniel. It's a reason we're tolerated, we of the Sixth Axis. The Council, and even the smaller councils, have the authority to execute others of witchkind. For high crimes, like murder. But it's hard to do it properly, without raising an angry, vengeful spirit. We can guarantee a proper Ending, not only to a life, but to all the angst around it. And we can hold an Ending in abeyance, at need. Such as, perhaps, your father's spirit, or even your great-great-grandmother's." She paused to let that sink in. "You done?"

I looked down at my breakfast plate, surprised to find it empty. Then I looked up at her, something loosening in my chest but not completely vanishing. Mother was already gone. There was no rush to do more right now. Right here, right now, I had work to do.

"I'm done. What's today's lesson?"

* * *

We returned to the workroom, where Kirmin drew another rune in the dusty tabletop.

"Gaubtas. The Shroud. The Sixth Axis's basic Form of Defense. There's a stronger Form, and that will be in your next lesson, but this is a good one to start with. It basically shields your body, perhaps one other person held close to you as well. No more."

"The other Axes have something similar?" I asked.

"They do, and it's smart of you to ask. First Axis can throw up a shield of water, provided there's sufficient water nearby. Second Axis, a wall of fire. Third, a wall of dirt and rock. Fourth, a wall of solidified air. They're all similar and all are considered basic, at least for adherents. Ordinary witchkind have smaller runes that can deflect or divert, but they're not as strong as a Form of Defense. What's important is that you'll actually be able to borrow their techniques, with some practice, because they're so simple and elemental."

"Can they borrow ours?" I asked.

"Yes and no. In theory, yes. But none ever would. Our Form of Defense isn't a shield like what they can create. It isn't tangible, I mean. It creates a..." she paused to think. "I guess I think of it as an area of Ending. An attack that strikes simply *Ends,* unless it can overwhelm your will to hold that End in place. The other adherents, like the rest of witchkind, fear Endings. They'd never try to use one, even in their own defense, and even if they could. I honestly don't know if they *could.* I'm not sure any have every tried."

"More Endings," I mused.

"That is what we *are* Daniel. I've said before that Endings are more than just death. As an adherent, you'll be able to End an issue simply by stating that it is Ended, and exercising the Axis's power to enforce your statement. Two people having an argument simply *won't* argue any more. Any dispute, any contradiction, you can End them."

I thought for a moment. "Then, why," I asked slowly,

"would we need a Form of Defense? If someone attacked, couldn't I just... End the attack?"

She smiled. "You're getting good at this. And yes, you could. But simply Ending an argument doesn't remove the underlying causes for it. Arguments, conflict, disagreements—those are healthy parts of life, when they don't get out of control. They let us examine situations, and *resolve* them. Sometimes, you may simply need to *dissuade* someone, rather than *Ending* them, and the Form of Defense can serve the purpose. Let the conflict play out to a natural conclusion, and keep yourself safe while that happens.

"In the past, the Sixth Axis has declined to offer Judgement on issues that *needed* to be resolved. Simply Ending them would not have served even the people who were demanding Judgement. And, in the past, the Sixth Axis has been attacked because it sought to End something, or because it refused to End something that someone else wanted Ended. And so we defend ourselves."

"So, just..."

"Wait," she said, chuckling and holding up a hand. "Let's go outside for this. It can get a little... messy."

* * *

Kirmin hadn't been joking. She'd instructed me to invoke the Shroud, and then tossed black spikes of shadow-power at me. As she did so, her fingers quickly elongated into sharp black spikes, and I remembered the lesson I'd experienced outside Great-Great-Grandmother's attic when she'd first handed me the Book. For that matter, the Shroud itself reminded me of that same lesson, where the dragon's fire had diverted around my body.

I said as much to Kirmin, and she grew interested. "A waking dream, then?"

"I guess."

"And a dragon. A big one?"

"Huge."

"Interesting. Dragons aren't real, you know."

"I hadn't really thought about it. Does it mean something?"

She chewed her lower lip for a moment before answering. "I don't know much about the Book, you know. It may have been testing you. Or preparing you. Or it might not even have been the book at all. The Axis itself could have been trying to show you something."

"Did it ever do that with you?"

"No. And to my knowledge—which I used to believe was extensive and infallible, although now I am developing doubts—it's never done that with any of us."

"So why me?"

"Why indeed. Let's resume."

I winced the first several times she flung the black spikes at me, instinct not quite trusting this invisible "Ending" in front of me. But each time, the spikes flew toward me, and then flickered and died a few scant inches from my body. Once I'd grown more confident, she'd had me drop the Shroud, and then invoke it quickly each time she attacked.

That took some practice, and at first I hadn't been quick enough. The little shadow-spikes bounced off my coat, though, shattering against the nearby stone spires. "I'm not making them to hurt you, but they have to hurt *something*, so this is more safely done out here," Kirmin said. The spikes did leave thin, sooty streaks on my coat, which I quickly banished using the cleaning rune I'd learned from my magic primers. Kirmin chuckled the first time I did that, and said, "Well, at least you haven't been idle with your time here." Eventually, I could snap my Shroud into existence fast enough to satisfy her. "That'll do," she approved after I'd flicked it into existence ten times in a row without fail. "Keep practicing that one in particular," she added. She paused for a moment, and spoke as quiet as I'd ever heard her. "I know it's lonely, Daniel. I came here at the same age as you. I *know*. But... someone has to be in this place, when someone's needed. I was sorry it was me, in the beginning. I'm sorry it's you, now."

"In the beginning?"

"What?"

"You said you were sorry in the beginning."

"Yeah. I guess in the end I was sorry, too. Some of the middle wasn't so bad." She chewed her bottom lip for a moment, something I'd never seen her do. Then she shook her head slightly and vanished.

* * *

I awoke the next morning fully intending to sink back into my waiting-for-Kirmin routine: practicing, spying on people in whatever town caught my eye, and occasionally trying to convince the Axis to let me hear Shura and Loran again. I'd mix in some library time, some exercise, and between all of it manage to hang on until my next lesson. Most importantly, I wanted to do *something* to learn more about my mother.

Could she still be alive, even now? Was it possible?

I hadn't even sat down to breakfast when an incredibly loud knocking sound rang through the Tower. I started, and just stood for a moment and listened. *Boom, boom, boom!* It sounded like someone was... pounding on wood?

The front door!

I dashed to the door and hauled it open. Before me was an older woman of witchkind. She had near-black skin that contrasted sharply with the pure-white hair that flowed down past her shoulders, and was wearing a flowing, diaphanous garment of light blue and silver. It hung gently from her slim shoulders, spilling down and puddling around her feet. Her eyes were bright silver, and her face was worn and kind.

"Hello," she said with a smile. "I'm Debesi, senior adherent of Sky. I thought it was time I introduced myself."

I nodded, awestruck and entirely uncertain what to say.

"May I come in?" she asked, her smile widening.

"Oh! Yes. Sorry. Please come in." I led her out of the foyer and into the public workroom. "Please, have a seat." My knowledge of social manners came entirely from the books I'd read, but she reacted as if I'd said the right thing. She slid out a chair, settled herself, and leaned her elbows onto the workroom table.

I sat opposite her, and we held each others' eyes for a few silent moments before she smiled again and asked, "May I know your name?"

"Oh!" I said again. How stupid. "I'm Daniel."

"Well-met, Daniel. How long have you been here?"

"I, ah... I'm not actually sure. A year at least. It was my birthday... yesterday?" I had no idea how long Kirmin had been here before leaving me again.

"I'm unfamiliar with how the Sixth's apprentices are trained, but I presume you've been working through the Forms?"

"Yes. I'm through four of them."

"Ah, a bit over halfway then."

"Yes." I then stared silently at her, waiting for her to speak. She stared right back, that same soft smile on her face, until I finally asked, "What can I do for you?"

"So formal!" she chuckled. "As I said, I mainly just wanted to meet you. We all felt it when you were Chosen of course, and it was indeed about a year ago, I believe. Our own apprentices move through the Forms in a year and start working alongside another adherent, but I suppose... well. The Sixth does things its own way. And with much more gravity, so I suppose it's no surprise you're still working through it all." She paused for a moment before continuing. "It's much too early to ask what kind of adherent you're planning to be, but have you given any thought to it?"

My mouth worked for a few moments as my brain tried to come up with something. Finally, I shook my head and simply said, "No. Not really. I mean... I know I'll be able to do a lot of good. I'm not planning to be a hermit."

"I should hope not. You've been handed a rather... desolate home."

"It's not so bad."

She laughed. "I didn't mean to imply otherwise. It just... well, it must be lonely."

I felt my spirit sink, all my feelings of isolation crashing back into my consciousness. "A little. I grew up alone, though. I guess I'm used to it."

She frowned. "Alone? How so?"

"My parents died when I was younger. They were my only family." No sense bringing up Great-Great-Grandmother.

"You mean to say you... you were completely alone? A child?" Her expression was aghast.

"We had brownies," I offered.

"You had... Axis protect me. You had brownies." She shook her head, incredulous. "And now you're here. Well. I have to say, I wish I could visit more often. I mean, I suppose I could. There's no law against it, no rule. It's just... not done. A courtesy call, certainly, but the tradition has been to... well. Putting it bluntly, I suppose the tradition has been to stay away from the Sixth as much as possible."

"Why?"

"More often than not, the Sixth only involves itself when *involvement* is needed. Meaning there's a problem to be solved. Again more often than not, by Ending something. Or someone. It's just... obviously necessary, but not something one... *courts*. But... Well. If you're ever in the mood for company, I'd be happy to visit with you here."

In my mind, Debesi took on a whole new appearance. She was suddenly a grandmotherly type, someone who'd... in the stories, grandmothers were always making treats, fussing over their grandchildren, making sure they were being raised properly by their parents. I couldn't see regal-looking Debesi *fussing*, so perhaps she was less a grandmotherly type and more... a friend?

"I'd appreciate it," I said.

She stood, offering a firmer smile. "I shall report back that I've met the new adherent-to-be, and that he's a polite, well-mannered young man who's all alone in his lonely, distant Tower. I'm sure my fellow adherents of Sky will be much relieved. In their minds, you know, they're all afraid you're going to be some world-Ending tyrant."

I'd risen from my chair as she spoke, and asked, "Has that ever happened?"

"Not once in all the centuries since the Axes were Forged, no." She laughed again, and it seems that humor was something that came easily to her. "But people will try to imagine the worst, won't they? It's been lovely meeting you, Daniel. I hope to see you again soon."

She led the way to the entrance, opened the door, and stepped through. "Be well," she said over her shoulder, giving me another friendly smile. Then, with a gust of wind, she was gone.

I realized in that moment that I hadn't actually learned how to summon her as she'd suggested.

Quarry

THE MOMENT DEBESI WAS GONE, I rushed up to the second level, and stood over the map table. "Show me my mother," I ordered.

The map... *jittered.* It slewed sideways, half the continent zipping off to one side. Then it jittered again, as if something was shaking it. Then sideways again, in the opposite direction. Then it zoomed out, showing almost the entire world, before zooming back in just as fast, focusing on a single tree. Then back out, then–

"Stop!"

It stopped.

I very much felt as if something was preventing it from working properly.

I'd promised myself to leave the new upper level unexplored for a while, saving the experience for when I grew truly bored. But now I felt that I needed every resource the Tower could provide, and so I rushed up to the third level, and then up the new flight of stairs that continued to the fourth.

* * *

The fourth level was completely empty. *Completely.* I peered into every shadow and didn't even see a shadow-being. The only item in the room was one of the heavy book-podiums, which was pointless because this level didn't even have–.

I stopped.

I was an idiot.

Kirmin had told me not to do this without her say-so, but I was past caring about petty rules.

I reached into my coat pocket and withdrew the Book. As I did, it returned to its original size, and I laid it gently on the podium. I *knew* this would work, but I held myself ready to catch it, in case it slid off as the journal on the first level had done.

It didn't slide off.

Instead, it opened itself, perfectly filling the slight depression in the podium's wooden top. Its pages ruffled as if in a strong wind, coming to rest a bit over halfway through. I looked at the page it had opened to. Everything was written in a neat, bold hand, the ink on the page dark and crisp. The runes and sigils looked to have been quickly copied out by someone who enjoyed a long familiarity with them, the pen-strokes quick and sure. They were not the perfect, almost artistic runes from the Disemstoke books, which had obviously been mass-produced in some fashion. Instead, these runes were... personable. They had character. I could sense the pressure of the pen in the varying widths of the strokes, almost feel the surety with which they'd been inscribed. They felt somewhat more precise than Kirmin's dust-runes, but they were no more formal or stuffy than her fingertip drawings.

On the page the Book had flipped to, I found a rune called *vaizdas,* the View. It was no more complex than many of the ones Kirmin had showed me to this point, consisting of just a few nested strokes. I studied them for several minutes, and then invoked them in my mind.

The walls came to life.

Where before there had been cold, empty stone, there was now... *everything*. It was as if the walls had simply vanished, leaving a panoramic view of the isle and the sea surrounding it. This high, I could see over and past most of the jagged spires that thrust toward the Tower. I was enchanted, and spent several minutes walking around the room. There was little enough to see, but this was the most breathtaking magic I'd seen yet.

I heard a rustling, and returned to the Book on its podium. It had turned a page, and revealed a section called *pasiskolinti skydai,* the Borrowed Shields. It seemed that my Shroud would become more powerful here, and as Kirmin had suggested, I would be able to invoke more powerful forms of the other Axes' Forms of Defense. Kirmin hadn't mentioned a couple of minor details, which the Book made clear:

On your own, the adherent may invoke the Forms of our brother Axes.

Doing so at length will attract those Axes,

Who will often dispatch their adherents to investigate.
Should your use of their borrowed power be just,
They will join you in your Defense.

So there was something of a cost for using other Axes' power injudiciously, but it could also be a way to summon them to my defense if needed. Interesting. I wondered if etiquette would permit me to summon Debesi for a social visit, but decided not to risk it just now. I flipped through the next few pages, and saw the runes needed to invoke the other Forms of Defense. Little point in practicing it now, I supposed. I was *very* eager to summon a huge wall of seawater, just to see what it looked like, but was mindful about using the other Axes' power without need.

I will admit that I did give into temptation later that evening, briefly summoning the beginnings of a sea-wall, but I let it crash back into the sea before it was fully formed, terrified of attracting the attention of an unknown adherent of Sea.

But for right then, I removed the Book from the podium. I did not, however, place it back in my coat pocket.

I had two other levels to re-investigate. Surely *one* of them could provide a clue as to Mother's fate.

* * *

I descended to the third level, walked to the dais, and placed the Book on the podium. It immediately opened itself and flipped to a page detailing *nuosprendžiu teismas,* the Court of Judgement. Another complex, multi-rune construct, this was the one Kirmin had mentioned. It would let me summon a court of litigants, witnesses, and anyone else I wanted, to conduct a Judgement here in the Tower. Once summoned, all the participants would basically be trapped in this room until I released them. The Tower would suppress most magics except my own. *That* explained the mini-library here, and the duplicate books I'd seen: they might be needed as reference material, and could be accessed conveniently without leaving this level. The Book even noted that the driežai would be able to come and go, to ensure meals and refreshments could be brought as needed.

I couldn't see myself using this court. It seemed so... serious. Formal. Kirmin's stories implied that she'd usually gone to *them*, rather than bringing them *here*. Still... it was useful to know what could be done.

I picked the Book up and walked down to the second level. I placed the Book on its podium, and let it open itself. It flipped to the Visitation rune, which I already knew. The following pages contained other simpler, minor runes: *surasti,* for locating things and people; *fizinis buvimas,* the in-person version of the Visitation rune that I'd presumably be able to invoke once I could leave the isle. Nothing as mind-shattering as the two levels above, but useful nonetheless.

I moved to the first level, and let the Book open itself. The Whisper was its first rune, followed by the one Kirmin had mentioned, which would let me listen in on other people. It was called *šnabždesys perklausė,* the Whisper Overheard, and it would only work here in the Tower.

This was exactly the magic that the Axis had used on its own, enabling me to overhear Shura and Loran all those months ago! I invoked it, once again holding my memories of their voice in my mind, but like all the other times I'd tried, nothing happened. Even with the rune blazing in my mind's eye, the Axis refused to make the connection. I sighed, and released the magic. Even now that I knew the rune, Shura and Loran remained stubbornly out of my reach.

Still. I couldn't resist trying again, just to see if I could command the magic as the Book described.

I sat in one of the room's comfortable-looking chairs, recalled the woman from the Testing office in my mind, and invoked the rune. Immediately, the room felt… expanded, some-how. Bigger. Not physically, but when I closed my eyes, it *sounded* like I was someplace else.

:I'm afraid not, dear,: the woman's prim voice said. It seemed to be coming from nowhere and everywhere all at once, fully surrounding me. *:Very few Test high enough to bypass First Cohort at Disemstoke's, though, so don't be disappointed.:* She paused. *:No, ma'am, we don't perform the Test twice. That will be all. Have–:* another pause. *:No, that will be quite enough. Good day to you all.:*

I realized that because I'd only invoked the rune on her, I could only hear her; anyone she was talking to wasn't audible. I suppose I could have Visited her directly, but she'd seen me before and I didn't want to risk that. Still, it was an amazing piece of magic. I released it, and the room's ambient sound returned to normal.

I closed my eyes, and once again held the rune for the Whisper Overhead in my mind. Beneath it I held the image of my mother, pale-skinned and lovely. I concentrated fiercely, pouring everything I had into the rune.

Suddenly, it felt as if the entire world had upended itself onto my head, and I passed out.

* * *

"You'll *have* to tell me what you did." I'd opened my eyes to find Kirmin crouched on the floor, leaning over me. "It's far too soon for me to be back, but I don't know that any adherent in this Tower has managed to pummel themselves with their own magic." She grinned. "What did you do?"

An almost overpowering sense of anxiety overwhelmed me, urging me not to answer. Instead, I asked, "Aren't you basically attached to the Axis? Can't you just tell what I did?"

"Doesn't work like that," she said cheerfully. "I only know what you can tell me. So what'd you do?"

More anxiety. But what possible harm could come of it? It's not like she could tell anyone. She was even more trapped here than I was, wasn't she?

"It's my mother," I said, my voice cracking slightly.

Her eyes grew wide, and she rocked back on her heels. "I'm guessing you don't mean you were just overcome with missing her," she said carefully.

"I think she's alive. I mean, she might be."

"You told me your mother died in Witchhold."

"I went there."

Her eyes grew even wider. "I... wow. I didn't think that would be possible for you. You used the Visitation?" I nodded. "That shouldn't have worked."

"It tried not to."

"I see. And?"

I sighed. "I actually went twice. The second time, I used *issiaiškinti* on the clerk. Mother's death certificate wasn't signed by their healer, it was signed by the warden. And she said a guard told her that someone carried Mother out. Alive."

"That's a lot."

"I know."

"It's a lot of hearsay, actually," she pointed out. "I can't believe you *voluntarily* went to Witchhold." Her expression... was it *respectful?*

"I'm trying to find out more. The map room... it couldn't find her when I asked. It kind of went crazy, sliding all over the place."

"That table has limitations I can't even begin to explain," Kirmin said, irritation creeping into her voice. "There are probably a hundred ways to hide someone from it. It acts weird if you ask it to focus on someone who's here-but-not, like your great-great-grandmother was. It goes totally bonkers if you send it after something or someone that sets the Axis off somehow."

"Like what?"

"There was a story of a woman who'd never harmed a single living creature. I asked the table to find her, because I wanted to ask her if it was true. It went crazy. Best I can tell, our Axis can't wrap its head around someone who has zero participation in any kind of Ending. I mean, I assume the woman ate plants, but that wouldn't get the Axis' attention. I'm sure she existed, because when you ask the table for someone who doesn't, it just sits there and does nothing."

"So my mother is alive."

"Maybe. Or not-alive, which isn't the same thing as dead. But she's probably not dead, not if the table was doing that."

"So how can I find out more?"

She sighed, and stood. "You can't. Not with what you know now. You're going to have to keep plugging away at this until you... well, until you know more. Until you're ready."

"So let's do the next lesson. Right now."

She shook her head. "Sorry, Daniel," she said quietly, and vanished.

* * *

I returned to the main library, frustrated and angry. All I could do now was attempt to continue without her. I decided to try and learn more about the Tower itself, and how it fit in with the rest of witchkind. To think that the Tower could be *attacked,* or that the Sixth Axis adherent—me!—could become embroiled in witchkind politics... it had my mind gently spinning. My role was far more than just the "death and destruction" I'd first thought it, and I needed to understand more. Perhaps, I thought, I could learn more about my abilities, without waiting on Kirmin to reveal them.

I found a history book that contained a long, involved accounting that ended with a session in the court room. I carried the book to the first level, and asked the shadow-librarian to bring me any journals from that time period. It did so, and I settled down to read. The phrasing in the history book was old, almost archaic, and I wound up returning to the main library to look up unfamiliar terms. It made for a long afternoon, but I was able to piece together what I felt was a pretty accurate story, corroborated by the Whispers of the adherent at the time.

It seems that two clans of witchkind were in a dispute over a marriage. A young woman of the Velas clan had fallen in love with a young man of the Troista clan, and they had asked their families' permission to be married. The Velas clan had agreed; from what I could tell, they had something of a reputation for being pretty open, and supported the idea of dual clan membership. The Troista clan was the opposite: highly insular, very exclusive, and very much opposed to the marriage. The

Velas clan leaders were insulted by the Troista's rejection, and offered to let the young couple marry and become Velas members. The Troista clan was infuriated, flatly refusing to let their member marry outside the clan, and insulted by the idea of him leaving to join another clan.

Other clans rallied to support one or the other. From what I could piece together, the older and more high-born clans supported the Troista clan's claims, while younger and less wealthy clans supported Velas. Fighting ensued, and some of that fighting spilled over into the human world. The great Council of witchkind grew alarmed at that, and ordered the clans to stop. Both insisted that they could never stop until the situation was fully resolved: they insisted that witchkind law clearly state whether or not cross-clan marriages would be allowed.

The Council—which seemed to be comprised of representatives from many different clans—had its own internal debates, but could never resolve the question. Rather than allow the situation to continue and potentially result in more fighting, the Council summoned the Sixth Axis to render Judgement and End the dispute.

The adherent of the time, one Ismin Norman, considered the request, and refused.

The Council was infuriated. I will admit that I am reading a lot between the lines here, but the author of the history book gave the distinct impression—without explicitly saying so— that the Council of the time was known to be heavy-handed, impressed with themselves, and demanding. But the Axes do not answer to the Council, and Ismin was within his rights to refuse. The Council didn't see it that way though, and again demanded his Judgement. Again, he refused. They summoned him to appear before them and explain himself; he declined.

And so they attacked the Tower.

Ordinary witchkind have ample means to attack and to defend themselves, but they pale in comparison to the great powers that formed the Axes. The Council sent a fleet of four ships to bombard the Tower with mundane cannons (I had to look up what *those* were), and they launched magical attacks as well. Ismin held the Tower, Reinforcing it (the wording in the text made it clear that was magic of some kind) and shrugged off the attacks. This continued for several hours, apparently, before Ismin finally Ended the attack, crippling the ships and sending them limping for the mainland.

The next day, Ismin invoked the *nuosprendžiu teismas*, summoning the heads of the Velas and Troista clans, the Council members themselves, and the two young lovers to the Tower's court room. According to the history book's author, Ismin listened to both sides for hours, even going so far as to use his shadow-bailiff (which I presumed was what the court room's shadow-being was called) to force the two sides to politely let each other present their arguments and counter-arguments. After almost a full day of debate, Ismin called a stop. "The Judgement of the Sixth Axis," he told them, "will always bring an End to the issue at hand. But you find yourselves in a case where there is no Judgement I can offer. Neither of you are objectively right. You both hold your opinions strongly, but neither is more worthy that the other. Your differences run deeper than this relationship, or even this marriage. The only way to resolve this is for one of you to change significantly, or both of you to change a little. But something Ended cannot change; there is no change beyond an End. This is why I refused Judgement in the first place, and it is why I refuse Judgement now. If you would stop the disagreement, if you would stop the fighting, then you must find a change that can do so." And with that, he ended his magic, returning them all to where he'd snatched them from.

In the end, the law of witchkind was changed. Any two of witchkind could be married, without their families' blessings if they so chose. But, the clan could decide whether to accept that marriage. If the clan did not, then neither of the couple could be members of that clan. If neither clan accepted them, then they would form their own clan, and be recognized by the Council. It wasn't a perfect solution: I felt sorry for the young couples who must have had to make such difficult and momentous decisions. But it kept the peace, and let the clans retain their power.

An idea sparked in my mind.

I handed the Whisper journals back to the shadow-librarian, bundled the remaining books up in my arms, and dashed down the stairs to the main library. I laid the books in a haphazard pile on a handy table—the driežai seemed to handle re-shelving in this room, and always cleaned up after I left. I walked directly to the section of the library containing record books, and looked at the tall, packed shelves. My spark of an idea began to gutter, then. Where to even start? "I need my mother and father's wedding announcement," I muttered. "I wonder where—" I started, but a flicker of shadow made me stop. The shadow seemed to scurry up the shelves, pulling out a book about halfway up. I pulled it down, opened it, and discovered it was a social registry of some kind. Estimating the date my parents would have been married, I flipped ahead.

There it was:

Messrs. Aboydne and Scratch,
the former of clan Karal and the latter of no affiliation,
are proud to announce the union of their children,
Beatrice and Neville.
Ceremony at the Village Hall at Noon.
Reception to follow by invitation only.
Aboydne was my father's original surname, then. And Karal

his clan, both of which he'd abandoned to wed my mother—a decision he'd apparently come to regret in the decade afterwards.

I finally had a *name.*

I ran up the stairs to the second level. The shadow-servant was standing patiently next to the map table. "Show me Shura of clan Karal," I said.

The image on the map table slewed and steadied, then zoomed in. It focused on a little hamlet named Hook. It was located on the western half of the continent, next to a turn in the major river on that side of the world. The map had zoomed in enough that I could make out the individual buildings of the village, and it had centered on what looked to be an old, dilapidated stable on the outskirts.

Without hesitating, I cast the Visitation magic, adding the mental twist that would let me be unseen.

I appeared outside the building, in a small patch of bushes. My head was pounding, and I felt like I'd been gutted by one of the black spikes that Kirmin hadn't yet taught me to cast. I immediately fell to my knees and started shaking, absolutely certain that if I'd appeared in person I'd have been vomiting. I fell forward onto my elbows, ignoring the sharp branches that were pressing into my sides, heaving and gasping uncontrollably.

I'd meant to appear *inside* the building.

Darting around the inside of my skull was a frustrated, angry sensation. It was a hot, stabbing feeling of anxiety and hate. I remained still on all fours for several long, almost excruciating minutes, willing my heart to slow and for the pain to subside. Eventually the shaking stopped, and I was able to push myself upright. The burning anger in my mind was still there, but it had cooled to a sullen ember, tinging my vision a deep red-black. I regained some control over my ethereal form, floating myself back to my feet.

The building was indeed an old stable, but it was less dilapidated than the map table had suggested. Someone had recently made some rough repairs, affixing new lumber over old in an attempt to patch holes and make the structure more sound. As the sound of my own heart began to quiet, I could hear soft, low moans coming from inside.

Ever so slowly, I floated myself closer to the building, aiming for a door that looked entirely new. Even the frame had been rebuilt. I intended to float through that door and see what was inside.

But I pulled up short maybe fifteen paces. Try as I might, I couldn't force myself to float further. I lowered myself the inch or two off the ground, but found that I couldn't so much as shuffle my feet forward, let alone take a step. It was as if I'd run into an invisible wall that—

No. No, it wasn't like a wall. As I analyzed what I was feeling, it was clear that there was no force blocking my way. Instead, there was something wrapped around me—wrapped *inside* of me—pulling me back. That something felt... *personal,* in a way. I half-recognized it.

I eased back a couple of feet, and the restriction eased immediately. I stepped forward, and it pulled me back again.

I realized that *my own magic* was holding me back.

"Shura!"

A man's voice, raised in anger, seized my attention. I quickly floated back into the bushes where I'd appeared. Just as I moved into cover, an old man rounded the corner of the building. "Shura!" he shouted again, making for the door I myself had intended to use. He was perhaps two paces away when he stopped cold—much as I'd done, although it seemed from his body language like he'd stopped himself, rather than found himself restrained by his own magic. He shook himself, took two steps forward, and pounded on the door. "Shura!" he shouted again, and then immediately backpedaled several steps, wrapping his arms around himself as if the air had suddenly turned bitter cold.

The door swung open and a woman stepped out.

The same woman I'd seen at the funeral service at Mother's mausoleum.

"Loran," she said easily. "Been a while."

"I don't know how you can stand it in there Shura, with all that iron," Loran snapped.

"It's not so bad if you can keep your magic within you." Her expression was a kind of superior satisfaction, clearly pleased that she could accomplish something the older man couldn't. "What brings you here after all this time?"

I blinked. In that moment, I realized why I'd never been able to use the Whisper to eavesdrop on them after that first time. I'd always focused on the *two* of them, since otherwise the magic would only let me hear *one* of them. And yet they'd simply never been together.

"We agreed not to do it this way," Loran said, his voice still roiling with anger.

"We didn't *agree* to anything, Elder," Shura snapped back. Her eyes were blazing, and she took another step out of the door, swinging it closed behind her. "You *demanded.*"

"We've a dozen machines in operation already," Loran said. "They're working fine. There's no harm to witchkind. There's no need for... for *this,*" he spat, waving one hand at the stable. "What's your plan for when they're dead?"

"I'll burn them. They're only humans."

"And you don't think their absence will be noted?"

"Not for some time. They're not from Hook. They were a

trading caravan, and I left ample evidence that they were attacked by road bandits. Once they're missed, there's an easy, familiar explanation for why they're missing."

Loran shook his head, frustrated. "And so you've built an iron cage to keep them in."

Shura took another step forward, holding eye contact with Loran. I longed to see the older man's face, but his back was still to me. "That's right. And I can drain them far faster, and far more completely, without risking any of witchkind in the area. The magic is contained. I'm producing more than your dozen other villages will produce in a season. Loran," she continued, her tone becoming friendlier, "we can have what we need in a handful of years, not decades! And none of our people will need to be at risk!"

"No," Loran said stubbornly, finally turning away from her. It was the old man from the funeral.

"No," he repeated. "This isn't the way. I want to complete the plan..." His voice trailed off, and I realized he was looking directly at me. "Again?" he said, almost to himself, as his eyebrows beetled together. He raised one arm then, his palm outstretched and held flat in my direction.

I didn't wait to see what was next. I cancelled the Visitation magic and snapped back to the Tower.

Fifth Lesson

KIRMIN WAS STANDING over me as I returned to my body.

"You okay?" Her voice was once again full of concern, and I realized that I was covered in slick, cold sweat. Clearly, whatever had affected my spirit-form had also had an effect on my physical one.

"Yeah," I said as casually as possible, my voice scratchy and strained.

She frowned. "Learn anything about your mother?"

I thought quickly before answering. "Sort of," I admitted. "But no, not really."

"Care to talk about it?"

I was roiling with emotion—and I suddenly realized that it wasn't all mine. The fear, certainly—I owned that. But I was also feeling... excitement. Anticipation. Anger. Distrust.

"Daniel?"

No. A clear, unequivocal sense spoke inside me. I didn't care to speak about this. "Not yet. You're back soon," I said, trying to change the subject.

Her frown deepened, but she didn't press it. "Your fifth lesson is closely related to the fourth. I figure we might as well get it over with. You'll probably want some lunch."

I followed her down to the dining area, where lunch had already been laid out. She gestured for me to sit and eat, "I thought it best to get this underway before you got too out of practice with your Shroud." I frowned, and wondered—not for the first time—if she watched me when she was "gone." I had practiced the Shroud only once since she'd left, although it was frankly difficult to practice defending yourself with nothing to defend against. "How've you been?"

"Good," I said, swallowing a forkful of food. I realized I was famished. "I did have a couple of questions for you, though."

"Oh?" Her eyes lit up with curiosity.

"Were you... before you came here, I mean. Were you... lonely?"

"Ah. Hmm." Her eyes unfocused for a moment as she thought. "Yes, I suppose you could say I was. I came from an unusually large family. Six children, and we lived in a very small village, and we were related to half the other witchkind there. We all lived in a giant warren of rooms tucked into the rafters of a human inn. I hated the noise, the crowding, all the bustling. So from the time I was big enough to get away, I did. The village wasn't far from the Great Northern Wood, and so I spent as much of my days as possible on the edge of the Wood. I liked the quiet, the solitude."

"So it wasn't a big change when you came here."

"As an apprentice? No. Not much of a change at all, I guess. Fewer trees," she said with a grin, "but still quiet. And with this whole place to myself, just as you have."

I nodded, chewing while I thought.

"You said you had two questions?"

"Oh. Yeah." I swallowed, and put my fork down. I was

famished, but lacked the appetite to finish the meal. "The Book. I used it in the upper levels. I was just wondering—you've never really mentioned it. There are spells in it that you haven't told me about. I realize I can't learn everything at once, but when–" I stopped, as she held up a hand.

"I will admit," she said with a sigh, "that I've never personally read the Book."

My fork dropped to the table and my jaw dropped nears as far. "How is that possible?" I asked.

"It was lost by a previous adherent. My own predecessor had never seen it, although he told me about it. It's probably been lost for, I don't know." She waved a hand vaguely in the air. "Almost two hundred years? More? Obviously we lost track of it. Frankly, I should remember everything in it anyway, but..." she paused for a moment, and then said, "I suppose memories have Endings, too. But," she continued more cheerfully, "I'm glad it's back."

I wondered why she felt she should remember everything in it, and asked as much.

"We'll get to that in due course," she said easily.

"Did... did you want to see it?" I asked, reaching for my coat pocket. I'd been careful to shrink the book back into my pocket whenever I wasn't actively reading it.

"No," she said shaking her head firmly. "I made it through my time as adherent without it. Although... well. Maybe not," she said, getting a faraway look in her eyes.

"What is it?" I asked.

"Hmm."

My stomach grumbled a bit, so I pushed another forkful of lunch into my mouth and waited for her to continue.

"It's like this. Your family is... well, was, I suppose, a little remarkable. And yet not remarkable. Almost *deliberately* not remarkable in some ways. They all but hid themselves, practiced some frankly borderline traditions, and finally created you. And then you show up here, with your name, and with the Book. It's all... it's all a bit *purposeful,* if you see what I mean."

I shook my head. I very definitely did not.

"Your family's True name, it means 'judge' in the True language. And your family is one of the only ones in witchkind that is fully matrilineal."

"What does that mean?" I asked.

"Your Great-Great Grandmother, Pranasa, married, but her husband took *her* name. They had one daughter, Patience, who married. Her husband took the family name too. They had one daughter, your grandmother, named Constance. Again, married, but the man took *her* name. They had one daughter, your mother, who married—and once again her husband took *her* name. And having only one child in a generation isn't unusual, but when it's in *every* generation... it's worth noting. And their magic was always a little... *odd.* The women, that is. And then for the first time, their only child was a boy. You. Daniel the Judge. And apparently your family has had the grimoire of the Sixth Axis all this time, even though as far as I can tell none of you have ever been adherents or even especially remarkable. Did you know your mother never even finished schooling? I know she married young, and she probably didn't know more than a handful of runes."

I hadn't known that, but it wouldn't have surprised me. Even before her... illness, Mother had always been disinterested in magic. But something Kirmin had said triggered a memory. "Before Mr. Nash brought me here," I said slowly, "I saw her— Great-Great Grandmother—one last time. She said something." Kirmin looked curiously at me, and motioned me to continue. I held up a finger as I tried to remember exactly what the old woman had told me. Fortunately, as I'd come to realize as I worked through the primers on magic, I had an *excellent* memory.

Sky and Earth, Flame and Sea
Cast adrift, their center lost
Until a Sixth might come to be
To join them all, or pay the cost

Kirmin's eyes had grown wide. "That's not possible," she said when I'd finished. "Although obviously it is. You're *certain* you didn't read that in one of the books here?"

"I swear it."

"That's a *very* old prophecy. From the time of—it must have been the second or third adherent, after... after Galas," she said. "It's one of the great mysteries of the Axis."

"What's it mean?"

She chuckled. "Witchkind has little use for prophesies, because they're vague and open to so much interpretation. The general consensus here in the Tower is that an adherent will one day End the separation of the Axes, reuniting them, as part of some great crisis that threatens to destroy us all."

I stared at her. She grinned. "It wouldn't be a prophesy if it wasn't overly dramatic."

"Cast adrift? Pay the cost?" I asked.

She laughed. "Don't take it personally. People who write prophecies like to be dramatic, like I said. And they like words that rhyme. Don't make too much of it."

We stared at each other for a few long moments before she said, "Well, you're not adherent yet, and you won't be if I can't get you trained up. Let's go for your next lesson and let this resolve itself another time."

I still wondered if I should say anything about Loran and Shura, but again something told me to keep it to myself.

* * *

We stopped in the workroom long enough for her to show me the runes we'd be using, and then moved outside.

My new spell was *smaigas,* the Spike, the little black thorns that Kirmin had thrown at me during our last lesson.

"I honestly think they're meant to call to mind the spikes around the Tower," she said, waving one hand around her. "Kind of as an ironic twist. I can imagine Galas being bound here the first time, and then deciding he'd make the symbols of his intended imprisonment into his own power."

There are three basic variants of the Spike: I was to start with the Little Spike, the *mažas smaigalys,* which could be deflected by any sufficiently heavy material. Cast against anything especially sturdy—a rock, Kirmin said, or even a stout table—and they'd simply shatter. Fragile as they were, they were all but useless as weapons, but I learned to produce them quickly and—much more importantly—cast them with a great amount of accuracy. Practicing with the Little Spikes made the next part easier.

That was the *skraidantis smaigalys,* the Flying Spike—the primary form of the attack.

"These will do some damage," Kirmin said. "Your Shroud will stop them. The Form of Defense for any of the other Axes will stop them. Some of witchkind's more powerful rune constructs, which not everyone can wield, will stop them for a *while*. They're good for a couple of hundred feet, once you get proficient at them. Honestly," she said, giving me a lopsided grin, "I've never been a great shot past a couple of dozen feet. We'll see how you do, prophesy-boy." Her grin grew wider. "Look up."

I did, and was surprised to see two shadowy figures descending at me from the air. Neither was as fully formed as the shadow-beings on the upper levels of the Tower: these were wispier, more like flying cloaks than people. "Get them!" Kirmin commanded, startling me into action. Spike after spike flew from my fingertips, and I was proud to see that I *did* have a greater range than she'd said she did. Each spike tore through a shadow, although sometimes it took a couple to shred one to the point that it faded. She kept them coming, creating new ones each time one vanished. After a bit, two more joined the fray, and then two more, until I was holding off a half-dozen of the creatures, coming from every direction.

"What are these things?" I yelled, breathing heavily. There

was no real physical effort here, certainly nothing as difficult as running, but the constant movement had my heart pounding.

"*Atspindžiai,*" she responded, her own breathing a bit heightened as she worked to keep up with me. "They're... shadows, of course. Reflections, I guess is a better translation. They're things that once were, but no longer are. They're not good for much more than target-practice, but we can call them back from the End long enough to serve that purpose. The Axis remembers them from their Ending, and can reflect them for a short while. They don't feel anything, if that's what you're worried about."

"I'm more worried about what happens if I miss one," I said.

"Then don't miss," she said, giving me an impish smile. "You can look up the rune for calling them in your Book if you want, although I'm not certain how fun it would be to summon them *and* dispatch them all at once."

I focused harder as she added two more to the mix. We continued for quite some time before she called a halt. "That's enough," she said at last. "I think you get the idea."

"I think so," I agreed. "You mentioned three variations?"

"*Didesnis smaigalys,*" she said. "Greater spike."

She held two hands together, and raised them to the sky. A huge black spike formed around her arms and hands, covering them both as it rapidly grew to around four feet long. It took a couple of seconds, but then it launched into the sky and flew out of sight. "Big deal," she said, lowering her arms. "It'll disintegrate once you separate your arms. Takes longer to form, but it can take out a ship, or punch through a building. You have to hold your arms together the entire time, though," she added. "Once you let them go, it'll vanish, even if it hasn't hit anything. Hungry now?"

"Famished." Although I kind of wanted to try the rune myself.

"Then let's go back inside. I'm sure you have some more questions I can try to answer."

* * *

Lunch had been replaced with a tray of sliced fruits and cheeses, and this time I dug in with gusto. "How is it that I'm not exhausted after all that?" Hungry, sure, but even my breathing had quieted by the time we'd reached the kitchen.

"The Axis is doing all the work. We're just directing it. Oh, don't get me wrong—you can get into some situations where you're directing it to do complex things for hours on end, and *that* becomes draining, let me assure you. But it's doing all the actual work."

I decided to try and fill in some of the gaps in my knowledge of witchkind. "So," I said between mouthfuls, "what can you tell me about the clans? I know Father had to renounce his, but I don't think I have a clan. Where do they fit in society?"

"Ah, you've been reading," she said approvingly. "And no, as far as I can tell your family kept themselves apart from the clans. I've obviously been out of it a bit, but they'd started to lose some of their importance even when I was out and about in the world. Originally, all of witchkind belonged to one clan or another. Basically not much more than extended families. Each had their own traditions, their own values, and most were entirely contained in whatever town or village they'd come from. You've read about some of the conflicts, I presume?"

"One with Ismin Norman."

"Yeah, I read about that one. Big to-do over a couple of kids who just wanted to get married. Stupid. But the Council of that time, they were big-time stupid. Confronting the adherent of an Axis like that? They're lucky it was the Sixth—we tend to not hold a grudge. Mess with Second and they'll burn whole villages to the ground just to make a point."

I shuddered just thinking about it. "So how does the Council get chosen?"

"They're meant to represent the different clans, really. Last I checked, the Council has a dozen of witchkind, so obviously not every clan gets a seat. But there've always been family alliances, and geographic proximity, and things like that. Any clan can nominate someone to a seat, but in reality they tend to band up to give their nominee a better chance. Each clan then gets a vote, and the dozen with the most votes sit on the Council for a decade."

"And they can summon us."

"*Summon*, technically. It's a specific magic. *Iškviesti pabaigą* is the rune. 'Summon the End' is a close translation. Any council can use it. Actually, any of witchkind *can*, although I don't know if it's ever done by individuals anymore. Whether we choose to respond or not is up to us. Summoning is a complex ritual and when it happens, you'll know it, and you'll have a good sense of why. The Axis... hmm. The Axis is attracted to certain things. Beginnings, to a degree, because they represent an eventual end. But it's especially attracted to endings. *Endings,"* she corrected herself, and I could hear the capital "E" in her voice. "So if someone casts a Summoning, the Axis starts sniffing around. You'll feel it." She paused for a moment. "And you know, you can kind of... kind of *direct* it as well."

"What do you mean?"

She looked away for a moment, and then turned back to me. "It's curious. I think it somehow feeds on Endings. Or is maybe just satisfied by them. But if you point it in a direction, it'll usually sniff out things that are nearing an End, or seeming to. And you'll be able to pick up details about it. Try it in the map room sometime, if you want."

"I will." I polished off the last of my lunch. "Are you leaving now?"

She grinned. "Not quite. The fifth lesson is a two-for-one. Let's head upstairs."

* * *

I followed Kirmin up the five flights to the fourth level. "Do you need me to put the Book down?" I asked, reaching into my pocket.

She thought about it for a moment. "I'll admit that I'm curious about whether it would make a difference. I don't have any memory of it doing so, but still. Personal experience beats a memory any day, right?" I was absolutely confused—if the Book had been missing for so long, how could she have any memories about it? "But no," she continued. "Let's do it the way I always have." She made a gesture, and the stone walls once again showed a panoramic view of the Tower's surroundings. "There's a variation on the Shroud. It's *sustiprinta gaubta,* the Fortified Shroud, or Reinforced Shroud, depending on how you translate the term. You can only cast it here, as far as I'm aware, but it fortifies the entire Tower. The entire isle, actually. It's how Ismin held off those ships for so long."

"Do I... just do it?"

"You do. It's actually the same rune, just behaving differently when you're here. It'll surround the entire Tower, although you can strengthen specific areas just by focusing on them. Go on."

I looked "outside" and saw dozens of shadows floating through the sky, arrowing in on the Tower.

I cast the Shroud in my mind, and *felt* the Tower lock itself down. I felt... sturdier, somehow. Stronger. Rooted in place. The shadows struck the invisible barrier and simply vanished.

"As far as I know, nothing can penetrate that. You need to *be* here to hold it, and you'll get tired if you do it long enough, but when you're here with that magic active, nothing can touch you."

I dropped the magic as the last shadow disappeared from the sky. "As far as you know? You've never used it?"

"Not personally, no. Not in... not in a battle. I've practiced it. I once had a... a colleague. An adherent of the Third Axis. I had him toss a huge boulder at the Tower one time. He agreed because he was curious."

"And?"

"It hit the barrier and instantly turned to dust. Its time as a boulder was Ended."

"Anything else?"

"You know there's not," she chuckled.

"When will I see you again?"

With a twinkle in her eye, she vanished.

* * *

It was growing late in the day, and I needed to do something to relax. But at just that moment, I also didn't want to be alone. Whatever Shura and Loran were doing was still roiling through my mind. I could still feel the burning pain from whatever had kept me out of that stable—it being lined with iron, as Loran had implied, was the likely cause. But regardless, I wanted... I wanted to see people, right now.

So I returned to the second of the Tower's upper levels, and walked to the map table. The shadow-being detached itself from the walls and drifted over to stand ready by the table. "Show me... show me someplace I've never visited. Someplace with people." It placed its hand on the map, which obediently swerved and twisted until an unfamiliar village was centered. I touched the map with two fingers, drawing them apart to enlarge the village until I could just make out individual people walking on the streets.

And then I cast the Whisper Overheard and just *listened.* I looked at the tiny people on the map, going about their little lives, and wondered what they were doing. Shopping? Going home from work? The map table gave no indication of time of day; I could be looking at a part of the world that was just at sunset, or just at sunrise, and I wouldn't know the difference. Were these people just waking, or were they heading home to an evening meal?

"Show me my family," I ordered. I'd tried this before, and just like every other time, the map didn't move.

"Show me someone who knew my parents."

The map slid until I was looking at Mr. Nash's office.

"Someone else."

Nothing.

I frowned in frustration. My mother may have left Witchhold alive, but I couldn't track her down. Kirmin had already confirmed that the table's behavior suggested Mother wasn't actually dead. But I could do *nothing.* I could find *nobody* who knew my family.

A cold breeze seemed to waft gently through me just then, cooling my frustration. I looked at the map table, and it zoomed out, showing a map of the entire continent. At this scale, I could barely make out the tiny speck that was my island, all alone in the Southeastern Sea.

"Show me people again. Someplace new."

The map slowly zoomed in on a village near the middle of the continent, closer and closer until I could again see little people scurrying about their day. I stared for several minutes, becoming absorbed in the scene playing out before me. *Here,* something whispered in my mind, and my eyes were drawn to a small cottage on the edge of the village. I touched the map, invoking the Visitation rune. I was in a room with two humans, a man and a woman.

"I'm sorry," the man said. "I understand what you mean. I'm just... I'm frustrated."

"I know," the woman said. "I just don't know what to do about it."

They regarded each other for a long moment, and then embraced. "We'll figure it out," the man said.

I dropped the magic and returned to the workroom, sensing the Axis' disappointment that I hadn't lingered a bit longer. But that hadn't been an Ending... it had felt like the Beginning of one.

I wanted something more immediate.

"Show me someplace else," I ordered. "Something... Ending. Show me something... *now.*" As far as I knew, the shadow-being was part of my Axis, so why not talk to it that way?

The image on the map table spun and slid, and focused on a new scene.

Over and over again that evening, I visited Endings large and small, traveling unseen each time.

One unhappy human couple finalized their divorce before a magistrate, both of them seeming relieved when the proceedings finished. Both were angry with each other, pained by the good times they'd enjoyed, by the love that had once filled them before it turned sour and foul. I felt a hundred little Endings all at once: their marriage, their attachment to each other, their sharing of possessions. Yet as both of them left the magistrate's office, I could sense something else: a dimly perceived sense of the future. Both would go on to love others, to form new attachments. Their many little Endings begat tiny Beginnings.

A family of witchkind interred their grandfather, full of mourning but also talking about all the fond memories they had from from their lives with him. The old man's life had Ended some days prior, but now his family's attachment to him, their expectation that he'd be there each morning... that Ended now. Through the Axis, I could feel their pain, their grief, the cracks in their hearts. But at the same time, I could feel the *relief* that the other Endings brought: they'd loved him, and he'd died, and with the ceremony the process was concluded. They would leave here and go about their lives. Hints of Beginnings traipsed through the air: a new great-great-grandchild was humming in her mother's womb, a new business venture might get underway tomorrow, a tiny dust-mite would find a new home and start a tiny family amongst the old man's bones.

A small child finished her first year of school, skipping happily home and whistling at her accomplishment. This was a happy Ending: she'd been anticipating this day for weeks now, and now that it was upon her she was brimming with joy. The air was thick with Beginnings: the things she'd do until school started again, the dinner she planned to help her father make that evening, the book she'd begin reading under her bedcovers that night.

A politician completed his term, satisfied with what he'd done, but frustrated he hadn't accomplished more. A staid Ending, one long expected, filled with joys, regrets, and a grim determination to somehow do more. Beginnings teased at the edges of the man's consciousness: he could seek reelection, he could strike out to try and effect change on his own, he could go home to his wife and try to make the second child they'd been talking about for four years.

Each of them was a unique End. I could feel the Axis's interest in them as each Ending neared and culminated, and then its disinterest as the End passed. It lingered briefly at small Beginnings, as Kirmin had suggested: the birth of a child, the commencement of a family's dinner. But its interest was fleeting, and it turned quickly away with a sense of, "see you later."

As these scenes played out before me, I felt something *twist* inside of me. A change of some kind. My own loneliness, my own solitude, my frustrated attempts to learn more about Mother, whatever Shura and Loran were up to... it all just merged into a single, unnameable emotion. That connected to the scenes I'd just witnessed, the Axis' fascination with Endings and the tidal waves of emotions that accompanied every End.

I felt cold inside.

No, not *cold*. That carries a negative connotation, doesn't it? This was... a relaxing feeling. Not pleasure, to be sure, but a much-needed *lack* of feeling.

I felt *cool* inside.

It was as if my own emotions had been warming me, and their fires had suddenly guttered and died. I'd seen myself in relation to the rest of the world, and I felt small. But with the Axis curling around me, I also felt *endless*. *This* is what being an adherent meant: witnessing these Endings, bringing many of them into being, accompanied by a dark, primal power that existed solely to facilitate Endings and... to *appreciate* them, in a way perhaps no-one and nothing else could.

I needed to rest.

* * *

I was woken abruptly the next morning, the thudding of the front door—which I was convinced was magically enhanced—booming through the Tower. Sighing, I pulled on fresh clothes and made my way to the door.

"Mesla, senior adherent of Earth," my newest visitor proclaimed. She was a brown-skinned, brown-eyed, brown-haired woman dressed in simple brown homespun clothing. She wore a serious expression, offering none of the small smiles that Debesi had graced me with.

"Daniel, adherent apprentice of... the Sixth Axis," I replied, stepping aside and inviting her in with a wave. I couldn't bring myself to say "of Endings," even if that was the proper form of address.

"I won't stay," she said quickly, taking a step back. I raised one eyebrow and stepped back into the doorway. The soul-numbing cold I'd felt inside last evening had softened to a gentle coolness, and I somehow felt years older and unconcerned about whatever fear she was expressing.

"Then how may I help you?" I asked. The sound of my voice surprised me: it seemed deeper somehow, and more resonant. It was flat, but not emotionless—the voice of someone in full control, although I certainly didn't feel fully in control of *anything*.

"I've come to pay my respects to the new adherent-to-be," she said quickly. "And to ask a question."

"Please."

"Will you be about in the world? Or will you hold here, at the Tower? Will you involve yourself in witchkind, or stay apart?"

"You mean, what kind of adherent will I be?"

She nodded.

"Debesi asked the same question."

"What did you tell her?"

"That I didn't know, but that I didn't think I could stay holed up here until my own Ending."

"Ah."

"Since then, I think my mind has clarified on the matter." Where were these words coming from? I felt like I was lecturing this dun-colored woman. But I felt confident and collected.

"Oh. And now?"

"I believe I'll be out in the world. I believe witchkind deserves the services of an adherent as a moderator between them and the Axis itself."

"Ah," she repeated, looking confused.

"I believe I'll be a bit more of an activist than some of my predecessors," I added.

"Ah. Yes. Of course," she said, growing more flustered. "Well then, I suppose that will do. Thank you for your time." My eyes widened as she began sinking directly into the earthen pathway that led to the Tower's entrance.

"May I ask you a question?"

"Oh. Yes, yes, of course." She stopped sinking, her feet and ankles embedded in the dirt.

"What kind of adherent are you?"

She blinked several times before answering. "The Axis of Earth serves, above all," she said slowly. "I encourage that service. We... we serve all of witchkind," she said. "However they wish us to."

"I see," I said, nodding gravely. "Thank you for your time."

She stared at me for a long moment before inclining her head in a slight bow and sinking fully into the earth.

What a strange woman.

* * *

I decided to pay a visit to Shura—but only if Loran wasn't around. His ability to sense me was uncanny, and I had no desire to discover if he could actually harm me. But the map table refused to focus on him, jittering and sliding about in much the same way it had when I'd asked it to show me Mother's whereabouts. It focused rapidly on Shura though, and so I cast the Visitation rune, taking myself a short distance from her so that I could determine if Loran was with her or not.

That wound up being somewhat more difficult that I'd imagined.

Shura was traveling between towns, riding in an enormous wagon pulled by six large horses. I appeared unseen well behind them, and caught only the cloud of dust that the wagon was raising on the dry roadway. Focusing ahead a bit, I empowered the rune again, appearing in the trees off to the side of the road, a good bit ahead of the wagon. As it passed, I saw Shura sitting on the vehicle's front bench, along with another of witchkind that I didn't recognize. Neither paid the slightest attention to me.

I paced them for a few hours, casting myself well ahead of them and then watching as they passed. I attempted to put myself directly inside the wagon, but the Axis' magic shifted and twisted, either unwilling or unable to accommodate me. Instead, I satisfied myself with studying Shura on each passing of the wagon.

I could see in her face that she was a confident woman. Her jaw was firmly set, her eyes casting ahead in anticipation of wherever they were going. I thought that I saw something of myself in her: the shape of her nose, perhaps, or the way her cheekbones jutted beneath her eyes. Features I imagined my father must have shared and passed on to me. Her skin was as dark as most other people's, my own rare, pale skin having been a gift from my mother.

Shura was not unattractive.

But she was clearly on unattractive business. I was mindful of her conversations with Loran, and firmly believed she was on her way to another small town to drain the humans their of their vitality and life. I frowned to myself, fully aware that I should continue pacing her and her wagon to wherever she was going. If I returned to the Tower, its way of messing with my sense of time would make it all too likely that I'd miss whatever Shura was about to get up to.

I did in fact pace them for a few more hours, until the sun was just a glimmer on the horizon, barely seen through all of the trees that this road twisted its way through. Then she and her companion stopped, pulled into a clearing off the side of the road, and began making camp. They tended to the horses first, as I crept closer and closer to the wagon. I made to poke my insubstantial head through the wagon's wall to see what I could see.

It was like ramming my head into a tree. Pain lanced through my brain, accompanied by a flash of dark light. My magic was cancelled, and I found myself back in the Tower, nursing a splitting headache.

More Time Passes

I NURSED my headache for the rest of the day, all night, and well into the next day. The driežai brought me cup after cup of *skausmo malšintojas,* a powerful, bitter-tasting painkiller, until the pain finally subsided. It was the first night in the Tower where I didn't sleep completely soundly, instead tossing and turning and pressing my aching head into my pillow.

When the headache finally passed, and I had for the hundredth time promised myself I would tread extra carefully where Shura and Loran were involved, I decided to take it easy for a few days. No Visitations.

Fortunately, I had a new level of the Tower to explore.

I immediately started up the stairs to the fifth level, which I knew would now be unlocked. Placing the Book on that level's podium, I looked around.

The room was mostly empty, just like the level below. On a hunch, I activated *vaizdas,* the View, and the walls sprang to life, showing the Tower's surroundings. I looked down at the Book, which had flipped to a new page. It explained that my Shroud would be stronger here than on the level below, surrounding the Tower itself, the isle it stood upon, and even the air surrounding it for a hundred feet out to sea. The rune was different on this level: *gaubiantis gaubtas,* the Enclosing Shroud, would cut the Tower off from the rest of the world for however long I held the magic.

Scattered around the room were a few model cannons, carved from wood but cunningly painted to resemble black, battered cast iron. Each had a rune-set carved into the top of the barrel. Consulting the Book, I discovered they were called *galingiausia ietis,* the Mightiest Spear.

I rolled one of the wooden cannons to the wall, pointing it

out at the sea. I laid my hand on the carved runes, and activated them in my mind.

The cannon rolled backward slightly as a thick, solid black spike flew from the Tower out toward the sea. My aim had been slightly off: I'd attempted to point at one of the few spire-tips that thrust this high up, but my spear flew past it instead.

The Book explained that these spears could completely destroy anything from a large dragon to a war-ship. I counted a half-dozen cannons in the room, and hoped that whatever I might be asked to defend the Tower against, they would be sufficient.

I practiced for what must have been two or three hours—certainly long enough for the sun to reach its zenith in the sky. Today the sky was unusually clear, one of the rare days when you could actually *see* time passing by watching the sun arc through the sky.

Irritatingly, I never did manage to hit one of the isle's rocky spires. My spikes always slid past them. So smoothly, in fact, that I knew it must be part of the Tower's magic, keeping me from damaging them.

As I stood and read the Book, I suddenly yawned. As I did so, the Book flipped to a new page. This one explained that the fifth level relied on my own personal energy to a small degree, helping to further direct the great energies of the Sixth Axis. I *did* feel somewhat tired, although the Book suggested that practice would help increase my endurance. That explained the seeming duplication of this level and the one below: I might be less powerful on the fourth level, but I could defend for longer. This level might end a battle more quickly, but it would come at a cost of my personal energy as well. Hopefully there wouldn't come a situation where I had to rapidly run up and down the stairs between the two, because that would *certainly* tire me out more quickly. Just thinking about it, I decided to add stair-running to my fitness routine. I also resolved to spend some time here each day, increasing my endurance as much as possible in the event of need.

For now, I needed to eat something.

As I ate, I tried to come up with better, more accurate ways of tracking my time in the Tower. Perhaps in a decade or so when all for this became routine, I'd welcome a fuzzier perception of time, but right now? I was fourteen, for pity's sake.

At least, I thought I was still fourteen.

I'd already tried a number of tactics that had failed. Attempting to carve notches into the wall of my bedroom had proven difficult, with several minutes' effort resulting in little more than a barely noticeable nick. The next morning, even that had faded, the stone restored by some magic of the Tower. A simpler version of the same idea—markings on a piece of blank paper I'd had the driežai bring—had lasted only a few days until vanishing. Assuming the driežai had "cleaned it up for me," I started over, voicing explicit instructions not to bother the paper. It lasted four days before vanishing. Using ink to mark the skin of my arm worked for a few days, although I had to be careful not to wash that arm each morning. But the ink itself began to fade far more quickly than I'd imagined possible, the first marks disappearing in just days. Refreshing each mark every day didn't change the speed with which the ink faded.

The Tower, it seemed, was pretty committed to turning the passing of time into an abstract concept.

* * *

I think, although I'd run out of ways to try and prove it, that Kirmin was gone for longer than ever after my fifth lesson. Another lonely Midwinter Feast came and went, followed not long after by another small birthday cake, this time presented without fanfare by the driežai. That brought me to fifteen— although it occurred to me that, should the driežai ever fail to bring a cake on a given birthday, the day would pass without notice. I could have been any age, at this point.

I eventually returned to my routines: studying in the library, exercising outside and in the exercising-room, and occasionally exploring the world via the second level's map table and my Visitation rune. I'd used the Overheard Whisper a few more times, but eventually gave up on it. Without a purpose to my spying it seemed... uncomfortable. Dishonest, even.

But spying on Shura and Loran didn't seem at all dishonest, and I visited them often and with great care, trying to understand what they were doing.

I had to be exceedingly cautious with Loran, because his ability to sense me was powerful, and because he seemed to be specifically on guard against me. Though the map table could never pinpoint him, now that I knew his name and face I could visit him directly. I did so twice, and on each occasion his head had snapped unerringly to me, and I'd returned myself to the Tower almost immediately.

So with the Visitation off the table, I tried the Whisper— which was fortunately undetectable. Its biggest problem was that I had to target *everyone* I intended to listen to, meaning most of the time I only got Loran's side of the conversation, punctuated by gaps where other people spoke. Since I didn't know who he was with, I had no way to add them to the my magical eavesdropping. It made for frustrating listening, sprinkled with half-clues about what was going on.

That's good. That makes what, a dozen villages?

I know, but we can't acquire the raw metal any faster. And you know we need to be cautious. There are... those who watch, you know. I believe I've encountered one of them already, on a few occasions.

Of course not, and it's been a while now.

Yes, but it would be all too easy for them to run across us, especially as spread out as we are now. They may focus on them, but they're not stupid. We stay the course: slow and quiet.

That's fine.

No, the second model is more efficient. All but empowering the rune, which is obviously the bottleneck.

Even so, it makes more sense to make more of those. They're less likely to attract attention. You know how much miasma the first one creates. Anyone more sensitive than a brick can sense it.

They're no more difficult, it's just that she–

No, it's just obtaining the materials.

And yes, obviously that. If we could work out a way to empower the rune without her, then of course we would. But it's a small price to pay for the result we're getting.

No, she's quite secure. I'm sure of it.

That kind of exchange, both tantalizingly rich in clues and completely devoid of useful information. Who was secure? And why was she a bottleneck? And what rune was he referring to? It was all maddening.

And yes, *of course* it occurred to me that "she" was Mother. But what could I do about it? Both she and Loran were untraceable by the map table, and so I couldn't find their locations. I could visit Loran directly, but he sensed me every time. I tried using Visitation to get to Mother as well, but the magic kept dumping me in the mausoleum. Maybe she *was* there, dead after all, and everything else was just... wishful thinking.

I'd taken to directing my attention to Loran almost daily, even though the majority of his time seemed to be spent alone, or in the kind of mundane conversations about finances, what was for dinner, and so on that became incredibly tedious to listen to.

Shura, on the other hand, was far less sensitive to my presence, and so I visited her still. I was still circumspect, as she'd started gathering more of witchkind to her way of doing things, and I could never tell when one of *them* might be as sensitive as Loran.

That's where I finally witnessed the full horror of what she was doing.

I found her in another hastily repaired building on the outskirts of a small village. I'd chosen to appear some distance away, ever cautious of her profligate use of iron. This location had obviously been in use for some time, because the narrow dirt road leading to the old structure had been well-trampled. In fact, as I arrived a cart was just pulling up to the building. As it rolled to a stop, its team of horses champing and nickering nervously, a heavy wood door flew open. There was Shura, carrying what was likely a dead human over one shoulder. She tromped up to the cart, dumped the body into the open back, and headed back in. Another of witchkind—a man, this time— was the next out. He and Shura went in and out a dozen times apiece, dumping more than a score of bodies in the back of the cart.

"Drive it to the ridge, just like last time," she said wearily after the last body was aboard. The man nodded, and climbed up next to the cart's driver. "Stay until they're burned this time. Last time, Gregor was lazy and the pile started attracting scavengers."

"Aye," the man said tiredly, gesturing for the driver to move on.

As the cart rolled past me, I got a good look at the poor bodies inside.

Men and women, all paler than possible, their normally dark skin drained to a pale, sickly gray. Even their hair had turned an almost unnatural white. They lay in an heap in the back of the cart, arms and legs sticking out of the pile. One of the bodies on top had been dumped on its back, and I could see its eyes, all color drained of the irises, staring miserably into the sky.

I could feel my Axis swirling around the area, sullen and angry. This wasn't the kind of Ending it wanted, and its fury was a cold, black hole in my stomach.

I shuddered, and took myself back to the Tower.

* * *

The sight of Shura's efforts put me off further visitations and eavesdropping for several days. Instead, I tried to understand *why* they were doing what they were. But the books in the Tower proved to be of little help. Nothing discussed anything like "draining" or any other word I could think to connect with what I'd seen. After a few days of looking, it all seemed gradually less and less urgent, a feeling I was starting to recognize as the Tower's way of blending the days together to minimize the sense of passing time.

When I wasn't trying to piece together clan Karal's plan, I spent much of my time in the Tower's library, trying to better understand the Axis and the world at large. I'd been so sheltered as a child, and so focused on adventure stories in my reading, that I found myself incredibly ignorant of witchkind's history.

I had come to realize that the library's section of history books were organized into two groups. The first group were general histories of the world, including notable people and events. The second and much larger group were histories of the adherents of the Sixth Axis. These were written from the perspective of someone outside the Tower commenting upon the adherents' actions, and they detailed most of the major public Judgements that the past adherents had made. Many of these narratives included information on those Judgements' outcomes and aftermaths, which I found especially enlightening.

One of the earliest adherents, Plaktukas by name, had become well-known for one particular Judgement, which the author of the history had named The Veil. It seems that back then, witchkind and humans mingled more freely. They knew of each other, and humans were aware of witchkind's special powers. Most small human villages had at least one or two families of witchkind, and they worked to ease humans' illnesses, helped to ensure the growth of crops, and so on. Back then, apparently, witchkind and humans got along just fine. But that started to end. The historian wasn't clear on the reasons—and I made a note to research the matter more fully—but humans at some point became jealous of witchkind. Or fearful, perhaps. Or maybe something else. Whatever the reason, they began to find reasons to cast witchkind out of their villages. In some regions, witchkind were hunted and killed. In others, they were shunned. In others, witchkind clearly got the message and made themselves scarce.

But even where witchkind withdrew voluntarily, humans remembered them, and would continue to attack them when they could. No small number of humans were caught up in the violence, either because they had associated too closely with witchkind, or because they were simply accused of being witchkind themselves.

The Council placed a Summons on Plaktukas and asked him to pass Judgement on the situation. This particular historian implied that the Council was really asking Plaktukas to punish the humans, but the adherent took the matter seriously.

He spent months considering the issue, and eventually called the Council to the Tower's court to hear his decision.

"I cannot simply End all humans," he said, according to the historian, "and I believe you understand that. However, I can End the relationship between humans and witchkind. I can End humans' memories of us. But I cannot prevent humans from rediscovering us, should some of witchkind be indiscreet and reveal themselves. So I will also End our coexistence with humans. We will no longer live alongside them in their villages. We will no longer pass them in their streets. Instead, we will retreat to the corners and shadows that they ignore. Witchkind will move away from the human settlements, and live in obscurity, or we will hide within the bones of their towns and villages, just as obscurely."

And it was so. The outcome was what the historian had termed the Veil: the ability for witchkind to live in and around human settlements, but never be seen. Our spaces would be within their walls, in their neglected spaces, and just out of their sight. Plaktukas' Judgement changed the very nature of space for witchkind. Our powers would be diminished in the presence of humans, to maintain the illusion that we were simply human ourselves. Humans would keep their stories of witchkind, but that's all they would be: stories. Over time, those stories would become further separated from the truth, helping to protect witchkind from discovery.

Plaktukas' Judgement was not universally popular, but one does not ask the Sixth Axis for a Judgement and then change one's mind once that Judgement is rendered. The Axis Ended the connections between witchkind and humans, apparently for all time, for the Veil persisted to this day.

Plaktukas' story was the first time I truly began to grasp the reach and power of my Axis. He changed part of the nature of the world, all to create an Ending. It was a terrifying power to consider, and I wondered if Kirmin would ever find *me* worth of wielding such a power.

Another history concerned an adherent named Silpnuma, whom the historian referred to as Silpnuma the Weak. Apparently, Silpnuma had gained a reputation for avoiding Judgements whenever possible. She would refuse to answer Summons, and on the rare occasion she accepted them, she would refuse to render Judgement. The Council of the time had become furious. The historian appeared to take the Council's side, but reading through some of the Summons they'd issued, I felt that they were simply trying to use the Axis to further their own political goals. Amongst the litany of refused Summons and declined Judgements, I found only one or two that—based on the limited information in the book—I'd have acknowledged myself.

The historian even included a quote Silpnuma had made at one of the few Summons she'd answered. "You seek not only to harness one of the most ancient and powerful of the primal, wild forces," she'd scolded the Council. "You seek to saddle it and ride it about to prove your mastery. But my Axis is not your mount, to be made to jump and trot and canter at your whim. It is the one wild force that is inevitable, that comes to us all, in a time of its own choosing." She'd vanished after making that pronouncement.

Almost as a footnote, the historian acknowledged the one Judgement Silpnuma had apparently conceded to make: a mother had managed to cast the Summons, and had begged Silpnuma to pass Judgement over her sick child. The child had suffered for years it seemed, and the mother wanted to know if her daughter would recover or be resigned to a life of pain. "Neither," Silpnuma had replied. Despite losing her child, the mother had thanked Silpnuma for her mercy. Silpnuma had passed from history shortly afterwards, and the world had lived without an adherent of the Sixth Axis for more than two decades.

* * *

I had long since exhausted the primers on magic that the library contained. I had leafed through some of the more specialized texts, but found most of them to be boring and esoteric. Strangely enough, the text that occupied much of my attention at that time was a book on kitchen-magic.

I have already related how the simple pantry in my family's house remained perpetually stocked, albeit with a lack of variety. Although most runes stopped working shortly after they were cast, the pantry magic was perpetual, provided it was given some kind of perpetual anchor. Sunlight upon a roof was a common anchor, from what I'd read. The complexity of the construct—and at a minimum, they often required hundreds of runes and intense concentration—determined the amount and variety of the food the pantry would stock.

The Tower's pantry had obviously been blessed with an incredibly complex replenishment construct. Although the driežai would frequently include favorites—they prepared a purple root vegetable mash that I was especially fond of—I would often go weeks without seeing a repeat of some items. I was especially impressed with the pantry's ability to replenish fresh food like vegetables; everything I'd read in the kitchen-magic book suggested that only non-perishable foods could be included. I decided to investigate. I'd recently taught myself another rune, *atskleisti pagrindą*, Foundation Disclosed, that would show me the runes underlying any perpetual magic. I was curious to see how the Tower's builders had achieved what they'd done.

Although I caught sight of them most often in the kitchen, the driežai were present all over the Tower. I'd seen them scurrying into my bedroom with fresh clothes, and I'd spotted them darting into the kitchen to clean up my dishes after a meal. A few times, out of sheer boredom, I'd attempted to communicate with them. I fixed my eyes on one—no mean feat, as their shadow-forms seemed to continually flicker in and out of existence—and spoke directly at it. Each time, the one I'd spoken to had paused, and briefly seemed to become more solid. But they'd never answered any of my questions, and I'd never managed to change their behaviors that way. Not that they weren't accommodating; all I had to do was voice a request aloud, and if the Tower could fulfill it, it would. When I'd first realized the Tower's generosity, I'd made myself sick on sweets after dinner one evening. I partook of dessert much less often now.

Today however, I had a goal that didn't require an answer from the shadowy little creatures. I walked into the kitchen, stood at the large table, and said, "I'd like a cup of *arbatos*, please." Kirmin had suggested it one time, and I'd grown immensely fond of the hot, slightly spicy beverage. Within moments, a driežai flickered into the room carrying a stone mug of steaming liquid. "Excuse me," I said to it, fixing it in my vision. It froze, the mug only an inch from the table top. "Could you take me to the pantry, please?" I asked.

For a moment, it flickered intensely, as if I'd asked it to do something impossible. I was about to retract my request when it lowered the mug to the table. Its form solidified into a deep, intense shadow, shaped almost like a miniature dragon. It moved toward the kitchen exit, gliding through the room more slowly than I'd ever seen one move before.

Just outside the kitchen, the driežai stopped and waited while a section of the stone wall swung open. My eyes widened. I'd always wondered where my food came from of course, but I'd never found anyplace. I'd more or less assumed it was part of the Tower's magic, but I'd never supposed there was a secret passage. Inside the doorway was a stone staircase, spiraling gently downward. Small torches in wall sconces flickered to life as I approached, causing the driežai to briefly vanish in their bright light. But we continued down, the shadow-creature and I, until we came to the bottom of the stairs. It was a substantial descent—I estimated we were descending the equivalent of two levels. I remembered the vast, empty space I'd discovered below the kitchen level. I'd never returned to it, but I imagined we were descending past it even deeper into the base of the Tower.

The stairwell opened into a broad, brightly lit room that... well, it was amazing. Even thinking about it now amazes me. The sheer audacity of the Tower's builders, or whomever had created this... wonder.

The room was more like a wide hallway, eschewing the upper levels' round floorplan for a simple, broad rectangle. It was easily eighty feet across, and probably triple that in length. Along the walls stretched shelves, each reaching to the height of the ten-foot ceiling and neatly packed with non-perishable foods. There was enough food here to feed a small army, and not a single shelf had an inch of empty space that I could see. I spotted salted hams, great wheels of cheese, bushels of dried grains, and stacks of fresh-looking bread. My joy at the hot, buttered toast I had each morning was doubled when I realized that this room must also have some kind of magic to preserve freshness.

But the shelves were not the true wonder of the room. Stretching down its center, aligned in neat rows, were hundreds of feet of rectangular wooden planters, each bursting with vibrant life. I saw tomatoes, onions, the purple root vegetables that I loved so much, and more. There were herbs, miniature fruit trees, and even the brightly colored squashes that graced my meals during the colder months.

The driežai scurried away, its mission complete, and I wandered through the food-hall in awe for some time. The light was as bright, and of the same quality, as the cheeriest summer day I'd known at my family's house, and seemed to emanate directly from the stone roof of the hall. Powerful magic indeed, and I was hesitant as I cast the *atskleisti pagrindą*. The text I'd learned it from had assured its readers that divining the nature of an active magical construct posed no danger but... well, this was clearly a set of runes out of the ordinary. But with the confidence of my youth, I cast the rune anyway.

The air in front of me flared to life with brightly colored runes, glowing in pinks, purples, blues, and greens. This hall wasn't maintained by a series of carefully made perpetual rune constructs; the *entire* hall was a *single* incredibly complex construct, consisting of *thousands* of distinct runes. My eyes widened in amazement. I stared at them all for several long moments, and then dropped the magic, allowing the runes to fade from the air.

The smells of the hall were so comforting, so... quieting. It occurred to me that there was one smell, one flavor from home that I'd never seen on a plate in all my time here at the Tower.

"Do you have *ramunėlių*?" I asked aloud. No driežai appeared, and I had an overwhelming sense of disappointment floating through the room. No, then. But I knew how to obtain the seeds: the book on kitchen-magic had gone on at length about the *sėkla iš tolo* rune, designed to summon seeds from mature plants anywhere in the world. I combined that rune with the one for *ramunėlių*, and a small pile of glossy white seeds appeared in the palm of my hand.

I walked over to the one of the planters. This one contained a miniature kartaus-fruit tree. The driežai had once prepared an after-dinner tart from the fruit, but I'd found it incredibly bitter and asked that they not serve it again. "Can this space be used to plant these seeds instead?" I asked.

Shadow-forms swarmed over the kartaus-fruit trees, and within moments they were gone. All that was left behind was a richly scented earth. I pressed my seeds into it, pushing each one in no more than an inch. "Thank you," I said. "I hope these do well, and if they do, the leaves of the plant can be steeped to make a calming tea at bedtime. Mother–" I continued, but then stopped. Already, green shoots were pressing up through the dirt, reaching for the gently glowing ceiling. I stared, entranced. Within minutes, the first wet leaves were unfurling themselves from the stem, and within minutes more the first blooms were appearing. The sudden growth—part of the hall's magic, I assumed—slowed and stopped once the plants were fully grown. "Thank you," I whispered. This would be a taste of home.

That brief pleasure was interrupted by the pounding noise of the Tower's front door.

* * *

"Greetings! I am Gilioj, senior adherent of Sea. You are Daniel, adherent-to-be of the Sixth. You're not yet sure what kind of adherent you'll be, but you're leaning toward being fairly active." The old man smiled, his brown, bald head wrinkling merrily as he did so. "Figured I'd get that out of the way. How are you doing?"

I blinked several times, trying to assimilate what was happening. "I'm well," I said at last.

"You're looking well," he agreed jovially. "I'd ask you to invite me in, but I'd honestly be more comfortable on the shore. Walk with me?"

I nodded, uncertain of what more to say, and fell in beside him as we walked slowly back toward the island's little beach.

"I know Debesi and Mesla have been here already. You'll have to excuse all of us for popping in on you as we do. It's just that we're mad with curiosity, and of course it's not like you have much of a social calendar where we could meet more casually. You're what, almost seventeen, now? Are you almost done with your apprenticeship?"

I blinked again and almost stumbled, rapidly trying to count birthday cakes in my head, but Gilioj carried on without waiting for a reply.

"It's just that the other four Axes have a... hmm. I guess you could say we have a balance with the rest of the world, humans and witchkind. We help when we can, we do what we need to get by, we have our little systems. The Sixth, on the other hand, is a bit of a wild card. You're all different, you know? No system, no little tribe of fellow adherents, just single, solitary you. Sometimes you just sink back and let the world run itself. But sometimes you *change* the world." He gave a little chuckle. "I think we're all just wondering which you'll be doing."

"I'm not sure I'm planning to change the world," I managed to get in.

"Ah, but plans can change, no? And we all dance to the will of our Axes, in the end. The Sixth especially, and it moves us all, does it not?"

I hesitated for a moment, and realized he was actually waiting for a reply. "How do you mean?"

We arrived at the little beach, and he gestured to the sea. "Take my Axis. Entire communities of witchkind live inland, and know nothing of the sea. They've never tasted fish, never smelled the salt air. Or take the fisherwitch families of the coasts, who spend so much of their lives on the waves that Earth is almost a foreign power to them. Not every Axis affects every person, you see. But the Sixth? We all know of Endings. We all experience death. When the Sixth exerts itself, it gathers up Earth and Sea, and even Flame and Sky, with it.

"I suppose we're all just wondering if the Sixth has taken an interest in anything, or whether it will let us be for another few decades."

"I... I don't know," I stammered. "I'm not even the adherent, yet."

"Of course not, of course not," he mused. "Still, it's unusual for so little to be known of you. Did you know that? Almost nobody knows anything of your family. The world of witchkind is not so large that an entire *family* can go unnoticed. So we know nothing about how you were raised, where you were from, what allegiances you might hold, what biases you might carry. Very unusual indeed." He looked at me gravely, the jolliness gone from his face. "So who *are* you, Daniel?"

I shook my head quietly, unsure of what to say.

"What do you know of the people to whom you will bring judgements and Endings?"

I shook my head again.

"Well, I suppose you've still some time to find out." He

nodded firmly, and a broad smile returned to his face. "It was good to meet you."

"I suppose Flame is next?" I asked as Gilioj stepped toward the sea.

"Zmogus? Perhaps. Prickly, that one. He might just stay away."

"Thank you for visiting," I said politely.

He gave me one last smile, and then vanished in a spray of salty water.

* * *

Gilioj's words hung with me over the next few days. What *did* I know about the rest of witchkind, let alone the humans we shared our world with? What I'd read in stories, mostly. What little I'd gleaned from Kirmin—over what had apparently been more years that I'd realized. What I'd seen and inferred in my visits to places like Twynsits and the little village near my old home.

I needed to get out more, and not just to spy jealously on happy families and couples.

I took myself to Chiton, the largest Northern city. As the Visitation magic faded and the city resolved itself around me, I almost cast a rune of warming on myself, before chuckling and realizing that the blowing, blustering winds couldn't affect me. Light snow flurried through the streets, and the sky overhead was gray and forbidding. I'd read about the winters in Chiton of course, but *seeing* it was another thing entirely. I was sure I'd get to visit in person one day, and vowed to try and make it during the summer.

I spotted a small witchkind-owned shop hidden in a rain-collection barrel on the corner of an alley. I watched a woman of witchkind gently rub the entry-rune that was carved into the side of the barrel, vanishing inside. I couldn't follow her directly of course, but I'd gotten a good enough look at her face to set the Visitation magic on her, taking me directly inside the shop.

It was a clothing shop, and every inch of space seemed to be stuffed with racks, each rack almost overflowing with clothing. Dresses, shirts, slacks, coats, scarves, and more all seemed to be jammed wherever they would fit, with no thought given to organization. The colors were mostly muted earth tones: deep oranges, browns, grays, dark blues, and the like. The only splashes of color came from the boxes of gloves and mittens, which were stacked in the very few spaces that weren't occupied by the hanging-racks. At the back of the store, stacked haphazardly against the rear wall, were bolts upon bolts of cloth, ready to be made into whatever clothing a customer might desire.

I just stood for a moment, taking it all in, when a voice behind me said, "Too cold to be visiting us in person then, lad?" I turned and saw a wizened old man before me, dressed in a neat suit the color of storm clouds. "Ordering then, I presume?"

"I'm sorry?"

"Can't very well be picking up like this, so I presume you're here to order something?"

"Oh, no—sorry. I was just—I'm new here, so I was just exploring. Seeing what there was."

He frowned, his forehead wrinkling heavily and his eyes going cold. "So awash in magic are you, then? Just pop out and go 'exploring' like this, instead of properly and in person?"

"I—I don't understand," I stammered.

"Don't understand," the old man muttered. "Explore all you like then, can't hardly stop you when you're as you are." He stalked toward the back of the shop, still muttering angrily.

"Don't mind Ebenez," a woman's voice said. I turned again and realized this was the woman I'd followed into the shop. "Only it *is* a bit rude to show off such."

"How am I showing off?"

"How much magic does this spell take, this apparition? Convenient as all, I don't mind telling you, especially given the weather, but at what cost, young man?"

"I—" I could exactly tell her I was the adherent-in-training for the Sixth Axis and that I wasn't using my own personal magic for this. "It's someone else's magic," I managed.

"Someone quite rich with it, then," she said with a sigh. "I suppose your the boy of some council member or something? Or one of the sea-merchants?"

"Something like that," I lied.

"Well, a word to the wise and keep your extravagance to the richer district. This is a working-class neighborhood, it is, and we spend our magic wisely." She shook her handbag, and I could hear the distinctive rattle of coins against each other. A *few* coins, at most.

"I'm very sorry. I didn't mean to offend anyone. It's just— this is the only way I'm able to leave the house." Close enough to the truth.

Her face softened. "Ah, one of those poor children. I see. Well, never you mind then. Wouldn't be in need of clothing, no matter how simple, then. So what brought you in?"

I had no idea what "poor child" she assumed I was, but if it settled the question of my non corporeal presence, I'd play along. "I was actually just looking for someone to talk to," I said. "I followed you in."

"Ah. Well... Ebenez' shop is probably not the best, might have chosen a cafe or an inn or something. But I have to tell you, much as I have sympathy for your... condition... I'll admit it's a bit eerie to be standing here speaking to you as if you were a ghost. And that beside, I've got to get back to my own shop. Just nicked in to pick up a shawl."

"It's right here," Ebenez' voice growled as he made his way back to the front of the shop. "Ah, you're still here."

"Now, Ebenez, he's no choice in the matter, you know. He's one of—"

"I'm sorry again, sir," I said quickly, before the story could get any more convoluted. "I'll go. Have a good day," I told the woman. I let the Visitation magic return me to the street.

A cafe or an inn *would* be a better idea. I wandered the street for a bit, being very careful to walk and not drift, and finally happened upon a small pub nestled between an apothecary and a trading office. Out in the open as it was, it was obviously a human business, but Gilioj had mentioned how the Sixth impacted them as well. I waited until another customer left, and then slipped inside as the door was swinging shut.

The room was dimly lit, the main source of light being the windows which were admitting the sullen gray daylight from outside. A few tapers burned in wall-mounted sconces, casting a weak, flickering glow. The place looked clean though, and a number of patrons were sitting at simple, sturdy wooden tables that were closely placed along the walls. A narrow aisle between those tables led to a bar that spanned the back of the shop. A human woman ferried food and drinks from the bar to the tables, while an older man worked behind the bar, pouring tall mugs of beer and shuttling food from the kitchen to the bar top.

I decided to talk to the bartender.

To the humans, I looked like I was physically present. So long as I was careful not to drift along, or to let anyone walk through me, the illusion was perfect. As I passed one table however, a middle-aged man sitting at it glared at me. I felt the soft tinge of magic that told me he was witchkind, not human, and I assumed he—like the old man in the clothing shop—wasn't pleased to see my profligate use of magic.

Ignoring him, I stepped up to the bar and struck up a conversation with the bartender, who turned out to be the proprietor. He kept the conversation going even as he filled more orders, promising that he'd get my order as soon as he caught up. As I obviously couldn't even pick up a mug, let alone drink anything, I told him to take his time.

We talked briefly. Business was good, the weather was poor as always, and his family was doing well. The city fathers' proposed tax on strong drink was concerning, but he doubted it would go through. I let him carry most of the conversational effort, only interjecting simple questions or comments to help keep it going, as I had no idea how to truly engage a human in small talk.

After a few minutes, I started to feel a heat on the back of my neck. When the bartender ducked back into the kitchen to retrieve a food order, I turned around. Two tables' worth of witchkind were glaring at me now, their looks openly hostile. I had a strong sense that it wasn't just my magic that was upsetting them: the fact that I was *talking to a human,* beyond the basic interaction needed to order a meal, was alarming them. Indeed, as I looked closer, their anger was layered over a very intense, very immediate fear. One woman looked almost horrified, and seemed ready to bolt from the shop at the slightest additional provocation.

I nodded slowly to them and abandoned the bar. I hurried outside, canceled my magic, and returned to the Tower.

"More exploring?" Kirmin's voice came from behind me. I whirled to face her, startled. She grinned. "Always glad to see you practicing." She laughed at my discomfiture. "I do so enjoy our time together, Daniel."

Sixth Lesson

"SO WHERE DID your explorations take you this time? Learn anything new about your mother?"

"No," I said with a sigh. "I don't even... I can't think about that all the time. No, Gilioj came to visit."

"I don't know that one."

"Adherent of Sea."

"Ah. You know, it never occurred to me that they'd come visit you. Has he been the only one?"

"No, Debesi and Mesla have already been here. Sky and Earth."

"I know Debesi. Or knew her. She was pretty young. She's senior now?" I nodded. "Interesting. What did they want?"

"Didn't the senior adherents of the time come visit you when you were apprenticing?"

"Hardly. They barely said a word to me the entire time I was adherent."

"Oh. Well, they mainly wanted to know if I was going to be an activist or a recluse."

She barked a laugh. "And what did you tell them?"

"That I don't know yet, but I was leaning toward trying to do some good in the world."

"Good for you. And what did they say to that?"

"Nothing, really. But Gilioj... he asked how much I knew of witchkind. Of humans. Of the people I'd be affecting, with... you know. Endings."

She tilted her head slightly. "You know, I keep forgetting that you grew up so isolated. You really *don't* know witchkind or humans, do you?"

"Not really."

"And so you went to what, meet a few?"

I blushed. "I guess so."

"And?"

I took a moment to find the right words. "They're just... people. They talked about the weather. They didn't like how much magic I was using." Kirmin grinned at that. "They talked about taxes. I don't know... I guess I thought..." I trailed off, uncertain how to finish.

"You thought you'd have some big revelation, some clue that would make all this Axis stuff worthwhile."

I nodded.

She sighed, and gave me a long look before answering. "It *is* worth it. Mostly. The world benefits from firm hands guiding these powers. Bringing reason to chaos. But that doesn't mean the world itself is especially... special. They're just people, as you said. But that... hmm." She thought for a moment more, looking into the distance. "Being *just people* is enough," she said at last. "If you'd had a more normal childhood, this probably wouldn't even be on your mind."

We stood quietly for a long moment. "Did you keep in touch with your family? After?"

"After my ascension? No. Not really. I visited for holidays, at first. But having an adherent around isn't comfortable. *Any* adherent, but especially of the Sixth. It's so much power. And it changes you. Changes *them,* maybe. So no."

"What about... relationships?"

"Meaning?" She raised an eyebrow, her face suddenly cautious.

"Were you ever in love?"

She frowned. "I think we should get on with the lesson."

* * *

"What I showed you last time was the Axis's Form of Attack," she said, her voice becoming businesslike and clearly marking an end to our discussion. "What I show you today is not technically an attack, although you can use it that way at need. Today, you're going to learn the Form of Purpose. This is the main expression of the Axis, its primary purpose in the world." She gave me a level, stern look. "You're going to learn to End," she said.

"This isn't a thing we do lightly," she said, her face solemn. "The Sixth Form of each Axis represents their fundamental natures, the powers they exercised most freely as wild energies. The powers that, at their greatest and most uncontrolled heights, triggered the Archons to bind them in the first place. You could argue that these powers are why we, as adherents, exist at all."

She looked intently at me, and I felt the gravity of her words. The air around us actually seemed to become more still, and more serious, as if it was waiting for me to acknowledge... my purpose. "I understand," I said firmly. "This is Ending things."

"Yes," she said, holding my gaze. "This is Ending things. This is why our Axis is feared so much more than the others, and it's ultimately why we were bound to the Tower in the first place. Nobody likes having an Ending forced upon them, whether it's a death or simply Ending an argument."

"I've been reading some of the histories," I told her. "Trying to understand the different Judgements."

"That's good," she said. "Ultimately, you'll come to have a much more personal level of understanding about those, but it's good for you to have that background. Good to have those perspectives.

"Are you ready?"

"I think so," I replied carefully.

"Well, let's leave all this then," she said, offering another grin as she gestured around the lush food-hall. I followed her back up the narrow staircase to the kitchen, and then up the spiral stone stairs to the main level. She didn't turn to her workroom, though, and instead continued to the first upper level, then the second. We passed the court-room, the viewing-room on the fourth level, and the fifth-level defense room. It seemed like yesterday that I'd first walked into that room, but Kirmin kept going. She'd unlocked the sixth level in advance of my actual lesson this time.

As we emerged into the round, almost empty room, she gestured at the book-podium. "You might as well," she said. "I've never seen it in action." I removed the Book from my coat pocket, and placed it on the podium. As always, it flipped itself open, this time landing on a rune that looked similar to the starting runes on the two levels below. I activated the rune in my mind, and a portion of the Tower wall turned into a window, rather than the entire room.

"Interesting," she said. "And convenient. This is *maty-damas*, the rune of Seeing. You don't need it to enforce an Ending, but it will let you do so remotely, as you're still bound to the Tower."

"If we were bound to the Tower out of fear of Endings," I asked, "then why was the Tower built to let us perform Endings at all?"

"Back then, witchkind knew that they needed us. But they didn't want us wandering around uncontrolled and unob-served. Their intent was the we would remain here, hold court below, render our Judgements, and come here to execute our Endings. We would be confined."

"Harnessed," I said, echoing Silpnuma's words.

Kirmin tilted her head at me. "Just so. But while the Axes bound the wild energies, the Archons didn't seek to *confine* those powers. Galas himself quickly understood how our restrictions could be bypassed. But by always being careful and diligent with the Axis's power, he and later adherents were able to allay most of witchkind's worst fears. They never really admitted that the Tower didn't confine us like they meant it to, but they didn't pursue the matter either."

She walked over to the magical window, and laid a hand on the wall next to it. The image blurred, taking away its view of the jagged spires and the gray sea outside the Tower, and re-forming to show a human encampment. From my reading, I recognized it as a small army, perhaps five hundred men. It was night wherever they were. "These humans are about to attack a nearby settlement," Kirmin said sadly, "for no reason other than their leaders' desire to control more land and more people. The settlement is poorly defended, but its people are proud. They'll resist. Many of them will die, and they'll be subjugated under their new masters' harsh will."

She turned away from the window and looked at me. "You can End this army. You kill them outright or," she said as I frowned, "you could End their ability to find their way. You could End their loyalty to their master. You could End their master. There are many ways for you to resolve this."

"No," I said without hesitation. I knew this was a test. "It isn't my place. Another leader like this one will arise. This one would send another army. Stopping this battle would make me feel better, but it would not resolve the situation. And I know nothing other than what you've told me. I couldn't render a true Judgement." Plenty of the histories I'd read had included situations like this one, and it was almost always better for the adherent not to act.

She smiled. "It's difficult for us all, in the beginning, not to use the Axis's power to resolve what we see as wrongdoing in the world. But you're right: that isn't our place, and it isn't our power. Too far down that path and we'd become despots ourselves, and finally justify the fear witchkind has had all along." She touched the wall again, and the window once again blurred and formed on a new image. It showed an old man, lying still on a narrow bed. I could tell that his breathing was labored. "He's dying," Kirmin whispered, as if the magic would carry her voice through the image. "And we would not normally interfere with that unless Summoned. His only child, his daughter, spends half her days caring for him. Once he passes, she will grieve, and then likely leave their small village for the larger town nearby. The man was an apothecary, and he passed all his skill and knowledge on to her. There's great demand for her skills in the town, but she's held herself back here. His disease is a slow, wasting one," Kirmin said, shaking her head slowly. "He's held on for three years longer than anyone might expect." She fell silent.

"I could End him," I said.

"It would probably be a justice. He will die regardless, and you would release him from his pain."

"But I have only your word on all this," I said.

She gestured. "Look at your Book," she said.

I hadn't moved from the book-podium, but I hadn't noticed the Book flipping to a new rune: *žinodamas*, it said. The Knowing.

"It will only work here, or if you are physically present with the person you are querying. It's actually a variation on our Form of Mind," she said. "It will verify all I've told you. But you must understand its limitations: it will *only* work on someone you're with physically, or that you're viewing through this window—it won't work if you're using the Visitation to be with them in spirit form. It will only work on someone who's End is already around them, who has attracted the Axis's interest. And it will only show you the current facts about their situation as *they* see it. Use it, and you'll see the man's own desire to pass on. You'll see *his* expectations for his daughter but you won't know her feelings on the matter."

I took a couple of steps toward the window, and held the rune in my mind. It confirmed everything Kirmin had said: in my mind, I saw the daughter toiling to care for the old man, struggling to make a living in their tiny village. I saw her, through *his* eyes, finally leaving and setting up a shop of her own in the prosperous town. I *felt* his pain, continuing and unending. I turned to look back at the book, and it now displayed a single rune: *galas,* the End.

The name of the Axis's most essential power, and the adopted name of the Archon that had bound it. I turned back to the old man, lying in his bed in the window. I held *galas* in my mind. He exhaled softly, and was finally still.

I released all the magic, and the window faded into the stone wall. "So I can just stand here all day and find dying people who need release?" I asked, some bitterness in my tone.

Kirmin shrugged. "You could. Look up Gailest the Merciful

in your histories. She was the adherent, oh, four hundred years past or so, at least. That's all she did, all day, every day. But it's not easy. You can't simply direct the window to show you people who are suffering. I had to search out this man myself, so I would be able to show him you. The window can only show you people you command it to. So yes, you could become a hermit, dealing out mercy as she did. How you conduct yourself as adherent is entirely up to you."

I thought about it. "No," I said at last. "I don't want to just be a... killer."

"It's your call." She paused. "I won't be gone as long this time. Your last lessons need to be finished soon." And with that, she vanished.

* * *

I sat in the library long into the night after Kirmin left. But for once, I wasn't reading.

I was thinking.

Could I not just End all of clan Karal? Everyone I'd ever seen with Shura wore the same medallion she did, one that I assumed represented the clan itself. Could I not simply seek out everyone who wore such a medallion and methodically end them, one by one? Or, based on some of Kirmin's comments and the histories I'd read, could I simply not End the *entire* clan, all at once, with a single statement? It seemed well within the Axis' power to do so, although I didn't know if —as I was still an apprentice, not the true master of the Tower —it would follow my instructions on something so significant.

I took myself to the second upper level, and stood in front of the map table. "Show me anyone of clan Karal," I ordered. The map lit up, small points of bright light hovering anywhere someone of the clan happened to be. I picked one at random, and used the Visitation to project my consciousness there.

If I'd hoped to come to some kind of definitive conclusion on clan Karal, then it was a long and unfulfilling night.

I saw families, mothers and fathers tucking their children into bed.

I saw a Healer, gently pushing magic into a man who'd been wounded on a fishing boat, reattaching a hand that would otherwise have been lost.

I saw a petty cutpurse using a stealthy magic to insert herself into a crowd, then using more magic to relieve several humans of their coins.

I saw a merchant and his wife, moving new goods from a cart into their shop.

In short, I saw all manner of people, all of clan Karal.

And no few of them completely undeserving of the fate that Shura, at least, was so *richly* deserving.

So what about Shura? I could End her easily, presuming the Axis let me do so without Kirmin's supervision. But that wouldn't stop the problem, would it? I'd already seen her with at least two accomplices, who would surely take up her work if she was dead. I could End them too, of course, but how many were there that I hadn't seen?

No. It was too risky. That was the lesson of all the histories I'd read: Endings must be careful, precise, and well-considered. The unintended consequences of hastily contrived Endings *always* resulted in trouble. If nothing else, it would show that the Sixth Axis was acting without reason or remorse, the exact fear that had caused this very Tower to be erected in the first place. I didn't know if the adherent of the Sixth Axis could, while standing in this Tower fend off all of witchkind, and I didn't intend to be the adherent who discovered the answer to that question.

I needed more information.

I yawned. Apparently I also needed more sleep.

* * *

I awoke the next morning feeling completely refreshed and relaxed, a state that existed for approximately one minute and was broken by the thudding sound of someone at the front door. I hastily threw on fresh clothes and took myself to the entry foyer.

The man standing at the door had jet-black hair tinged with red highlights. His eyes were a red so dark as to be almost black, and his ruddy black skin was flushed with deep red. He was dressed entirely in heavy, scarred black leather, as if he was accustomed to working at a forge.

"Senior adherent of Flame?" I asked, after he'd stood staring silently at me for several moments.

"Zmogus," he snapped. "I won't need much of your time. I've spoken to the others"—by which I assumed he meant the other senior adherents—"and I'm not here to quiz you. I'll simply offer you a warning, and then go."

"A warning?" I asked, ire beginning to rise in my back.

"A warning," he repeated. "I know you're to be the all-powerful adherent of the Sixth. Fine. Stay in your Tower, roam the world, do as you will. Nobody can stop you. But restrain yourself from becoming a world figure. You're no emperor. You're no ruler. You've no right to bend the entire world to your will. Refuse the judgements they'll ask you to make— don't be their crutch. Let the world take care of itself. Stay out of it." He clamped his lips shut, as if he had surprised himself by saying so much.

In as polite a voice as I could manage, I said, "I appreciate your warning. I'll definitely think hard about what you've said."

Or rather, a half-wish that's what I'd done. Instead, I found that my manners had deserted me. "And this is the directive from who, the mighty adherent of Flame? Or is this the consensus of the four of you? Because let me be clear: you are on *my* island, standing before *my* Tower. I will do my best to guide the powers of my Axis, as I presume you do with yours. I will bend it to the good of the world as best I can, as I presume you and the others do. I will *not* see myself as a dictator, although you clearly have some work to do in that area. And I will thank you for your visit and bid you good day." And with that, I slammed the Tower door in his face. I waited in the foyer for several long minutes as my nerves reacted to what I'd just done and I began shaking uncontrollably. I forced myself to breath deeply, and eventually settled.

I took myself unseen to the island's little beach and drifted back to the Tower to confirm he'd left.

At least the other three hadn't been jerks.

Seventh Lesson

"TOLD you I wouldn't be gone long," Kirmin said from her usual perch on the kitchen table the next morning. At least, I think it was the next morning. I had become increasingly convinced that the reason I woke so refreshed every morning is that the Tower was somehow keeping me asleep for days and weeks at a time. It could have been a month since I'd last seen her, and I'd have no way of knowing.

"You did," I said cooly. I wouldn't admit it to her, but I'd become accustomed to the long periods of solitude between her visits, and I'd hoped to spend more time researching the histories in the library. Not to mention investigating the food-hall downstairs to see what other wonders it might hold. And although I did enjoy seeing her, and I was excited for what I assumed would be my final lesson, I still hadn't decided if I actually could be the adherent, be an all-powerful killer. "Is it time for my seventh lesson?"

"After breakfast," she said magnanimously, gesturing to the food that had been laid out. I sat and began to eat. "I want to talk about this one a bit before we actually get into it. There are some... unpleasant memories around it for me, and I've never really had to talk through it before."

"Oh?" I asked around a mouthful of food.

She sighed, thought for a moment, and began.

* * *

I was lucky enough to become the adherent during the reign of the worst, most selfish, most power-hungry Council that I think witchkind has ever seen, *she said*. They'd managed to rig the selection process, packing the Council with a group of truly small-minded, ambitious, un-empathetic bastards. That alone was bad enough, but before long they started ignoring the Council's own long-standing policies and coming down hard on witchkind. Entire families were hauled off to Witchhold on spurious or trumped-up charges, just so the Council members could add the "criminals'" properties to their own personal estates. They dusted off obscure laws that carried the death penalty, and started having their foot-soldiers enforce them. It was an ugly time. They didn't seem to care at all about the survival and protection of witchkind, which was their job. Instead, they seemed intent on amassing as much wealth, property, and power as possible.

One of their most offensive projects aimed to move all of witchkind into larger towns, fully apart from humans. They wanted to rip witchkind out of their traditional homes, even from behind the Veil, and concentrate them into what they called "hidden cities." It was nothing more than a baldfaced attempt to get as many of witchkind as possible under their personal control. They executed it by depriving witchkind of their traditional family homes, shutting down businesses in smaller villages and rural areas, and more. That Council is one reason witchkind tends to prefer to live in smaller, more remote places now—it's a long-standing reaction to that time.

Witchkind in several larger towns tried to put up some resistance, even going so far as to put together a no-confidence petition. Under witchkind law, a sufficient number of signatures would have triggered a new election, ousting the current Council. But the Council caught wind of it and had most of the organizers either killed or imprisoned. The petition faded away, and everyone who knew of it quickly learned to keep to themselves.

The adherents of the other four Axes, typically considered outside Council law, tried to intervene. One adherent of the First Axis actually tried to destroy a ship that was carrying two Council-members, in an effort to open up at least a couple of seats on the Council. That wouldn't have worked; these people had plenty of like-minded colleagues they'd have filled those seats with, rigging the elections just as they'd rigged their own. Regardless, the attempt didn't succeed: you don't get on the Council, rigged elections or no, without being pretty powerful. The two Councillors simply rescued themselves. Short of unleashing their fill Sixth Form and basically declaring outright war on the Council, there wasn't much the adherents could do. You have to understand that the first four Axes play a crucial role in witchkind society, and they couldn't afford to lose the trust and respect of ordinary people in some kind of coup attempt. They *could* have crushed the Council, especially if all four had aligned themselves to a single plan, but they'd have cast witchkind into chaos. It's honestly doubtful that our people would have survived that kind of plan, and I think they all knew it.

So it fell to the Sixth Axis. Everyone's already afraid of it, and it's pretty much considered the last resort.

I called the entire Council into the court-room. We can't

really enforce that power unless there was someone accusing them of something, but I'd found one of the petition-organizers who'd managed to survive, and she was more than willing to level charges against the Council. She stood right here in this Tower, along with all of them, and accused them of... well, basically of everything they'd been doing.

There's no doubt they were guilty. But I don't apply the law; that isn't what the Sixth Axis's Judgements are all about. And I was in a tricky position: I could have Ended them all, but their rise to power wasn't a fluke. Kill them all and more of their faction would have taken their place. It's like you've learned from the histories: you can't solve underlying problems by simply wiping out the current incarnations of them. I needed to do something more forceful. More... dramatic. Something that would demonstrate to *all* of witchkind that the Council's actions wouldn't be tolerated. Something that spoke beyond the law, and touched on the basic truths shared by all of witchkind.

And yes, I see the question on your face: I could have killed this set of Councillors, killed the next set, and kept on going, but the underlying problems—the assumption that the Council could be bought or stolen, or that the Council was above its own laws—would still exist. I had to do something to clearly demonstrate that the *attitude* would not be accepted, and would never be successful. I had to do something... forceful. Something to remind all of witchkind that something more powerful and eternal than themselves existed, and was watching.

The Council's chambers are in Evermore. It's one of the few towns that belong entirely to witchkind. There, our people don't need to hide in the corners, keeping behind the Veil. They can walk in the open, do magic anytime they please, and live however they want. It's an expensive town to live in, which is one reason all of witchkind doesn't simply move in. More importantly, it is the *Council's* town. All of the Council members live in lavish homes at the center of the town, surrounding the actual Council Hall. And they're defended by the Council Arms, the only armed force in all of witchkind. Nominally, the Arms keep order in the city and enforce the Council's edicts. Of course, they'd been completely subverted by the Council—one of their first acts upon being seated, in fact, had been to put their own people in the Arms' ranks of officers.

What I felt I needed to show was that the Council, even with the force of the Arms behind them, couldn't just discard centuries of witchkind law and tradition. So I did something that no adherent since Galas had done: I mustered demons.

The Seventh Form of the Axes let us call up a group of magically constructed creatures, designed to execute the Axis's will *en masse.* It lets us act on a larger scale than we could on our own, and it's a pretty visible sign of our power. It's the closest we come to taking the Axis off its leash and letting it act as a wild power again. The First Axis summons kraken from the depths, the Second calls up an army of fire-beasts, that kind of thing. In our case, it means calling up a Horde of terrifying creatures whose sole purpose is to End those we've directed. Once the Horde is called into existence, the only thing that can stop them is the completion of their directive. The Axis itself becomes largely unavailable to us during that time as it gorges itself like it did in the old days. It's... it's horrific.

My Horde marched into Evermore, willing to ignore anyone who wasn't on the Council or in the Council Arms' officer's corps. They destroyed most of the Council residences, and almost all of the Arms' barracks and other buildings. They slaughtered the entire Council and all of the Arms' officers, although they all put up a strong fight. The thing about the Horde is that it's literally unending: until it completes its mission, you can kill all the demons you like and more appear to take their place. One Councillor tried to bring down the Council hall itself on the Horde, and succeeding in destroying hundreds of demons. But hundreds more simply appeared in their place and tore the man to pieces.

Once the Council and a quarter of the Arms' men and women were dead, the demons vanished, their mission complete. Witchkind recovered from its collective shock, and new Council elections were held. The old Council's remaining cronies stepped back, afraid that they'd meet the same end. And they would have. Archons help me, I would have done it again.

You won't find this story in any of your histories, Daniel. At least, not the full story. You can certainly read about the demon horde that destroyed the Council of witchkind, but you won't find me or the Tower mentioned. None of witchkind even knew it was me. None of them even know the Sixth Axis can *do* that. As I said, it's been done only once before, and Galas summoned the Horde to stop a grand army of humans bent on destroying witchkind. Even then, he attributed the Horde to something else, saying a group of witchkind must have summoned it. So witchkind feared the Sixth Axis no more than it ever had, and we helped bring a terrible, terrible time to an End.

But at such a price.

* * *

My eyes were wide as Kirmin finished her story. "I hope you never have to use our Seventh Form," she said, her eyes moist. "If our Sixth Form is a precise, surgical way to End strife and suffering, the Seventh is a blunt instrument. Innocent people died under the claws of the Horde," she went on, her eyes taking on a faraway look. "They got in the way. They tried to protect the Council, the same Council that had been standing on their necks. Witchkind came together, forgetting their disputes with the Council for that moment. You would normally be proud of them, right? Putting aside their disagreements to face what they thought was a common foe bent on destroying them all. Those that stayed home, that stayed inside, survived. But plenty didn't." It was several long moments before she looked directly at me again. "Let me take you to the seventh level," she said.

I followed her out of the kitchen and onto the great stone spiral staircase for what I assumed was the final time. As we trudged up the stairs though, something occurred to me. I hadn't used my Visitation rune in a long while, having grown bored with Visiting random villages and towns. I recalled my second lesson with Kirmin:

"It lets us leave the isle?"

She smiled. "No, and if you tried, the spires of the isle would catch you on their tips and hold you here. Initially, you'll be able to send your spirit, not your body, and only for a limited time. As you grow stronger and more used to it, that time will grow longer and longer, but your body will remain here."

But I wasn't leaving the Isle, was I? I was staying right within the Tower. I summoned the rune in my mind, and pictured the sixth level with its wooden model cannons. With a rush of wind, I was there, standing on the staircase that now stretched upward an additional level. I climbed that level, only to find Kirmin waiting for me. "I wondered how long it would take you to try that," she said with a small grin. "Frankly, I'm surprised it took this long. You must really like climbing stairs."

"Good exercise," I muttered, drawing the Book from my

coat pocket and placing it on its podium. This level was completely empty, the only notable attribute a large circle carved into the stone floor, completely surrounding the staircase. A second, larger circle encircled the first one, with about five feet of space between the two.

"The Seventh Form can only be exercised when you're standing in that ring," Kirmin said, pointing at the space between the two circles. I looked closer and saw that the stone there was a slightly different color—rather than the usual gray used everywhere else in the Tower, this stone looked reddish. Stained, even. I swallowed heavily at the implication.

The Book, which seemed to have taken a moment to settle itself this time, finally flipped open. As I'd expected, the rune it showed was *demony minios,* the Demon Horde.

"If you use that rune," Kirmin cautioned, "make sure you have extremely specific and finite goals in mind. Remember, they won't end their carnage until your directives are fulfilled. You need to set them a clear mission with a clear, objective ending. Otherwise, you run the risk of them continuing forever." I shuddered at the thought.

"There's more," she added, "which I see is not written in the

Book." She took a deep breath. "You'll be trapped in the ring until the demons complete their task. The Axis will stop answering to you, and the Tower itself will stop functioning. You'll be vulnerable—completely defenseless. The driežai won't serve you. If your mission carries on too long, you'll starve." She gave a slight shrug. "That won't matter, of course. You won't die from it, but it isn't pleasant, let me assure you."

I turned a page in the Book. "What's this one?" I asked. The rune was *giltinė*, the Reaper.

"I... I don't know," she said, shaking her head and peering at the page. "And I don't know how that's even possible. This says it's another expression of the Seventh Form, our power to temporarily unleash the Axis. But... I've never heard of this one. I don't remember any other expressions of the Seventh Form. That... that shouldn't be possible. How can I not remember?" She fell silent, still staring at the Book.

Memories have Endings, too, she'd once told me. I turned the page again. Or tried to: the Book firmly refused. It was as if the remaining pages in the Book—perhaps a tenth of its overall thickness—were fused together into a single mass, and could not be separated. "I can't turn the page," I told her.

"There's more, then," she said softly. "More, but not for you. Or perhaps not for me."

I looked again at the Reaper. "A flight of bringers of death, it says," I said. "To simultaneously bring an End to those who deserve it. It says you can assign each Reaper a target. This..." I paused for a moment, and looked up at her. "This is a more precise way to End several people without unleashing the Horde."

Her eyes were wide in horror as comprehension sank in. "Why?" she asked, her voice thick with emotion. "Why wasn't I told about this? I could have..." she stopped, looking away from me. I understood. This was the tool she should have used, had she known about it. She could have Ended the Council, the officers of the Arms, and spared all the innocents who put themselves in the path of her Horde. "After the Horde," she whispered, "I stayed here. I was so afraid to use my power again. Thirty years... was it forty? I don't remember," she said, shaking her head. "I rarely left the Tower. I... all that time. All those people." She fell silent. Then she looked back at me. "I'm sorry," she said, and vanished.

* * *

I stood in that room for a long time after Kirmin left. This is what it came down to: could I unleash the Horde? Or even the Reapers? The latter would clearly be a way for me to deal with the death clan Karal had been unleashing on the humans all these years. I'd simply need to track down everyone involved, which wouldn't be that hard. I could assign a Reaper to each, and the task would be done. I obviously couldn't do it *now;* the Book was specific that only the actual adherent could access the Seventh Form. But my choice of whether or not to accept the mantle of adherent couldn't be far off.

Was I a killer? A mass murderer, even in the name of a good cause?

I had never missed Mother so much as I did in that moment.

I had never felt so completely and utterly alone.

Final Lesson

KIRMIN'S STORY sat heavily in my heart for a day or two. *All those people.*

I had no obligation to the humans that clan Karal was... killing. Draining. Whatever. I technically had no *obligation* to any of witchkind, even: the Sixth Axis' adherents did more or less as they pleased, and the minimum I was required to do was to simply *exist,* to give the Axis a physical form that could be directed.

But *all those people.*

I needed to see more of what Loran and the rest of clan Karal was doing. I needed to see what their supposedly less-destructive efforts led to.

I focused on one of the villages where I'd tried to visit Loran. I wouldn't try to appear to him, if he was even still there, but I could at least get a sense for what the humans of the village were experiencing.

Farreach in the North was a cold, windy, uninviting town in the summers, but this was the thick of winter, and I had never been more glad that my spirit form wasn't affected by the weather. Everyone bustled through the city bundled in blankets and furs as snow blew nearly sideways through the streets.

I could easily pick out those of witchkind: they wore a bit less clothing, relying instead on small magics to help stave off what was obviously a biting cold. That much, I could perhaps have expected. What I did not expect was to see how hale those of witchkind seemed to be, compared to the humans all around them.

Those poor souls limped and staggered through the streets, clearly tired. *Drained of energy,* even. I followed one couple, supporting each other as they trudged along the snow-dusted cobbles, until they arrived at a physicker-shop. They managed to push their way in, and I floated through after them.

"You'll have to wait, he's with someone right now," a harried-looking woman was telling the couple. She was standing behind a small desk, guarding a door that doubtless led to the physicker's work area in the back. Her dark hair was frazzled, her long white work coat smudged, and her expression frustrated. The couple merely nodded, shrugging out of their heavy coats and blankets and taking up places on either side of a small fireplace that was set into one wall.

I drifted through the door that led to the back of the shop.

The back room was a cramped affair, the walls lined with shelves and cabinets containing sachets, bottles, boxes, and books. A sturdy bed occupied the center of the room, and a man lay on it. His face was drawn and wan, although not the sickly, unnatural gray of Shura's victims. Two other men stood on either side of the bed, examining the prone man. The first was clearly the physicker, dressed in the same kind of long white coat as the woman out front. The second was an older man, dressed entirely in black, a heavy white chain hung around his neck.

. . .

"It's nothing in his humors," the physicker said. "I smudged an entire pot of bane-leaf, and that should have removed any dark humors. But he remains weak."

"Abel, when did you last eat?" the black-clad human asked.

"I've eaten regular, Father," the man on the bed mumbled, his voice hoarse and tired. "Breakfast and lunch today. Three meals yesterday. Three afore that." He shook his head weakly, the heavy bedclothes crinkling slightly at the movement. "Doesn't help. The missus started feeling it yesterday. The two boys are still fine, but my Davvi was looking tired this morning, despite she having slept well all night."

"It's why I called you, Father," the physicker said. "He's the tenth one this month, and the other shops have had a like share. I spoke to Tunny yesterday and he said this whole neighborhood has come down with it."

"Not unlike the mountainside quarter a month gone," the man in black said.

"Aye," the physicker agreed.

"Vermin then? Those small biting insects? Sheffenton last year had an outbreak—"

"But that would *spread* from one neighborhood to the next," the physicker disagreed. "This *moved*. Mountainside's fine now, almost everyone recovering."

"Recovering?"

"All but the elderly," the physicker said. "Takes a few weeks, but eventually everyone was right as rain. That lets out a sickness of the blood—one doesn't recover from those so readily. And it lets out anything vermin-spread. Even aether-spread, to my thinking."

"So what are you suggesting?"

The physicker looked left and right, as if checking for eavesdroppers, before speaking in a low voice. "Magic, Father."

"Mag– are you mad?" The man in black made an odd hand gesture over his chest, his two hands quickly twisting together then untwisting, a movement I'd never seen before. "I pray to the Three you've not mentioned that to anyone else."

"Wasn't my notion, Father. Tunny brought it up, and said Mullen had brought it to him. We spoke: it's the only answer that fits the symptoms. Nothing else we've done has helped, and yet to see mountainside recover? And lakeside, a hundred people came down with similar symptoms a month ago, and they're all now starting to show the same signs of recovery."

"Which means we can expect the same here, once this runs its course?"

"Likely so, but it'll strike someplace next."

"But *magic*." That last word came out in a hiss. "There's been no sign of magic in the world for millennia. After the Time of Sundering, the Three put an end to magic." A pause, followed by a firm shake of the head. "No. It can't be. I'll consult the books of course, but no. Continue to treat these people as best you can, and lay to rest your thoughts of magic. It's... it's heresy. And it's *ludicrous.*" He fixed the physicker with an even stare. "Do you understand?"

"Yes."

"Good. I'll speak with Tunny and Mullen as well. Good day."

The man in black saw himself out, pushing past the couple I'd followed in as well as another woman who'd apparently just entered.

I floated outside, following the man for half the block before stopping. I had a sudden feeling of anxiety, of fear. Helplessness, even. Something in the back of my brain was screaming at me to hide, to curl up into a ball in the deepest hole I could find. I shook my head for a moment, wishing for just a second that I could *feel* the freezing winds blowing around me, just to snap me out of it. This was the Axis I was feeling, its emotions again bleeding over into my own.

Then the town vanished.

* * *

I was floating hundreds—no, it must have been thousands, *tens* of thousands—of feet above the world. I could see the sharp folds of the mountains, the deep blues of the lakes and rivers, and even the blue-gray of the ocean. I could see forests, villages, and towns.

And laying over all of it was a pale, translucent white gauze.

The world suddenly flew closer, and I descended into a small village near the center of the continent. I found myself standing on a street, humans and witchkind walking about their business of the day. The humans moved freely, unimpeded by the gauzy film that I could still see, laying gently over everything.

But those of witchkind... they were *covered* by the gauze. It draped over them, moving easily with them as they walked along the street. Where the humans seemed to simply walk *through* the gauze, it *hung* on my people.

A small child of witchkind, holding her mother's hand as they walked along, laughed brightly as she cast a small magic from her free hand. It was little more than a spark, the harmless experiment of a child still delighted by what it had learned to do, but the reaction of the world was instant.

Her mother immediately reached down and clamped both of the child's hands together. The two came to a stop, and the mother crouched down, speaking to the child in a low, urgent voice, their noses nearly touching. The child's expression was hurt, disappointed, and confused, not understanding why she was being scolded.

But the gauze...

It had snarled at the exact moment the child's magic had been unleashed. In that brief moment, the child had been brighter, *clearer* than before, her true colors shining through the twisted, separated fibers of the gauze. Even as I watched, those fibers knitted themselves back together, suppressing the child's bright hues, damping her and her mother back into subtle, gray-tinged normalcy.

This was the Veil, I realized. The great working that had Ended humans' memories of witchkind and magic, and that separated and protected us still. It was delicate, ever so fragile, and it depended entirely on magic being kept *out of humans' minds.*

Except that at least some humans were now proposing magic as the cause for whatever ailment clan Karal's plans were causing.

I withdrew my magic, and let myself return to the Tower.

* * *

I stayed up long into the night, the implications of clan Karal's actions, and their possible impact on the Veil, foremost in my mind. Their works, whatever they were for, now stretched beyond making some humans sick, or even killing a few. The Veil itself, the fundamental magic that let humans and witchkind live safely together, was threatened. Something needed to be done.

I slept little that night, napping briefly in my chair in the library, before my stomach finally prompted me to seek out breakfast. As I descended to the dining room, I saw that Kirmin had finally returned.

"Happy eighteenth birthday," she said from her customary spot on the kitchen table, in front of the small cake the driežai had made for the day.

Eighteen years, I thought. Five years I had been in this Tower. It hadn't felt like... even the birthday cakes didn't add up, did they? That is the moment when the full weight of the Tower's manipulation settled over me. Five years of my life lost, broken only by Kirmin's lessons, my vague memories of studying, exercising, and practicing, the futile attempts to find my mother, and the clearer memories of my encounters with Shura and Loran. This explained why, each time I managed to visit them, their plans had seemed to accelerate more quickly: *they* had been living those years at normal speed, while I'd been skipping through them.

Then I remembered that eighteen, for the young adults of witchkind, was a major milestone. It marked a graduation from schooling and a passing into adulthood.

Was my apprenticeship done, then?

Was I finally ready?

"You look terrible," Kirmin said, shaking me from my thoughts.

I sat at the table. "I feel terrible," I admitted.

"Want to talk about it?"

I hesitated, but decided to finally confide in her. I told her about clan Karal, about Shura, and about Loran. I told her about the dead humans, and the sickly ones in Farreach in the North. I told her about the Veil, and about the Axis' anxiety. I told her about Mother again, and how I'd found nothing to confirm her continued existence.

She said nothing the whole time, listening carefully until I finished. "Well," she said when I'd finally come to the end. "I suppose that explains your side project."

"And it's been going on these past five years? All while I could have been doing something?" I picked up my fork and stabbed the cake in frustration.

"To be fair," Kirmin said quietly, her voice calm, "you couldn't have done *anything.* You are not the adherent, Daniel. Yes, you can direct some of the Axis's smaller powers, but your ability to take action in the world is *very* limited. You can observe, which you have done. You can plot and plan, which I imagine you'd done. But *doing something?*" She shook her head. "No."

"Am I ready, then? Is that why you're here? Can I do something *now?*"

"You're close," she admitted. "Closer than perhaps I realized. Hmm." She fell silent.

I waited.

"Do you remember the story I told you, the last time I saw you?"

I nodded.

"Do you understand why it upset me so much, to tell that story?"

"I think so. Are you... better?"

"Yes. We never truly understand the Axes, you know. I have to remember that. They reveal themselves slowly, over centuries. And with only one of us at a time, and not even one of us *all* the time, we probably know less of our Axis than the other adherents know of theirs." She paused. "It doesn't make it easier, but it doesn't make it my fault, either."

"That army you showed me," I said, referring back to her sixth lesson. "They were human, but the Axis would still have Ended them, if I'd asked it?"

"Yes. Humans and witchkind are more alike than many

would like to admit. We came from the same stock, in the beginning. Witchkind simply surrounded itself with the world's energies, while humans spent their time trying to conquer their environments. But we live much alike, don't we? We live in houses, not caves. We mingle with humans in their villages and towns, although the Veil keeps them from realizing. And like it or not, both humans and witchkind are subject to the wild forces that were bound into the Axes. Humans might not believe the Axes are real, but they can't simply disavow primal forces with such power. Where we see the adherents of the First Axis releasing the earth's tension, humans see an earthquake and a tsunami—natural events, never recognizing our hand in managing those for the good of all.

"In some ways, the Axes are the last common bond between humans and witchkind." She paused. "And that's why it's important for witchkind, at least, to know of the ascension of a new adherent, particularly to the Sixth Axis."

"What do you mean?"

She looked at me for a moment before answering, "Do you remember your grandmother's prophesy?"

I nodded, closed my eyes, and recited it again:

Sky and Earth, Flame and Sea
Cast adrift, their center lost
Until a Sixth might come to be
To join them all, or pay the cost

Kirmin's face grew solemn. "I think there's something coming," she said. "You're young, but I think the Axis senses something. Something that may be an Ending, one larger than any before. One that will need *managing.*"

"Meaning what?"

She looked grim. "It's not for me to say. Or even know. But the Axis may have been sniffing at you and your family for longer than either of us think. It Chose you for a reason." She frowned. "It almost feels as if..."

"What?"

"As if you were *made* to be its Choice." Then she shook her head. "But that's not possible."

"I'm not sure I understand."

"Prophecies are stupid. And it's time for your final lesson."

We returned to Kirmin's workroom then. "I thought there were Seven Forms within each Axis," I said. "Wouldn't your last lesson have been... well, the last lesson?"

"That's true." She sat at the dusty work-table. "But the Fifth and Sixth Axes—had the Fifth ever been bound into an Axis—are different, as they are different in so many other respects." She sketched a rune on the table. "*Mantija.* The Mantle. It's a rune you might not even find in your Book, as the tradition has been for it to be passed to each adherent personally. Try it."

I did. I held the rune in my mind, as I'd done for so many others. I could feel its power begin to build, suffusing my limbs with a cool energy. It felt pent-up, something ready for release but being held back. I concentrated more, but nothing happened.

"Stop," Kirmin ordered quietly.

I stopped, and realized I'd closed my eyes. I opened them and looked at her. "It isn't working."

"It isn't ready, yet. Or *you're* not ready, to be more precise. You've a decision to make, and a place in which to do it."

A Truth Come to Light

"LET'S do this the hard way this time," she said, and led me out of her workroom. We started climbing the stone staircase, one slow level at a time. I quickly understood why she'd wanted to do it the "hard way:" at each level, she stopped and asked me a question, or made a comment.

"There's a reason our Forms are taught in the order they are," she said. "Communication is the foundation of the direction we provide to the Axis. Asking questions, listening to the answers. Truly *hearing*. Always remember that you probably know less than you think. Be humble, and *listen*."

Second level: "Being there is important. Actually going out and seeing people, grasping the full context of the situation. Yes, you can become more vulnerable on someone else's home turf, but you can see them in their element. You feel *who* they are, not just what they are telling you."

Third level: "Even when you don't bring people here, remember that your position always needs to be neutral. We don't take sides. Our job is to take a powerful, destructive force and direct it to more subtle outcomes that benefit everyone on this world, human and witchkind alike. Our Judgements must reflect that. And Daniel, if you're doing it well, you'll rarely climb higher than this."

Fourth level: "This is where you defend yourself and the Tower, and maintain your independence and neutrality. You *can* be hurt. You *can* be subverted. But here, you have the opportunity to defend while doing the least amount of harm in return."

Fifth level: "This level is where you know things have gone wrong. This level's use of your own personal energy is a message, telling you that things have gone too far. Avoid ever having to climb this high, and if you must anyway, be merciful."

Sixth level: "This is the heart of what we do. Ideally, no End would need to ever come from our hands. But... well, that rarely seems to be the case."

Seventh level: Kirmin said nothing. She just looked at me sadly. I saw that the stairs now went one level higher. We emerged into the topmost room in the Tower, and this level had four real windows, each carved into the wall at the cardinal directions of the compass. Two comfortable-looking chairs faced each other, and Kirmin directed me to sit in one as she seated herself.

"It is time for a Truth," she said evenly, looking deeply into my eyes. "I am not here with you now, and never have been. No," she said, holding up a hand to stop my protest. "I, *Kirmin,* have not been with you. I am simply the last adherent that the Sixth Axis experienced, and so it takes my form to train you." I blinked. "Keep in mind that we rarely have an adherent in the Tower continuously. The Axis... takes breaks, as I've mentioned. But I will leave you soon, leave you alone in this Tower. You have a decision to make. You may stay here as long as you wish, exercising what power you've gained these past five years. You already have the power to do some good, to direct the Axis toward beneficial outcomes. But if you want to leave, if you want to truly become the adherent of the Sixth Axis, then you must become something more than you are.

"There is only ever one adherent of the Sixth Axis," she continued, "because we become *part* of the Axis. It holds our memories and experiences, from the time Galas bound it. It's why we thought we didn't need the Book anymore," she said with a small shrug. "We have all of our memories within us, all the time. That was apparently short-sighted," she said, her eyes once again sad. "But if you would leave the Tower, if you would assume your full power, if you would take what I believe may actually be your *birthright,* then you must choose to End yourself.

"Not to die; an Ending is so much less, and so much more, than death. But when you are ready to make that decision, if ever you are, then come to this room. Hold that decision in your mind, and cast the Mantle. You will End, and you will join an unEnding line of adherents. You will *become* Galas. You will become *me.* And you will remain yourself. All of witchkind will feel your ascension. Even those humans sensitive enough will feel your power, although they'll likely attribute it to a story or myth they create to explain it. And because you are Ended, past death itself, you will be able to leave the Tower at will. Those great spikes will no longer hold you here."

"I... I'm not sure what I'll decide."

She gave me a sad smile, nodded, and vanished.

* * *

I hadn't expected her to disappear, but she'd made this into a solemn moment. It was *my* decision, perhaps best undertaken alone. But I hadn't been truthful with her: I *had* made my decision. Perhaps the first real decision of my life. A decision I'd clearly been *meant* to make.

I held the rune for the Mantle in my mind then, closing my eyes to concentrate. This time, the power flooded me, built up, and then... nothing. Again.

It didn't make sense. I'd made my decision. I was on the eighth level. What was the matter?

I have nothing to lose. I'd said that to Kirmin when I'd first come here. I also had nothing to gain. Aside from the medallion around my neck, I was a nobody, a nothing. A barely-adult with no family, who didn't even have a family name I could publicly lay claim to. Trapped on a tiny island in a stone tower with an imaginary friend.

I closed my eyes and leaned back in the chair. I held the rune for the Mantle in my mind, but didn't try to invoke it. Just as I'd done in the map-room so long ago, I tried to quiet myself and *listen* to the Axis.

I'd had plenty of practice in being quiet these past five years, and relaxed peacefulness settled over me after a few minutes. I did nothing, and tried to think nothing. I tried to just *be.* And before long, a sense of... *something* wrapped around me. Even now, ages later, it's hard to describe. It was like a... a dragon, or a great snake. Cold, smooth, and considering. *Ancient.* It coiled itself around my body, around my *soul,* and *considered* me.

After what seemed like an eternity, I thought, *Am I the one? Is this what I was born to?*

Maybe, but...

I didn't want this.

I stood up, and started walking back down the stairs.

The feeling of ancient, cold, consideration faded away as I walked.

* * *

I trudged slowly back to the second-level map table, Kirmin's words—today, and over the past five years—rolling through my mind. Her stories, and all the stories of former adherents I'd read in the library. The people I'd seen in Twynsits, Chiton, and all the other towns and villages I'd visited over the years. My own solitude, the loneliness I'd felt so keenly so long ago, and that had settled into a constant companion over the years.

I could become the adherent. Become a killer, in effect, an all-powerful judge who could End... anything. An eighteen year-old judge with powers that made him seem omniscient— even though he was still a mere eighteen year-old.

Or... I could ask Kirmin to End me.

Or perhaps I could simply stay in the Tower until I grew old and died, forever an apprentice.

There was much good I could do in the world, guiding the Sixth Axis. According to Kirmin. The senior adherents of the other Axes clearly weren't as confident. And Gilioj...

What did I *know* of witchkind and humans, even now?

I knew they cared about the weather. And taxes. And wasteful uses of magic.

But did they care about Endings? Did *they* feel the Axis could do good in their world? The humans obviously didn't; they didn't even know the Axes existed. Witchkind? I wondered. If adherents never or rarely went home to the families they'd left... how welcome *were* the Axes and their adherents?

I stopped as I reached the second level.

I didn't want this.

But the Axis' powers were my only hope of finding my mother.

I walked to the map table. "Show me my mother." As always, the table slewed and slid, unable to focus. "Stop." I waited for the image to stabilize. "Show me Shura." This time the map slid smoothly to a town called Withring. I pulled the image apart with my fingers, zooming in until I could see Shura. She was at a warehouse on the edge of the town, her death-wagon parked outside. She was speaking to someone older...

Loran.

Without thinking, I cast the Visitation rune, appearing unseen around the corner of the building.

"They were first-generation machines, Loran, due for replacement anyway. They were scarcely better than the ones Neville developed."

Father! I thought excitedly.

"You've no right to them, Shura," Loran said tiredly. "Not after what you've done. A half-dozen villages are closed to us now, thanks to you."

"You know I've stopped draining them to death, Loran. A year ago, more even. They just get sick, blame it on some illness passing through, and we move on. And you know I'm producing more energy than any five other villages put together. With four of the newer machines–"

"And you thought to just come take them."

"I didn't know you'd be here, so I–"

"Exactly. You didn't think to ask, you just thought to take."

Shura was quiet for a moment. "I didn't think–"

"No, you didn't. You *know* the difficulty in empowering the machines' runes. And you know we don't do it here. Not without her."

"No, but you keep the finished ones here. That's all I needed."

Her, I thought, hope blooming in my heart as I heard him say the word. *Does he mean Mother?* But she wasn't *here.*

"We've only one finished machine here," Loran said with a sigh. "Beatrice has taken a turn. We're behind."

Mother! I cried out in my mind.

"How? You must have produced dozens of these over the years."

"They break down," Loran said, frustration in his voice. "They're good for eighteen months, twenty at the most. This entire past year, we've been barely keeping up with replacements. I was hoping to reuse your older machines, in fact. They're... sturdier."

"It was a fierce storm."

"I know, and you were lucky to make it out with what you did. The loss of the machines is regrettable, but I understand. But it's why I don't have the machines to replace the ones you lost."

They were quiet for a moment, and then Shura spoke. "I'd like to see her."

"You know we never let—"

"I know, and I'd like to see her. You know... we have a history."

Another long moment of silence.

"I'll take you," Loran said.

My mind was whirling faster than it ever had before. I returned my consciousness to the Tower, my decision made.

I needed the Axis' full powers.

I would take up the mantle.

* * *

I returned to the eighth level, sat in the chair, and reached out again for the cool feeling I'd had before.

It returned slowly, as if it didn't trust me not to leave it again. But then it came in more eagerly, wrapping itself loosely around me again, considering me. It *knew* me, I sensed, knew me from long, long ago somehow.

In my mind, I reached for it.

The feeling reacted. It drew closer around me—not crushingly, but... lovingly? Possessively? *Bred to this,* it said to me in a wash of old, relaxed emotion. It was the feeling of a power that was never in a hurry, that knew it had all the time in the universe. That *was* all the time in the universe, and just a moment after. That was always hungry, yet always fed just enough. That hated the idea of being chained, but had become endeared to the idea of being guided. *Like few others,* it said. *For reason.*

I suddenly had a great sense of space and time, as if I could see and feel the entire world, for all of its existence past and future. The world was a tapestry, dotted with knots and frayed threads. One knot in particular... it tore the tapestry apart. A knot that pulled on all its adjacent threads, gradually unravelling the entire work. *This,* the power said in my mind. And a sense of a knife, thin and sharp, cutting the knot out. Leaving in its place an empty, yawing gap, but also leaving the rest of the tapestry... damaged. Damaged, but intact. In time, the loose threads could be woven back together. *You,* the power said. I had a sense of fear and unaccustomed urgency. Fear of an Ending of self. Urgency, because the forces arrayed against it were younger, faster, naive. *Us,* it said.

But you are *Endings, aren't you?* I asked.

If Endings End, what remains? it responded.

I understood. If I accepted its offer, I would not be a normal adherent. I would not live out some number of days until I tired, or grew politically inconvenient, or simply wished a true Ending. Something was coming, something that threatened even the powerful forces of the Axes.

Another vision filled my mind: the Six Axes, each darting in its own direction, but at their center, the common Origin from which the world itself sprang. And around that Origin, a binding, a common desire—but one that was faded and frayed. The

Axes' centers strayed from the Origin, permitting the knot that threatened the entire tapestry. Then, a hand, strong and merciless, grasping them all, pulling them back together and rebinding them. *We,* it said, and I had a sense that it meant more than just me and the Axis itself. In my vision, the hand was scarred and burned, yet still it held the Origin in place. *We,* it repeated.

I accept, I thought to it. *I demand it. I* cast the *mantija* rune in my mind.

I Ended, and I Began.

My sense of the Axis uncoiled around me, and dove headfirst into my mind. It remade me, spinning throughout my body. I felt new, and old; incredibly young and indescribably ancient. I felt suffused and empty, my mind parched and overwhelmed, all at once.

In a daze, I opened my eyes, reached up to my neck, and removed my medallion: I was no longer the apprentice of an adherent; I *was* the adherent now. As I pulled it over my head, free of it at last, it disintegrated into a fine mist, and blew away through the Tower's open windows.

Almost instantly, my body convulsed. I lurched forward out of the chair, falling to my knees on the stone floor, retching violently. My head was suddenly pounding with pain, dozens of different voices screaming inside me. I imagine I screamed aloud, because the world felt full of nothing but pain and burning. In the midst of it all, a rune surfaced clearly in my mind, standing out amongst the chaos and pain: *atmintis,* a rune for Memory. I held on to it like an anchor, wrapping myself around it, trying to find *myself* amongst the chaos.

Everything went dark and cool. I was no longer in the Tower, but was instead in an endless darkness that was blessedly free of noise and pain. An old man appeared before me, his face brown and weathered, his long white hair gathered into a tail, much as Kirmin's had been. "Galas?" I asked. I needn't have asked; somehow I *knew*.

"This is a memory construct we developed to help us cope. Suddenly receiving the memories of dozens of adherents, and merging those with your own original memories, takes some time, and is painful. This helps."

"What is this place?" I asked.

"It isn't a place," he said. "This is your own mind. A quiet corner of it, someplace you can reflect on your memories without pain. This brings some order to the chaos, until your mind fully settles."

"Are you real?"

"I am how you remember me, through the memories you have inherited. I never died, any more than you have or ever will. A quirk of the Sixth Axis is that while it loves Ends, it fears its own End more than anything. When I bound its wild energies into an Axis, I helped ensure that it never *would* end. We, its adherents, help it persist, and we never End either. And that is why there is only ever one of us: we *are* it, in a very real sense, and in a way that is unique amongst the Axes. There is only *room* for one of us. And that is also why it sometimes goes decades without an adherent: when it desires rest, or feels quiescent, it simply declines to raise another of us. It is only when it needs or wants to act more fully in the world that it must anoint a new adherent, giving itself direction and form."

"Kirmin—you, I guess—suggested the Axis had been grooming my family for this moment."

"Something is coming. A Beginning, perhaps, which always teases the Axis's attention. But more likely an End, one the Axis perhaps wishes to hold off. Perhaps something that threatens the Axis itself. But yes, you remember hearing rumors and whispers of a family of witchkind that held themselves apart, that was part of no clan. Wealthy beyond reason, but restrained to having only one child in each generation. Always a daughter. Rumors," he repeated with a shrug, "and whispers. Nothing more, but clearly all true."

"Father always hated that he'd had to take the family name," I said. Thinking of him made me recall his machines, the dark runes etched into the shiny brass surfaces.

"That," Galas said, referring to our shared memory of Father's machines, "is very likely the problem we face."

* * *

Galas and I had talked for some while longer. Well, I suppose I technically had spoken to myself in my own mind, but the magic had helped me explore my new memories and past lives. After a time, I sensed it would be safe to return to myself, and I ended the magic. I used the Visitation to return to the library on the Tower's main level, knowing the driežai would clean up the eighth level for me. While there was plenty of work ahead of me, I had one small task that needed doing.

The handwritten book that contained the names of the Sixth Axis's past adherents still lay open on the podium where I'd left it years ago. Flipping through the pages, I found that I could now read them. I knew the language now, the tongue called *Endurian* that was no longer spoken in the world, and had not been for hundreds of years. Past its End, it had become the private language of the Sixth Axis's adherents.

Each page had been written by the adherent themselves, beginning with their name, and containing no more than a few pages of notes and comments. Each was a piece of advice or caution to their successors, and as I read each, I found myself remembering having written them. It was an odd sensation, to be sure.

I turned to a blank page. No ink had touched the pages of this book. Instead, I cast *rašalas,* a rune of Marking, and inscribed my own name onto the top of the page.

Not Daniel Scratch.

The bold, black marks at the top of the page read *Daniel Teisėjas.*

Daniel, the Judge.

The New Adherent

A NEW SENSE of power flooding my mind, body, and soul, I used the Axis' magic to take myself to the map table. "Show me my Mother," I ordered. Again, the map table slewed and jittered, but I concentrated, forcing energy into it. Slowly, ever so slowly, it stabilized and zoomed in, showing me the mausoleum where Mother was purportedly buried. "No," I told the table, shaking my head. I looked at the shadow-assistant and said, "Show me my *Mother.*"

It flickered and the map table slewed and shook again. Eventually, it came to a stop, zooming out to show the entire continent. The shadow-assistant shook its head, unable to comply.

"Then show me Shura of clan Karal."

This time, the map table complied quickly, eager to obey. Shura was in Withring still, but on the other side of the sprawling town. She seemed to be... yes. It was a section of town given over to warehouses, an area where trade goods came and went. She seemed to be alone, although a section of the building she was in was... blurry. Indistinct.

Good enough.

I cast the Visitation rune, leaving the Tower physically for the first time, and appeared just outside the building.

Its large wooden doors were hanging open, one of them swinging gently back and forth in the subtle breeze that blew through town. I stepped inside, letting my eyes adjust to the dim light. Fortunately, it was a sunny day, and several panes of grimy glass lined the upper portion of the walls, admitting a sickly, grim light.

The large space intended for storage was empty. But it was clear to me it had recently been full and had been rapidly abandoned: small pieces of debris lay everywhere. Chunks of wood from broken transport pallets, short lengths of rope and twine, scattered pieces of broken glass, and more were all cast haphazardly about the room. The dirt floor showed where heavy equipment had recently been dragged about, and thin, parallel ruts showed where carriages and wagons had been brought in, loaded, and rolled back out.

There were two doors on one of the far walls. One sat next to a small glazed window, perhaps an office for a warehouse manager. I checked that one first, and found it as empty as the main area, the only remnant of the former occupants a battered old desk.

The second door led to something more interesting.

As soon as I stepped through, I could feel the Axis hissing in my mind, pulling me back. I stopped in the doorway and cast *apšvietimas,* immediately lighting the room with an intense white glow. The room was fairly large, with another set of large doors on the far side—perhaps this was intended to hold additional merchandise. But whatever it had once been, it was now a prison.

A series of flat iron strips had been folded and bent into a cube perhaps six feet on a side. The strips were as broad as my hand, the spaces between them equally broad. In all, it was an iron latticework clearly designed to contain someone of witchkind. Even at a distance of a dozen feet or more, I could feel the iron tugging greedily at the Axis' power, and feel the Axis glaring and pacing, eager to be away from this threat.

A small pool of dark, dried blood lay in the loose dirt in the center of the cage.

I knew it was Mother's.

An icy fury rose in me. I turned and walked back into the main area, scanning it again for clues. *Anything* that could help lead me to my mother. I pulled the illumination magic with me, brightly lighting the entire open space. A glint on the floor caught my eye, and I quickly walked over to examine it.

It was a scorched piece of metal. It didn't pull at me as the iron cage had, so I reached down to pick it up. Brass, from the weight and from the color of the one undamaged side. Turning it slowly in my hands, it seemed as if it had been ripped from some larger piece: three sides were jagged and blackened. An explosion, perhaps?

As I turned it in my hands, I saw that a rune had been carved into its surface:

A memory slammed into my mind: I'd seen this before, etched into the medallions of the mourners, whose ceremony

I'd interrupted so many years before. The mausoleum where my mother was ostensibly buried, and where I'd first laid eyes on Loran—though I hadn't known it at the time.

But what was the connection to my Mother?

I slipped the fragment into a coat pocket, and continued looking for more clues, anger still pumping through my body. There wasn't much else to see, just pieces of wood, rope, and glass everywhere.

"I see Loran wasn't just being paranoid."

I whirled, hands up and ready to cast magic, and saw Shura standing in the broad, open doorway where one door still creaked lazily back and forth in the breeze. "Shura," I growled.

She raised one eyebrow at that. "You have the advantage of me," she said carefully. Her fingers twitched, and I knew she was preparing magic of her own.

"I do," I agreed, not offering her my name. "You held a woman prisoner here. Where is she?"

Her face registered confusion for a brief moment, before settling back into an even, confident expression. "*That's* what you're worried about?"

"I'll have time to worry about the rest of your crimes after you've returned the woman to me."

Too much. Or at least too much of the wrong thing; I'd never played this role before and the look on Shura's face told me that I'd given her something. "Are you with the Taryba?" asked. "The Council has nothing to worry about here."

"Kidnapping a woman of witchkind? Draining humans in groups until they die, and then burning the bodies? I think the Council had plenty to worry about."

"You said *return.* She's no Council member. She's no relation to a Council member. She's no relation to *anyone.* What do you mean by *return* her to you?"

The anger finally grew hot in my stomach, boiled up

through my chest, and burst out of my mouth: *"She is my mother!"*

Shura's eyes grew wide, and her fingers twitched toward me. A lance of hot, burning pain stabbed through my right thigh. I cried out, falling to the ground. Kirmin would have been furious with me, furious that I hadn't spent more time snapping the Shroud into place as quickly as possible. I brought it up now, just in time to watch a second attack splash against it and fade into nothingness.

I cast *smaigas,* three tiny black spikes of power launching from my fingertips. My aim was poor, hindered by the throbbing pain in my leg. All three spikes went wide, missing Shura completely. I laid one hand on my injured thigh and cast *išgyti,* a simple but powerful rune that would begin to slowly stitch my flesh back together. It required an immense amount of magic, but little in the way of concentration or attention, so it was perfect in a case like this.

Shura's expression had turned to guarded surprise at both my defense and subsequent attack. She took a step backwards and muttered something, but she was too far away to hear. I longed to End her, longed to scrub her from the face of the world along with everyone she was in league with. But I couldn't: the iron cage is clearly what had hid Mother from my map table, and Loran—the only other member of clan Karal I could identify—seemed to be similarly obscured. Shura was my only link to them, and I needed her alive.

She turned and ran back through the doorway into the street.

I roared, dropping the Shroud and taking a step to run after her. But the healing magic hadn't yet had time to do its full job, and with a stab of pain in my leg, I fell to the dirt, bits of glass gouging my hands as I caught myself.

I roared again, and some dark, buried instinct took over,

lashing out. But I was no mere eighteen year-old boy: I was the adherent of the Sixth Axis of power, the embodiment of Endings. Another young man my age might have screamed curses, or even hurled a last, futile attack against the fleeing woman. But me? I lashed out with the ancient, bitter power of my Axis.

The building Ended.

Its walls didn't so much crumble as they did blow away in a cloud of dust. In less than a moment, the only thing left was the iron latticework cage, now showing a fine layer of orange rust on every surface. I could feel the iron grow hot even at this distance as it pulled some of my magic into the ground, nulli-fying it.

I felt a... *cracking* in my soul. It was the strangest sensation, and one I've never been able to fully describe. Imagine that you are standing on a thick bed of granite, and a quake comes. The ground roils and shudders, hard enough to crack the very stone upon which you stand. And the crack continues upward, split-ting you through the spine, rolling up until your very skull cracks.

That's approximately how I felt. Disoriented and hurting, I looked up, casting my eyes around for any sight of Shura, but the streets surrounding the building were empty.

I closed my eyes, took a deep breath, and let my magic whisk me back to the Tower.

* * *

My home was in chaos.

Shadowy driežai were flickering everywhere, scurrying around the Tower as if they were a hive of bees who'd had a stick shoved into their hive. The building itself was shaking, and I could dimly sense the sea outside chopping and frothing.

"What's happening?"

A memory smashed into my mind.

I was Baldochowska, an ancient adherent of the Sixth, asked to render judgement on a young couple who wished to marry across clan lines. Jealous of the young man and enraptured with his bride to be, I denied their claim, fully intending to seek the woman's favor for myself.

I was Jeramy Kuziakow, a more recent adherent, asked to End a virulent plague that had all but laid waste to the witchkind of a small inland village. I learned that the plague was spread by humans, who weren't affected by it themselves. Full of arrogance, I simply Ended the entire village, murdering almost five hundred humans and a hundred witchkind, but stopping the plague in its tracks.

I was Duena Salomon, who Ended the family who'd been so mean to her before her Choosing and ascension.

I was Lucerne Zdunowski, who Ended the tenure of an entire Council because they'd refused to let her build a residence away from the Tower.

I was every adherent who'd ever Judged selfishly, every adherent who'd ever taken the Axis' power for themselves, every adherent who'd ever unleashed an Ending without just cause.

As the memories faded and my senses returned, I could feel a throbbing deep, deep below the Tower. Something that cried out in pain and remorse, something that was broken and could never be fully repaired. Wearily, I took up the Visitation magic and took myself deep into the Tower's roots.

I found myself standing in a deep, dark, damp cavern. I could feel the pressure in my ears, telling me I was well below the ocean floor. The sound of gently trickling water surrounded me. It would have been peaceful, had it not been for the sharp keening sound that cut through the space, drilling into my ears and vibrating my teeth.

The space was lit with a dim, diffuse blue light, revealing a soaring pillar rising high above me and vanishing into the darkness. When I say 'pillar,' you may imagine some decorative structure perhaps four or five feet across, but no. This pillar was as wide as the Tower itself, and it was only because I was standing so far back from it that I could perceive the curve of its surface.

I took several long steps closer.

It was made of what appeared to be utterly seamless black granite, shot through with thin white marbling here and there. It gleamed with wetness, and as I stepped up to it and laid a hand on it, I could feel the cold, salty water coating it.

Something caught my eye. A jagged edge of sorts, an imperfection in the otherwise flawless surface. I ran my hand over it, and could feel the hairline crack.

I was Galas, Archon and First Adherent of the Sixth Axis. I bound the Axis, and then used its power to take revenge on the humans who had killed my family.

I looked up, and realized that the pillar was full of these small imperfections, these tiny cracks, these minuscule monuments to abuses of the Axis' power. A thousand memories teased at the back of my mind, offering to drown me in my predecessors' mistakes, but I pushed them aside as something else caught my eye. It was a faint gleam, a place where newly raw granite caught the dim blue light, reflecting down on me.

The keening sound faded and the cavern grew peacefully quiet, the sound of trickling seawater the only thing breaking the utter silence.

I knew that the new crack far above was mine. My mistake. My moment of rage. My indiscretion.

I stepped back and looked at the pillar with new eyes. Its flawless surface, its implacable strength, was riddled with a web of mistakes and faults, each one a consequence of an all-too-human adherent who, for a brief moment, played the role of a god. In time, with enough such mistakes, this pillar would shatter, and the Tower above come crashing down.

I—we, all of the adherents—could do wrong. And there were consequences for our mistakes.

The need to find my mother, to exact revenge on Karal, still smoldered in my heart. But it was now tempered with the weight of my position, the consequences that would outlive even me. I still needed to find her, needed to End what the clan was doing—but I needed to do it right.

Sobered, I took myself back to the Tower above.

I COLLAPSED into a chair in the main workroom, wondering what to do next. A trip to the map table was probably in order, to see where Shura had gotten off to, but for the moment I just felt exhausted.

I felt something digging into my side, and remembered the metal fragment I'd stashed in my coat pocket. I pulled it out, turning it over and over again in my hands, running my fingers through the engraved lines of the rune.

I'd *seen* this before. Not just on the mourners' medallions, but... someplace. Where?

Another memory crashed into my mind.

* * *

I must have been five, maybe six years old. My head was just above the doorknob that I was turning, opening the door that led down into Father's basement workshop. That young, Father still tolerated my visits now and again. Barely.

As I carefully climbed down the steep, rickety wooden staircase, I could hear Father's voice. Was he talking to someone? I didn't pay any attention: I was focused entirely on holding the worn wooden handrail with both hands, easing myself down sideways one step at a time.

In stories, basements are always dark, damp, scary places, full of dust and bugs. Not so in the house: Father had scattered dozens of *amžinai ryškus,* globes of semipermanent magical light, all over the place. His basement was brightly lit, carefully organized, and ruthlessly clean. Through the lens of memory, I could almost smell the *švarus* runes working, eliminating dust and tiny pieces of debris, leaving the basement almost spotless.

To a child's eyes, Father's basement was a wondrous place. His machines were tall, shiny cylinders of brass and bronze, each one sporting a dozen or more elegantly shaped rods and levers. Meticulous engravings picked out the cylinders' curves and indentations, making them seem even more magical and mysterious than they already were. Highlighted on each cylinder, carved deeply into the brass atop each one, was a series of runes. My adult eyes, reviewing the memory as one might review the books of a shipping company, picked out the most prominent rune on each. It sat in the middle of a complex rune construct, and was filled with a shiny black substance, lending it a stark contrast against the brass around it:

The same rune I'd seen on those medallions. The same rune that was on the piece of brass I'd picked up in Withring.

"I'm telling you, it's driving me mad."

Father's voice, coming from a far corner of the basement. My six year-old self rounded a workbench and caught sight of Father's back, but ventured no further. He'd been growing angrier of late, less willing for his son or wife to visit him in his domain. He was hunched over a smaller bench that was tucked up against the stone wall of the house's foundation, his body mostly blocking a flickering glow that came from whatever sat on the bench in front of him.

"Stick with it, Neville. Your designs are almost perfect. The machine you brought us last month is working perfectly, in fact." Another voice, this one an older man's.

"What do you mean almost perfect?" Father's voice was irritated, now.

"We're having trouble duplicating your work," the other voice said.

"Your clumsy workers, Loran," Father snapped.

"They're as precise as you, Neville, but we can't get the central rune to empower. The entire construct is absolutely lifeless. It refuses to take any energy. We've had a dozen people try, including myself."

Father was quiet for a moment. Then: "It's her."

"What do you mean?"

"The central rune... it's hers. *Her* rune. You know of her... hobby? Her disgusting pastime?"

"The humans?"

"Yes, the humans. They're all twisted, the women in this family. My mother-in-law communes with animals, Loran. Keeps a flock of birds about the place at all times. Says she can draw magic from them, more than she could Gather on her own."

"What's that got to do with your wife?"

"Beatrice *always* loved being around humans. Dressing like them, going out to parties with them. Once we married and they—you!—forced me to come live here though, Beatrice has been... lethargic. Barely stirs herself. Won't even try teaching runes to the boy."

"I'm not following."

"She draws magic from humans, Loran! Don't you understand? I don't know how, don't know how it's even possible, since humans ground magic. But somehow, she does. When she's around them, she's full of energy. Full of *magic.* Not that she knows how to use it, ignorant lazy cow that they raised her to be."

"Sacred vows, Neville, she's still your wife."

"Only because you arranged it. Only because you suspected something about their magic. The women's magic. Only because you *wanted* it."

"And because *they* wanted *you.* This obsession they have with lineages and matches. Is the boy remarkable in any way?"

"Quiet and bookish. Stays out of my way mostly, thank the powers. She fusses over him constantly, first boy-child the family has had in a dozen generations."

"No sign of... odd magic?"

"He's six, Loran, of course not."

"So the rune is tied to her, then."

"It would seem. I can empower it, but she's just upstairs when I do so."

"So we'll have to have all the machines... made there?"

"Don't be ridiculous. You know that old woman's spirit is still here, and the house obeys her alone. You'd never find the place, and I can't keep lugging them down to the village for you. Besides, I can't produce these things in any kind of quantity, I'm working in a basement."

"I see." Both voices were quiet for a long while. Then: "What are the chances we could get her out of the house?"

"With the old woman still here? Practically zero," Father snorted. "Though I'd welcome the quiet, especially if you could steal the boy away as well."

"No chance?"

"Not without a team of Proctors," Father scoffed.

"Hmm. They'd need a warrant. Has she done anything illegal?"

"*You're* the one who—ah, never mind. No. She's innocent as a child. Just... I'll keep working. Maybe I can modify the rune somehow, come up with a variant that doesn't require her presence to empower."

"Yes." Loran's voice was thoughtful. "You do that. I have... another idea in mind. I'll work on that on my end. Tell me... has she been *stable?*"

"Stable? I suppose. She just cossets the boy, reading him stories, and sleeps all day. She's not dangerous, if that's what you mean."

"I'm going to have Lystia send you a rune construct. It may... *unbalance* your wife. She shouldn't become dangerous, but it might be enough to open some other opportunities."

Silence. "Ah," Father's voice said at last. "I see where you're going."

"Keep working on the rune."

"I will."

I shifted my weight, *crunching* on a stray bit of wood that the cleaning magic hadn't yet eliminated. Father turned. "What're you—I'll speak with you later," he snapped. He stood and walked toward me, his face twisted in anger and menace.

The memory ended.

* * *

I blinked as the memory faded. Was this always going to happen to me? How had any prior adherent managed to stay sane, with their brains constantly running away from them? I thought about it for a moment, and then cast the Memory rune again. The world faded slowly to black, and Galas appeared before me. He said nothing, looking evenly at me, waiting for me to speak.

"This memory thing... how does it work?" I asked at last.

"The Axis contains the complete memories of every adherent. Well... mostly complete. There are gaps, somehow, but I don't know how. But when you experience something, when you need to remember something, those memories will surface."

"Will it always be so... much?"

He laughed. "No, once the memories have integrated with you in a few days, it'll feel more natural. They'll only be overwhelming if it's something significant or especially strong."

"But what I just did, what I just saw—those weren't the Axis' memories. They were mine."

"Your memories *are* the Axis' memories. It contains all the memories of *every* adherent. Including you."

"*I* don't even remember those things, though!"

"You do. When we're alive, our memories are... difficult. You don't remember being born, right? Don't remember your first tooth falling out, don't remember the first time you fell down. But the Axis does. It remembers all of it, and it can share those memories with you. Everything Ends, Daniel. Everything except the memories of the Axis. It's a record of us all." He paused for a moment, and then frowned. "Or it should be. We never should have been able to lose track of your Book, for example. So now I... wonder."

His frown deepened, and he faded away. The blackness faded with him, leaving me alone again in the library.

Food. I needed food, and then I needed to find my mother.

A Clan Obsession

MY MAGIC TOOK me to the map-room. It had all finally come together: the reason behind Father's constant anger and abuse. The reason for Mother's distractedness and lethargy. The rune that clan Karal had based their entire enterprise around. And the reason they'd somehow arranged for Mother to be taken to Witchhold, where they could abduct her.

Now I just needed to find them all.

Fortunately, I'd just been given the key to doing so.

"Show me everyplace this rune appears on anything larger than a medallion," I ordered, picturing the rune in my mind.

The map table zoomed out, showing the entire continent. Small green motes of light lit up, strung across most of the continent. They followed the trail of the humans' iron roadway, crossing the continent from east to west, designating all of the tiny hamlets and villages along the way. They traced out the coasts, highlighting all the small fishing villages and coastal settlements. Not a single green light appeared over any major city or town, save one: Withring.

They'd been there all along.

A collection of bright green dots were clustered in a single building near the center of the town. As I zoomed in, I could see it was a human structure, used for some sort of government function. They'd retreated to a hidden space, then.

No matter.

Nothing could stop me from getting to Mother.

* * *

I appeared in Withring a block or so away from my target. I came in person; accessing private hidden spaces in my incorporeal form was problematic unless I knew someone specific I could target. Since neither Mother nor Loran qualified, obscured from my magic as they were, I'd have to enter the same way as anyone else would. Besides, the leg still throbbed from where Shura had hit me, and I had a new sense of caution about the whole situation.

The street was busy this time of day, government functionaries and ordinary citizens scurrying to and fro on their business. The building I was after looked to be the offices of several local trade councils, and a steady stream of human guildsmen and merchants streamed in and out. I scanned the building quickly, and spotted the discreet entry-rune carved into a wall, above what looked like a document deposit box of some kind.

I didn't approach the rune immediately, though. Instead, I stood for almost half an hour, watching closely. Two people entered the hidden space in that time, both dressed in simple working-man's garments that blended in perfectly with the crowd around them. Both simply strolled up to the deposit box as if they planned to walk right by it, reached out at the last minute to touch the entry-rune, and vanished.

My heart was pounding. I had no idea where that rune

would land me, but I had to assume Shura had already alerted the rest of Karal. Still, I was the adherent of the Sixth, wasn't I? Attacking me certainly felt like a valid reason to aggressively defend myself, if not End my attacker outright. And at this point, with Mother all but in my grasp, I had little reason not to just End everyone who stood in my way.

No *little* reason. I did have a huge reason though, in the pillar that held up the Tower. I wasn't sure what how much more damage that could weather, or what the consequences would be if I passed that limit. I wasn't especially eager to find out.

Avoid unnecessary Endings, then or at least unjustified ones. I gathered my power around me, prepared to cast my Shroud, and walked across the street. Nobody paid the slightest bit of attention as I strode up to the deposit box, touched the rune, and found myself whisked inside.

I was met by two guards, both of whom launched attacks at me almost immediately, shouting for assistance. Both attacks withered and died against my Shroud, and both attackers went down in screams as black spikes pierced their kneecaps.

They'd live.

The entry foyer led to a single hallway that looked to run the length of the hidden space. I could see doors almost evenly spaced along the right-hand side, with a single door on the entirety of the left-hand side. That door opened and four more people spilled out. They'd apparently practiced for this, because two of them immediately dropped to their knees, casting low attacks, while the other two cast high attacks over the comrades' heads. All died on my Shroud, and I saw four sets of eyes widen in surprise and sudden fear.

They had no idea who they were dealing with.

A single Greater Spike flew down the hallway, filling most of the space and bowling all four of my attackers over. Smears of blood on the walls and floor told me they'd been seriously injured, but I didn't feel the Axis respond to anything like a death. Fine. I lowered my arms and panted—Kirmin hadn't been kidding, the Greater Spike took a bit of effort—and strode down the hallway.

I Ended the first two doors on my right, blowing them away into dust, but they contained only small offices. Next was the door my most recent attackers had come out of. It was a vast, dark space, and so I cast light into it.

It housed a half-dozen of Karal's brass machines, each in various stages of completion. They were circled around another iron latticework cage, in which lay a pale, honey-haired woman dressed in a ragged blue frock. Her head rose at my entrance, her expression quickly changing from dull and tired to hopeful and surprised. As she took me in, her eyes grew wider and wider, seeming to fill half her face. Those dull, purple eyes slowly brightened as Mother recognized her son.

"Daniel," she whispered. She struggled for a moment, and then finally raised herself to her knees. I saw the reason for her struggle: she was missing a hand.

"Your hand," I said slowly, taking a step toward the cage. The Axis moaned and tugged me back, wanting nothing to do with the deadly metal.

"Taken, and buried in a mausoleum," she whispered, her voice cracked and weary. That explained the map table's behavior, and why the Axis had kept taking me there. With Mother obscured by iron, her hand had been the only thing the magic could connect to.

"I'm taking you out of here," I said grimly, dropping the Shroud and focusing my concentration and will. I ordered the Axis to End the iron cage, putting as much determination and intent as I could into my thoughts. The Axis howled, battering itself against the iron. The metal rusted instantly, but it held.

Twice more I lashed out, insisting the Axis End this construct of my enemy, and twice more it hurled itself against the bars and drew back, fatigued and afraid.

"You can't, Daniel. It's iron. It draws magic into itself. They have to take me out of here to even use me, but you can't—"

"I am the adherent of the Sixth Axis of Death and Endings," I growled. Her eyes managed to widen more, and her mouth gaped. "I will not be told what I can and cannot do." This time, I smashed at the bars with all my fury, all of the Axis' pain and anger, and everything else I could muster. I screamed as power rushed from me, pouring into the unforgiving iron. I could see the metal glowing red in some places as my magic heated it, and then—

Nothing.

It wasn't enough. I put my hands on my knees, bent over and panting. "Let me–" I started, and then something smashed into my back.

I caught myself, wrenching one wrist painfully, and then rolled onto my back to face my new attacker.

Attackers. Four more had pushed through the door, their hands raised toward me. I could sense their magic building as I again threw up my Shroud for protection. Eight invisible attacks thudded against the Shroud, their kinetic energy Ended by the Axis' power. I half-formed a thought to End them all, when a voice in my head objected.

They've done nothing wrong, you broke into their property.

I panted slightly, the wind still knocked out of me. I looked up at them as they readied their next attack. "Release the woman," I ordered.

"Never!" one of them cried.

I smiled. "Then I judge you guilty of kidnapping her," I said, and unleashed the Axis. All four crumbled to dust in a sudden, cold wind.

I turned back to Mother. "I need to get something to physically break the cage," I said. I reached behind me and with a flick of magic, closed the door leading into the room. Another quick thought Ended the separation between door and wall, sealing the two of us in. "That will hold them for a bit, until they break through," I said. "But–"

"Daniel, no," she said softly. She reached toward me, careful not to touch the iron, but even so it was clear that it was robbing her of her life. "Forget about me. I was dead to you years ago, let me remain that way. But stop them."

"I'm not even sure what they're doing, other than draining humans," I said, levering myself back to my feet. "These machines–"

"The rune that powers them is my soul-rune, Daniel. Something the women of my family, clanless as we are, all possessed. Mine connects me to the humans, somehow. Your father"—and here, both her voice and expression grew bitter—"learned it from me, learned to use it to make his machines. They take power from humans, Daniel. Not sips, but great amounts. They're storing it, hoarding it for some purpose." She shook her head and slumped back onto her heels. "The iron kills me a little more every day, Daniel. This," and she held up the stump where her hand had been, "has been infected for years, taking what magic I could hoard to keep it from killing me. But I'm tired. I can't go on much longer."

"I'll End the building," I promised, although I knew I couldn't. It would kill countless innocent humans at the same time.

"You have to *go*, Daniel," she said. "Those were only the workers they had *here*. They have many, many more. They–"

A sound like the tearing of rock shattered through the air, and I whirled to see the entire wall coming apart. As the dust settled, I saw a dozen or more grim-faced people, all dressed in black leathers, all eyeing me cautiously. I sensed their magic, poised and ready to strike.

"Daniel!" Mother shouted behind me.

I reactivated my Shroud.

Blasts of light burst forth from a dozen pairs of hands, flying—

Past me.

I looked to one side, wondering how they all could have—

A searing pain blasted through my left shoulder. The Shroud didn't surround me! Their attacks had rebounded off the wall behind me, or been steered somehow, to hit me from behind. Even as I realized it, another pierced my right calf, another my left thigh, and a fourth my abdomen. I screamed, collapsing to the ground. I felt the Shroud snap out of existence, my concentration boiled away by the pain that was tearing through me.

I spared one last, agonized look at Mother, and let the Axis take me home.

* * *

I collapsed onto the floor of the Tower's entry foyer, the driežai swarming over me in a solid mass of shadow. I could feel them directing the Tower's magic, felt a cool, soothing power flow through my wounds. *Restauravimas,* a memory told me. The Restoration, a magic rarely called upon, but designed to restore an adherent to full physical function. I couldn't be killed exactly, but I could be incapacitated and potentially even kept that way, which was worse.

Rarely used?

Few adherents act so rashly, my memories suggested.

True enough. I'd forgotten that while I had access to effectively unlimited power, I had no experience. No skill. No *abil-*

ity. Things my attackers had in abundance, despite their sharply limited access to magic. Experience and skill trumped power every time, a truism I'd read in tale after tale all my life, but evidently hadn't taken fully to heart.

Well, there'd be no more mistakes like that. As the Tower's magic finished its work, I pushed myself off the floor. The driežai began silently scouring my blood from the pale stones, and I withdrew my Book from my coat pocket. I flipped to the page that covered the Shroud, read the crabbed handwriting that covered the page, and shook my head. I'd thought as much.

I put the Book away and took myself to the very top turret of the Tower.

I needed help.

The Conclave

ON YOUR OWN, *the adherent may invoke the Forms of our brother Axes.*

> *Doing so at length will attract those Axes,*
> *Who will often dispatch their adherents to investigate.*
> *Should your use of their borrowed power be just,*
> *They will join you in your Defense.*

Taken right from my Book, something I'd learned shortly after Kirmin's fourth lesson. I withdrew the Book now, opening it to that passage, and reviewed the runes that invoked the other Axes' minor Forms of Defense.

First, the *potvynio siena,* the shield of Sea that could stunt almost any physical attack. I faced North, and summoned its rune into my mind, feeding it the Axis' power:

The sea roared up before me, forming a wall of water that foamed and sprayed at its edges. Next, *priešgaisrinis skydas,* cast to the east. The Axis of Flame's Form of Defense, it took the form of a cyclone of fire that darted back and forth, ready to intercept any attack.

Next, the defense of Sky, cast to the south: *audra,* the deceptively simple and almost invisible shield of swirling, spinning air. In the event of attack, it would condense into an all-but-impenetrable wall of protection.

Finally, the Axis of Earth: *moliné siena,* cast to the west. Rocky spires jutting up from the ocean floor, braiding through each other to form a literal wall of earth.

My island was now surrounded by raw elemental shields, and the sound of roaring water, rushing air, and crackling flame almost drowned out my own thoughts. They did not, however, drown on the magically amplified sound of four hands hammering at the Tower's front door.

My company had arrived.

I dropped the magic and took myself to the foyer to greet them.

* * *

"This is ridiculous. It's exactly the sort of high-handed *meddling* that we all feared the Sixth would engage in!" Zmogus had been largely unsupportive of offering me any help, which I'd expected based on what he'd said during his visit. "This puts every Axis in danger, puts all of witchkind in danger!"

I'd taken a few moments to seat my guests, explained that my concern was quite urgent—I felt certain they'd already moved Mother to another location, and tracking her down again might be difficult—and that I desperately needed their help.

I'd explained the situation with clan Karal, and how they'd created machines that drained power from humans, storing it for some unknown future need, and in at least some cases killing the humans involved. In all cases, making humans sick at the least. I'd explained how my own mother's soul-rune was the key to it all, and how they needed her physical presence to fully empower their machines.

"End your mother," Zmogus had snapped. "Seems simple enough."

I'd held my tongue and my considerable anger in check, and told him that Karal had been doing this for at least five years, probably closer to eight, and had doubtless amassed incredible stores of magical energy—all for reasons unknown.

"Witchkind store magic against future need all the time," Mesla had informed me, a dour expression on her face. "So one clan got good at it, big deal." This from someone with effectively unlimited magic, who didn't see that the problem wasn't the storing of power, it's where they were getting it, and what they planned to do with it all.

I'd pulled out the last argument I could think to muster, one that had seemed to impress at least Kirmin and Mr. Nash:

"Do any of you know anything about my family? Not just me. Not just my mother, Beatrice. My grandmother, Constance. My great-grandmother, Patience. My great-great–"

"Nobody cares who your stupid family–" Zmogus began to interrupt.

"–grandmother Pranasa," I shouted over him.

The room got very quiet.

"You said soul-rune?" Debesi asked softly, the first thing she'd said since arriving.

"She said it had something to do with being clanless," I said. "I don't understand it, but–"

"Clan members identify themselves primarily with a clan rune. It's part of their being, and part of what binds them together deeper than blood ties. But the clanless obviously don't have them. Clanless people of witchkind are— unattached, in a very literal way," Mesla supplied.

"But some identify themselves as... something else. More than themselves, but not part of a clan," Gilioj mused, stroking his chin.

"They have a soul-rune," Debesi finished.

Even Zmogus seemed subdued.

"People said that the women in my family had *odd* magic," I offered.

"I can see that," Debesi said. Then she shook her head. "But I still don't see the need for our involvement. Or even yours, although that's your decision obviously."

"We don't interfere," Zmogus growled, his attitude returning to normal. "We aren't the Taryba, we aren't the Proc-tors, we aren't the Inquisition." He slapped the workroom table. "Take this to them."

"There's really nothing we could even do," Gilioj said. "We're not... antagonists. We don't fight battles."

"Especially when *humans* are the only ones being harmed," Zmogus muttered.

"Fine, I'll End them all," I said, my voice cold and flat.

Debesi paled slightly, and said, "That's within your bailiwick, Daniel. But I don't think you will."

She was right. "Gilioj, you asked me what I knew of witchkind, what I knew of humans. If I knew anything about the people I'd be impacting. Right?" He nodded, but refused to meet my eyes. "I know they'd rather not be dead. Rather not be sick. I was in one village where the sick humans were already starting to blame magic." Everyone's heads snapped up at that. Ah, that had their attention? "That's right. One of their *priests* suggested it." The human church had always been one of the driving forces behind the Hunts.

The other four adherents exchanged glances with each other.

"I could see a need to at least understand the potential impact of what Karal is doing," Gilioj said slowly, looking to his colleagues to gauge their reactions to his words.

Zmogus shrugged and frowned even more deeply.

"A threat against the Veil is the domain of the Proctors," Debesi said, although she sounded uncertain.

"A threat against all of witchkind is the domain of us all," Gilioj said softly. "If this suspicion of magic has spread, Thornwaithe's may already be aware."

I pounced on their concern. "Mesla, you could draw the building down into the Earth, draw the iron away from my mother, without even touching it. Zmogus, you could defend us with fire, or Debesi, you with Sky. Any of you could–"

"We're back to your mother, *boy,*" Zmogus barked, startling Debesi enough that she almost tipped her chair over. "So is this about your mother, or about the Veil? About witchkind, or the humans? Hmm?"

I ground my teeth. "I won't End my own mother," I said, my jaw still clenched.

He shrugged. "Your call. It's her soul-rune that caused all this, from what you're telling me."

And my father. And even my grandparents, with their obsession on managing their family tree. And even–.

Wait a minute.

I stood, and gave each of them a hard stare before saying, "Thank you for your time. I apologize for summoning you out of turn. It won't happen again." I turned to leave the room, figuring they could find their own way out.

"Daniel, what are you going to do?" Debesi asked, standing and taking a step toward me.

I turned to face her. "I'm Ending the rune." And with that, I concentrated, ordering the Axis to ensure the thing no longer existed in any form. I felt the Axis spin away with a feeling of... glee? as it removed every trace of the rune from the world. I felt nothing more than a brief shudder.

"That's probably a bad–" Mesla began.

"It's done," I snapped. "Now if you don't mind, I'm going to go see to my mother."

Mother

SWIFT AS THOUGHT, I returned to Withring, taking myself directly to the room where Mother had been caged. Miraculously, she was still there, although there were four guards around her. My Shroud snapped into place, and I raised one hand to fire spikes at the guards. They reacted more quickly than I'd thought possible, throwing up their own glowing shields and firing bright lances of energy at me. Their attacks died on my defense, but their own defenses managed to deflect my spikes. One of the guards pointed a finger at Mother, and his intention was clear: they couldn't touch me, but she was defenseless.

Something *thumped* me in the back, knocking me forward a step but doing no damage. I turned, and saw two more guards moving through the rubble that had once been a wall. My Book had confirmed that the Shroud could cover me completely, but it required constant visualization on my part to maintain. I'd never practiced that, and with my blood pounding hot in my ears, this wasn't exactly the easiest time to master the skill. I sent more spikes toward these two new attackers, forcing them to dodge and raise their own shields.

A lance of pain burned in my back—insufficient to seriously injure me, but enough to distract me. I'd let the Shroud go thin behind me, and three of the guards near Mother's cage were advancing slowly, their shields still raised. Snarling, I reached for the Axis' power, holding the rune for Ending in my mind.

Suddenly, a rush of cold wind from behind me blasted the four of them to the floor. A moment later, the rock of the floor itself curled up around their heads, holding them fast.

I turned and saw Mesla and Debesi standing there. "We have mothers too," Debesi said softly. "Even if Zmogus was born of a dying worm," she added in a mutter. Debesi had already turned to the other two attackers, another blast of wind pushing them back through the broken wall and into the hallway.

Mesla gestured toward Mother's cage, a look of intense concentration on her face. "This isn't easy, even at a bit of a distance," she forced out between gritted teeth. Slowly, the stone of the floor reached up and grasped the iron bars, pulling them slowly apart. Then, all at once they finally let go, the cage ripping in half with a fierce clanging noise.

"That'll attract some attention," Debesi said calmly. Mesla nodded, gestured behind her, and rock debris began crawling up to re-form the walls. Debesi waved her arms and I felt a wall of solidified air establish itself between us and the reforming wall.

"Thank you," I said softly. Then I turned toward Mother.

"Ah-ah," Debesi said behind me, and a softer gust of wind blew through the remains of the cage, carrying Mother clear of the iron and settling her at my feet.

I knelt beside her. Her face was waxen, her eyes dull, and her breathing shallow. "Mother?"

"Daniel," she whispered, her lips attempting a smile. She coughed, and a mix of blood and spittle was lost in her dirty, torn, stained frock. "You came back."

"I Ended the rune, Mother," I said, tears starting to stream from my face. "They can't use you any more."

"Ah," she said with a small cough. "That explains it. It felt like... it felt like my very center went missing. My magic is gone. The iron... the iron took what was left."

My heart almost stopped and I felt something icy and hard clench at my guts. "Mother..." I choked, my eyes filling with tears. "Have I killed you?"

"No, no, my dear," she said, coughing harder this time. I could see flecks of blood on her lips. "The rune was part of who I am, but not all of me. But... I was already dying, my love. I've been in their cages for years, drugged asleep whenever they needed to move me. Drugged more when they needed me out to empower their machines. Using what little magic the iron left to me to keep the infection at bay." She waved her stump weakly. "Daniel, I've longed for it to end. Ending my rune may have sped it up, but I wasn't long anyway."

"I'm sorry about Father," I sobbed.

She shook her head. "Don't be. The man pretended to be something he wasn't just to get into our family. For our secrets. And Mother—your grandmother—wanted him for what she thought he could bring us." She smiled weakly. "You. Turns out she was right." She coughed again, and this time the blood was a thick gloss that pooled on her lips.

"I missed you," I said softly through the tears.

"And I you, my love. But you've become what you were born to be. The boy I was born to bear."

I cried for a few minutes more, my tears falling onto her face and mingling with her own.

"Daniel," she said eventually, her voice cracked and weaker. "Daniel, it's time."

"I can't, Mother." I was shaking now, and I could sense Debesi behind me starting to push at her air-shield a bit more. Karal was attempting to get back in.

"You can, my dear. For me." She smiled again, and for a moment her face was filled with the gentle, pure beauty I'd remembered. Her eyes glowed again, bright and dancing. "I love you."

I nodded, to choked for words. And, with a nudge to the Axis, I Ended her life. She drew one last ragged breath, smiled gently, and closed her eyes. She was, finally, at peace.

Debesi and Mesla said a short, respectful goodbye, and then left.

I knelt there for several long minutes, looking at my mother's tired, drawn face. Behind me, I could hear more people arriving and beginning to batter at the rock wall that separated us.

A hot, boiling anger began rising in my chest. This clan and their machines had taken *everything* from me. They'd kept me from having a father who loved his family. They'd taken Mother from me, caged her and ruined her magic. They threatened all of witchkind.

There will be regret, a voice inside me said as I began to picture *demony minios,* the rune of the Demon Horde. Kirmin's memories flickered through my mind. *Imprecise,* the voice said. It wasn't discouraging me, just reminding me. It was the voice of memory, not of judgement. I had no one to guide me now, no one but myself.

Then I remembered. The rune Kirmin hadn't known, the one I'd found in my book.

Giltinė, the Reaper.

I forced my mind to be clear, ruthlessly pushing aside my fiery hatred and anger. I held the rune firmly in my mind's eye, ensuring it was the only thing in my consciousness. "End the ones who made these machines," I ordered, my voice ringing like the iron that had caged Mother. "End anyone who ever carved her soul rune. End anyone who ever touched her."

The Axis swelled around me, a dark-winged predator and impassionate judge. I could feel sharp, shadowy shapes separate themselves from it, hurtling off to obey my commands. There would be no mindless Horde today. Instead, there would be sharp, precise instruments. Not of death, but of pruning, carefully slicing out a disease from the body of witchkind.

I *felt* them as they set off on their task.

I *felt* them as they sliced through the first of Karal's brasssmiths, one who'd crafted the bodies of the machines.

I *felt* them as they lanced the hearts of the engravers who'd now forgotten the very rune that they were being punished for once knowing.

I *felt* them as they cut into the mind of a young girl of witchkind, who'd done nothing more than help wash Mother's wounds, who'd brought her food and showed her kindness.

And *touched* her.

I howled in dismay, Mother's lifeless body slumping gently to the battered stone floor as I stood and screamed. *This isn't what I meant!* I roared in my mind.

Precise, a calm, disinterested voice said in my mind. *Targeted.*

The Reapers moved swiftly, spreading across the world in the blink of an eye, bringing Endings to everyone I'd named. Even as I felt those lives stopping, I could feel the shadowy creatures returning to to the Axis, their missions complete.

I howled again, but the passion had drained from me. My cry cut off halfway, ending as a choking sob.

I'd taken up the mantle. I'd become the adherent of the Sixth. I'd exercised the fullest, most terrible of my powers.

But what else had I become?

I gathered up Mother's still form and let the Axis' magic take me away.

Master of the Tower

I RETURNED to the mausoleum where Mother had allegedly been interred, and the witchkind there helped me open her crypt and gently place her body in it, as it was always meant to be. They'd retreated respectfully, leaving me on my knees to pour out my emotions on the ageless, unfeeling stone. I'd stayed for hours uncounted, great wracking sobs alternating with an exhaustion so soul-deep that I'm sure I must have passed out for some time.

Eventually, I'd emptied myself, growing so numb, so tired, that I could actually feel the axis' presence swirling lazily around the hole where my love had once been. *This will pass,* the voice in my mind said. Again, not a voice of reassurance, but a voice of experience. Time and time again, this *had* passed, for untold numbers of adherents before me. It would pass for me as well.

I took myself back to the Tower.

The driežai were even more subdued than normal, sensing my emptiness and giving me space. It was three days—I think; it was hard to tell in the Tower, as always—before I summoned the courage to take myself deep into the Tower's roots again, to look at the damage I knew I must have caused.

The deep new fissure was probably no more visible than any of the others that the Tower's foundation had taken over the millennia, but it stood out to me. This one was *mine*. My mistake. My overreaction. My untimely Ending of those who'd given no cause. The sensations I'd gotten from the Reapers had come too fast, too hard, but I knew that more than just one innocent, kind young woman had been Ended. It had almost felt like *disappointment* from the Reapers, as if they knew what they'd been asked to do was not wholly right.

I ran my fingers over the fissure, and the sensations returned. More slowly, this time. More deliberate. It gave me time to contemplate every mistake, regret every imprecision.

I will tell you now that I returned to that pillar many times in my life. I ran my fingers over that very fissure again and again. Always, it served to remind me of the terrible, horrific power I directed.

It was a month or more before I ventured forth again.

In that time, a small measure of my soul seemed to return. *This will pass,* the voice had said, and it was correct. Particularly inside the Tower, I could feel even recent events becoming a little fuzzier, a little less present. This was the Axis' magic, its gift to its long-lived, suffering adherents: the gift of distance.

The other adherents contacted me, offering their condolences. Gilioj had reached out to the Taryba, the great Council of witchkind, and filled them in. They'd expressed dismay and fear at Karal's enterprises, and asked all the adherents to help discover what had become of the clan's amassed power, and what they'd intended it for. The others had agreed to hold a monthly conclave at my Tower, and to have all of their fellow adherents keep their eyes and ears open for any clues as to Karal's plans.

I took some time to officially move into the Tower. Now its master and resident, it fell to me to redecorate the large, empty, slightly-charred basement level that would be my private workroom. I created a small sitting area with several bookshelves full of books and a very comfortable chair, but left the rest of the room empty. I had no idea what to do with it.

I'd begun accepting requests for Judgement from the councils of the world, hearing them in the Tower's third-level courtroom. I was rapidly learning more about witchkind society and government, and used the Axis' powers as best I could to benefit everyone.

And I tried to keep track of Loran. It galled me that they were still alive, but apparently they'd never *made* the machines, never actually carved the rune, and never touched Mother. I'd discovered their survival almost by accident: One night, I'd settled in my workroom and idly invoked Whisper Overheard, holding Loran's face and voice in my mind. I'd fully expected the magic to reach out and find nothing, but it had latched on immediately. As it almost always was with the Whisper Overheard, I found myself eavesdropping on a one-sided conversation.

You were right, of course.

No, not a single one. It's clearly an empty spot in the rune sequence, and it's on every machine. And no, nobody remembers anything about that rune. It was clearly... removed. And everyone who'd worked on the machines, everyone who'd cared for her, they're all dead. Across the continent.

No, I don't think anybody knew that was possible. Forgetting, of course. Runes have been forgotten. But taken? Ended? No.

No, I'm aware. I've never heard of the Sixth doing anything like that, have you?

Obviously, yes, a terrible time. But I'm not sure what we could have done to mitigate it. Our guards, those few left alive, swear it was adherents, how were we to expect they'd involve themselves all of a sudden?

Yes, they'll be disappointed. There will be... repercussions.

Yes, well, it's two problems isn't it?

Of course. That's probably the first to deal with.

Well, because it's the only thing in the here and now I think we can *deal with. The machines will require a new rune. It took almost a century to stumble across the one we lost, we know that much. Runewrights aren't common, and there was only ever one woman that we know of with that soul-rune, aberrations that she and her family were.*

No, he had no idea he was a runewright. That family would never have accepted him if he had known, or if they had found out.

It's hard to say. I wasn't there, but the few survivors—once we chipped them out of the floor—claim it was the new adherent of the Sixth. The black spikes are a tell.

Yes, I know.

It's impossible to say. There isn't–

That's never been successful, but of course. We can try.

Clearly, he understood my role in undoing his clan's work. And just as clearly, they were planning to take some action—likely against me, although in all my memories, ordinary witchkind had never *successfully* countered an Axis in the long term. I toyed with the idea of Ending him, but he was my last link to his clan, and I knew I'd need him to discover their broader plan.

I suspected that Kirmin's distaste for being an investigator was not going to be reflected in my own experience as an adherent. Something was still coming—my Axis had settled somewhat, but I still sensed an anxiety. The disposition of whatever had been taken from the humans, the power collected by Karal's machines. But it all felt as if forces within witchkind were moving to disrupt the world, attempting to shift its very Origin.

I moved myself to one of the Tower's uppermost turrets. They were small, barely more than ten feet across, but they each featured a large, true window. The sea-breeze blew evenly through them as I stood overlooking the sea. I felt the memories of all the adherents before me, who'd shared this same view. I smelled the sea-air for the hundredth time in my life, and for the billionth time, all at once.

I had much ahead of me, and much of that was unknown. But in the past few days I had gained confidence in myself as adherent of the Sixth Axis.

As Master of the Tower.

Epilogue

YES, *well I did tell you that it was quite long.*

No, there's a good bit more. But don't you think that's enough for tonight?

Yes, parts of it are sad. But it all worked out.

It's close to dawn, you know. What if we continued tomorrow?

Hah! Yes, I did. Or I thought I did. For a moment, at least.

Yes, I'll tell you about her. Tomorrow.

Of course. I'll see you then.

Pronunciation

AXES IS the plural of *axis,* and is pronounced, *acks-ease,* not *acks-ehz* like the weapon.

Most of the words in the True language are Lithuanian, or close approximations of Lithuanian words. A pronunciation guide is available at https://omniglot.com/writing/lithuan ian.htm if you'd like to sound them out. In my mind, the story was never set in any place on Earth; Lithuanian simply had the right look and tone for me. It's an old language, and to English eyes appears somewhat ancient, especially with its unusual (for English) diacritical marks. It sounds ancient too, and to my ears it's a language that might have been spoken in secret by wise mystics. Google Translate supports Lithuanian, although if you actually have it translate most of the words I used, you're going to be underwhelmed. Some words were deliberately misspelled simply to accommodate my personal aesthetic preferences.

About the Author

Don Jones spent two decades writing tech books before he finally penned his first sci-fi novella, *A History of the Galactic War*. His well-reviewed novels now span fantasy and science fiction, with a focus on world building and relatable characters. He lives in Las Vegas (and sometimes in Southern Utah).

Connect, get free novels and short stories, and learn about upcoming releases by joining the author newsletter at DonJones.com.

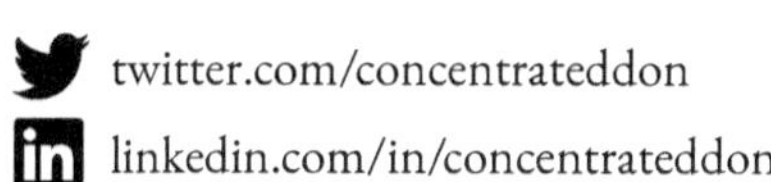

twitter.com/concentrateddon
linkedin.com/in/concentrateddon

Also by Don Jones

Daniel Scratch, a story of witchkind®

Endless Sky®: Truthsayer

The Never: A Tale of Peter and the Fae

* * *

Free eBooks!

The Achillios Chronicles trilogy, *The Prime Wave Accounting* duopoly, and *short stories of witchkind* are all available by joining the author's newsletter at DonJones.com.